CIRCLE OF DEATH

Felix Flores, Jr.

CIRCLE OF DEATH

By Felix Flores, Jr.

Published by
MIDNIGHT EXPRESS BOOKS

CIRCLE OF DEATH

ISBN-13: 978-0692444368 (Midnight Express Books)

ISBN-10: 069244436X

Disclaimer: This is a work of fiction. All characters are totally from the imagination of the author and depict no persons, living or dead; any similarity is totally coincidental.

Published by
MIDNIGHT EXPRESS BOOKS
POBox 69
Berryville AR 72616
(870) 210-3772
MEBooks1@yahoo.com

CIRCLE OF DEATH

By Felix Flores, Jr.

Felix Flores, Jr.

I would like to dedicate this book to my sisters, Lena, Priscilla and Katrina... Also to my beloved mother Diana, who I keep in my prayers each night.

Thank you Rogelio Vasquez for your help on the cover art.

My warmest thank you go out to Victor and Linda Huddleston of Midnight Express Books for helping my dreams come true; without you, I would still be daydreaming. God Bless both of you.

No matter where you are, never give up on your hopes and dreams. Everything is possible with faith in your heart.

I hope you like this book and more to come.

Felix Flores, Jr.

Felix Flores, Jr.

CHAPTER ONE

Carlyle Winston Causey, better known as Woody, was only fifteen years of age as he sat shotgun on his family's wagon. Looking for a better life, his father and mother had spent their last hard-earned money on a wagon trail. The wagon master and his men had promised each family on the wagon train, a new life where a land of new hopes and dreams would await to unfold. Twenty-four wagons lined up behind each other ready to roll out. The excitement on Woody's face could easily be seen, as the young man on the first wagon had a clear view of the open country's beautiful mountains. Which seemed so far away.

As the echoes of the wagon master yelling, "Roll 'em out!" went into the ears of Woody; the excitement was way more than he could bear. For Woody himself stood straight up from the wagon's seat and yelled at the top of his lungs, "Roll 'em out!" He then smiled as he sat next to his father and mother and held their hands. Then again from the wagons behind them, another child with the same feelings Woody had experienced yelled, "Roll 'em out!"

As the young child's voice was heard, his pet dog barked at the sound of his master, for "Roll 'em out!" kept echoing down the line from other wagons on the trail.

The morning was young as the cool wind gently blew the wagons' canopies, sending dust flying into the open land. The sky was clear blue as clouds slowly floated in the distance, yet so far away. The sun once again slowly made its dance across the open country, which promised a beautiful day. But still, somewhere else closer to the mountains or on the other side, had been said would be like living in heaven itself.

At the sides of the wagons, the wagon master and his men rode in silence yet each seemed to know of a destiny where to go. Thick black handlebar mustaches with dark black eyes, told Woody these men were meaner than rattlesnakes. At times some made eye contact and didn't, let go until the other person's eyes watered and blinked first. None ever seemed to laugh or even smile, which made Woody wonder what kind of life these men may have lived. Most were thin yet looked to hold their own and on each one's side, some wore double holsters for the sparkling kept Colt .44 pistols. On their saddle scabbards, each packed a Winchester .44-.40 on its ready to use.

Up at point, one rode ahead even camped out alone. The wagon master with crow's feet around his eyes was the only one with light blue eyes and clean-shaven. He wore his gun to draw cross-cut and also had on his hip a bone-carved handle knife in its long thin leather sheath. Dark brown chaps hung from both sides of the wagon master's saddle, because it was too hot to wear them. The white shirt, which now looked a dusty gray from years of use, had gotten worn out and thin. Yet it seemed to feel and fit pretty good on his broad shoulders. The vest hung open and a pocket watch laid within its pocket as the chain dangled from side to side. He also wore a handkerchief around his neck and at times when he rode close by. Woody could swear he'd seen a scar. Yet maybe it was only dirt, as each man seemed not to have bathed in weeks. The straight, dusty, round, black-brimmed hat the wagon master wore allowed the wind to blow his thin blond hair, which seemed to only be long at the back of his head. No sideburns or mustache, only a small mole on his face. Whenever rest periods arose, Woody noticed a limp to the left side of the wagon master's foot. On his right wrist, he wore an earth tone beaded band with three claws which seemed to be on an eagle.

Woody's excitement overflowed his thoughts as he spoke out loud, "Wow!"

Next to him, his mother spoke softly. "Woody, you need to pay attention where and how far we travel because some day, my son, you may become a great leader yourself." Hugging Woody, she smiled, as the excitement on her face had long been overdue. For many years Woody's father, Frank, had promised Maggie a new life. Somehow, the years had piled up after she had married Frank and had Woody. Living in a small one room wooden shack next to the town named Lubbock, which only had a small courthouse, a bank, and a general store. The town's hotel, jail, saloon, and more shacks now stood empty as the wagon master and his men had ridden in with promises no one could turn down. The families that stayed behind were the ones who could not afford the price of the wagon master and his men, at least not yet.

Slapping the reins upon the horse's back, Woody's father, Frank, told them, "Getty up!" He began to speak to Woody and his wife Maggie, "You two seem to be happy we're leaving this little old town."

At the same time, Woody and his mother both said, "Yeah!" as they both laughed aloud. Then Woody pointed to the mountains and asked. "Which way is that?"

"Northwest," said Frank as he reached in his pocket and handed Woody the reins to guide the wagon along. The small cloth bag that fit in Frank's front pocket contained, dry tobacco along with some rolling papers.

As Frank lit the cigarette, Maggie said. "Frank, you really need to stop smoking, cause you have been coughing more each time you stick one of those in your mouth."

"Every time I smoke, I send smoke signals to our Maker and let him know where we're at," Frank said with a chuckle, rolling his eyes upward to the sky.

Woody giggled as Maggie reached over his shoulders and hit Frank on his arm. "Frank, you also need to stop speaking like that.

She was right, he did need to stop smoking, but it seemed like she was talking to a rock because he was not about to stop.

If he ran out of tobacco in the small cloth bag, he kept more in a tin can somewhere inside a wooden chest with all his stuff.

As Woody looked on, his mother Maggie let loose of her ponytail and began to brush her curly waves of reddish gold shiny hair. She was a beautiful redhead with a sprinkle of freckles on her face and light green eyes. Every time she smiled, two dimples appeared on her rosy cheeks. Her voice was soft, but she spoke her mind when she knew she was right. "Oh, Lord!" she said as she fixed her ponytail back up. "It's very hot today. I pray we run across some water so we can get cleaned up."

Frank blew a ring of smoke and said, "I heard the wagon master last night tell his men, a lake laid out close to our trail and we'd get to it in a day or two."

Maggie hugged Woody once more smiling, "That will be very nice." Puzzled, she asked."Will we be able to swim?"

Frank threw the butt of his cigarette on the floorboard of the wagon, as he put his boot on top of it and twisted until it was completely out and said, "A lake could be huge or it could be small, But I'm sure we all will be able to swim and get cleaned up a bit."

He leaned over and placed both elbows on his knees as he took the reins and guided the horses through a small path of rocks on the trial.

Maggie made her way into the back of the wagon. "I'm taking a nap and leave you two alone a while."

Woody slid over to the right side of the seat and nearly hung over the side looking back at the other wagons.

Gently on Woody's side, Frank tapped him and motioned him back over to his side. "Son, I got something I want you to know in case you need a gun, knife or rifle. Under the boards of the wagon, I made a secret place only you and I know.

Woody's thoughts danced in his mind for not only the excitement had meant a lot to him, he now had a secret of where to find help if he needed it. "Yes sir. I promise I won't tell anyone."

Frank leaned back on the seat saying, "You're a man now and I expect you to be a good one, my son."

Woody looked at his father and promised to be good and said, "I love you, Dad, and I love Mom as well. You don't have to worry. I'll be good in life, OK?"

Frank smiled at his son and told him, "And don't pick up my bad habits like smoking cigarettes, OK?"

Woody giggled and promised not to ever smoke a cigarette.

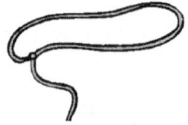

Going into a week, the wagon master rode out in front of the wagons and hadn't been seen all day. The day had almost come to an end when up ahead, a silhouette of two riders on horses stood next to each other. The one who'd been the point man rode away as the wagon master waited for the wagons to catch up.

As the moon's light cast a dim glow over the open country, the sparkling lake's water danced its music to the eyes of the people on the wagon train. The wagon master motioned his men to form a circle with the wagons as he dismounted his horse and moved closer to the lake.

Woody's eyes never left sight of the point man as he asked his father, "Why does that rider stay away from us, Dad?"

Frank looked at the point man and said, "His job is to point the way and not to mingle with us."

Woody scratched his head and raised his eyebrows as he told his mother, "Mom, that man has a lonely life. I don't think I'd like that kind of leadership."

Maggie smiled at her son saying, "Leadership in this world comes in many ways Woody. All you have to do is pray something good comes along." She hugged Frank as Woody jumped off the wagon looking back at the point man who no longer seemed to be anywhere. Not a clue of how the point man may look, only the waves of his hands toward the wagons lingered in Woody's mind. As his eyes searched the outline of the lake, he wondered if the point man was young or old and what his name could be.

The circle took a while to form with the wagons as the children kept jumping off the sides and running to the lake to freshen up a bit. Still on their horses, the men all rode to one side of the circle as to choose a spot to camp out for the night.

Woody's eyes lifted up in amazement as the rugged cowboys dismounted their horses and removed the saddles of their horses to use as pillows for the night. Each rolled out their bed rolls and sat down pulling off their boots and hats.

The night was still young as the women began to cook in big iron kettles. The fire beneath the kettles gave light within the circle of wagons. The aroma of chili and beans made Woody forget about the rugged cowboys and headed next to his family's wagon to eat. "Woody," his mother spoke, "I want you to get cleaned up a bit before you go to sleep, OK honey?" Frank looked at Woody with a smile because he knew the water would be ice cold. Maggie handed Frank a bowl of chili and beans then said, "And that goes for you too, Frank."

Woody returned the smile to his father with a little chuckle added to it.

The thought of moving to a new place where new hopes and dreams would await to unfold lingered in all the women's minds. Each seemed to be happy as they cooked extra chili and beans to serve the wagon master and his men. None of them spoke.

Woody looked on as the women gave food and coffee to the rugged men only nodding their heads in appreciation. It was hard for him to understand the wagon master and his men. In his mind, he thought not only should everyone searching for a new life be happy, but also all the rugged cowboys, for they were the ones who held the scenery of this new land which awaited for everyone. After everybody was cleaned up, the wagon master and his men took turns going to the edge of the lake to do the same. As Woody looked on, his eyes focused on the wagon master. Getting cleaned up, he sat on a rock, he pulled up the left pants leg over his knee and unwrapped a cloth four to five inches wide and about two feet long. What Woody saw next made him crawl back out the other side of the wagon and look straight up at the stars in shock. The wagon master had pulled off a fake leg just under his knee.

"Woody!" His mother called for him from inside the wagon.

"Yes Mom," he returned standing at the wagon's tailgate with both hands on top of the edge.

Maggie always had seen to everyone else's needs first, then she cared for herself. "Here Woody. Use this blanket for the ground and this one to cover up with."

He caught both blankets and placed them under his arm and called out to his father, "Dad, do cowboys always use saddles for pillows?"

Frank smiled within the wagon as he remembered back in the days when he was young and spent many nights alone with a saddle for a pillow. "Real cowboys do. Why do you ask?" Frank replied.

Woody just needed to change the subject in his mind of what he'd seen moments ago and asked his father. "Well, what do I use? "

Frank kissed Maggie on her cheek and told her, "Honey, I'll be right back." Jumping out of the wagon, he reached back inside and grabbed his horse's saddle that hadn't been used since the wagon trail had taken place. His horse had walked behind the wagon tied around the neck and the rope was tied to the wagon. "Here you go, cowboy," Frank told his son.

Woody smiled from ear to ear and said, "Wow! Thanks, Dad." He dragged the saddle under the wagon. Now Frank and Maggie could get some sleep and Woody could play cowboy for the night. As he laid under the wagon, he thought about the wagon master and his men. In Woody's mind, these men were real cowboys and knew all about the frontier. Rifles, guns, and spurs brought excitement to Woody's life. For all that, he had really seen growing up was his father plowing fields and wearing coveralls. But, at times, he spoke of his past life before marrying and settling down. The stories Woody was told of gunmen and how they tried to tame the wild country now began to show. So many times, he had told Woody to be real careful who to trust and also that anyone could make a mistake.

The sparkling stars upon the lakes' water glittered as the moon sent its dim glow over the land. Rest would provide clear thinking for everyone and Woody could still hear the words his mother had told him. "Woody, you need to pay attention where and how far we travel

because some day, my Son, you may become a great leader yourself."
The lake would be easy to remember as it laid three weeks away from
Lubbock going northwest and the mountains to the left.

The dawn's light seemed to come so fast as Woody turned to the other
side. Looking at the wagon master and his men where they had
camped for the night. Not moving anymore, he looked on as the wagon
master gave out orders to his men, each with a nod walked away and
began to saddle up. The wagon shook as Woody's father jumped out
onto the ground. Looking under the wagon, he smiled at Woody and
asked him, "How did you like your pillow, cowboy?"

Woody smiled at Frank and said, "I loved it, Dad."

Frank stood up as he reached for Maggie to climb out of the tailgate.
Before Woody could crawl from under the wagon, Maggie told him,
"Woody, dust out those blankets before you put them back into the
wagon."

As Woody dusted the blankets out, the wagon master made his way
over to Frank and told him, "Frank Causey, I believe," and reached out
to shake his hand.

"That's me," Frank replied.

The wagon master looked at Woody and gave him a nod then looked
at Maggie from top to bottom and back up again and said "Good
morning, ma'am."

She walked over to Frank's side and returned with, "Good morning,
Wagon Master."

He took off his hat and placed it over his chest and said, "You folks don't have to call me Wagon Master. You can call me Jerry Wheat from now on." He put his hat back on and said, "We're staying here all day and night. In the morning, we'll head that way," pointing straight to the mountains.

It was a big relief to rest and camp out in the open land. The wagon master walked around the circle of wagons telling everyone the good news. They all began to cook their breakfast meals and mingle with each other.

The whole day through, the wagon master and his men sat apart from everyone else. Woody sat under his father's wagon looking and studying each and every man. For each one was unique in its own way. Woody couldn't place it or just maybe his mind was playing tricks on him, but it seemed something wasn't right . . .

All day the wagon master and his men had been cleaning their guns. It was then and only then that each one had been laughing and smiling. As they stayed their distance, no one could hear a word they spoke. Searching once more at the edges of rocks which laid far away, Woody kept looking for the point man. And in the distant morning mist, a slim silhouette of a man stood next to his horse. The point man was ready to ride out farther on, into the trail as he mounted his horse and rode on . . .

Felix Flores, Jr.

CHAPTER TWO

The splashes of water from the lake sent ripples of waves as the young children ran off the edges into the lake, swimming the day through. Woody had gotten cleaned up earlier as he now sat in his favorite spot under the family's wagon. Each time Frank passed by, he spoke to Woody asking him, "Woody, how'd you like to go fishing on the other side of the lake?"

Woody only nodded back to his father saying, "No thanks, Dad. I like watching the wagon master and his men." Coming from under the wagon, Woody asked, "Dad, do those men seem strange to you?"

Frank placed an arm around his son and told him, "Son, those men are paid to do whatever the wagon master tells them. And any man may seem strange if you don't know him or them."

Woody smiled as an idea came to float in his mind. Frank rubbed the top of Woody's head with his hand and walked away and spoke once more, "Boy, get that idea out of your mind and stick around here." He knew his son better than the back of his own hand and he knew Woody wanted to go meet the men. He looked at his father and scratched his head in amazement of how he knew so much about him. He turned around to look for his mother Maggie who seemed to know he was looking for her. She stood next to the kettle cooking supper, but kept her eyes on him as she smiled at him.

Under another wagon, a young boy played with his pet dog. Woody could hear the young man call out the dog's name "Tippy." The dog barked at his master as it wagged its tail and jumped at the young boy.

"Woody!" Frank called out from the wagon. Woody took one more look at the wagon master and his men, all of them stood up and started to walk over to the circle of wagons.

He stood next to the tailgate looking in the wagon and answered his father, "Yeah, Dad. What's up?"

Frank tossed him a pair of leather riding gloves and told him, "You can have these. I used to wear them on trails like this many years ago."

Woody caught the gloves in mid air, then told his father, "Dad, the wagon master and his men are headed this way."

Frank jumped out the back of the wagon and stood next to Woody saying, "The men are hungry. So, we got to feed them."

Woody crawled back under the wagon and sat on the grassy patch that hid him from view. Each man was handed a plate with chili and beans with a cup of pure black coffee as they looked at everyone mingle together. Stepping out of the circle of wagons, the wagon master and his men sat in a circle of their own staring back at everyone.

The night was still young as the stars loomed in the distant sky. The dim glow of the moon light stood its silence, which denied a pitch-black cast over the wagons, that had not moved all day or the night before. This night now taking its turn would never be the same, for Woody's life would be turned upside down in the moments to come.

Setting aside their plates the wagon master and his men finished their meals; each began to clean their guns once more as the wagon master spoke to them. Each nodded at the orders given. They walked in twos around the wagons. Woody looked on and wondered why this was taking place. As the last two men made their way around the wagons. The women and children sat around talking, the men sat apart telling each other how they planned to build small ranches on the Promised Land. Some spoke as well, of how they would plow the land and plant their seeds.

Woody sat back against the inside of the wagon wheel to try on the pair of leather gloves. The wagon master and his men walked into the circle of wagons; Woody looked on.

Suddenly the night was filled with gunshots as the women and children yelled for mercy, which had ended their cries for life in an awful shock. The men also had no chance to fight for their lives. They were all gunned down until no one was left alive.

Not understanding, Woody laid in silence as his father had been gunned down without a chance to defend himself. Yards away his mother had been shot to death, Woody could see with the moon's light that she knew he'd been under the wagon all along.

The echoes of her voice sent chills through Woody's body, but quickly crawling out the other side away from the circle of wagons, Woody ran for his life.

As Woody ran away, the sounds of gunfire began to subside, which meant everyone had been killed. Slowly the dawn's light started to form its dance to a new day. Woody knew in his mind that the wagon master and his men would get a count to see if anyone would be missing. The word, "Run!" lingered in his mind and kept going as fast as he could. Woody's mother had saved his life, because if she had not yelled, "Run!" He would still be laying under the wagon in shock or even dead like everyone else.

Into the wooded area, Woody made his way deep into the darkness of the forest, which held yet another danger. No man should be caught alone especially without a gun or knife. Climbing high up into a tree had taken almost all of his energy. The leather gloves had come in handy and made the climb much easier than it would have been without them. As Woody had been running he'd picked up some rocks and stuck them into his pockets. He knew he had to outwit the wagon master and his men. A game his father once played would now save Woody's life. For the wagon master now below the trees spoke to his gunmen, "Find him and kill him." As the wagon master sat atop his horse, Woody above the tree sat as tears rolled down his face and on to the edge of his chin.

As the tears dripped off his chin, they made their journey downward as he cried even more. He tried to stay focused and reached into his pocket for the rocks. Tossing them into the air, a teardrop fell onto the top of the wagon master's horse's ear. Flinching and backing up, the horse knew something was above it.

The crackling of the rocks Woody had thrown hit bushes and more trees. The wagon master motioned in silence that something was up ahead. Scattering out the gunmen looked on with their guns at the ready to shoot anything that moved. As the bushes rocked back and forth, the wagon master and his men opened fire into the moving bush. The sounds of laughter echoed into the forest along with the shots of guns. The wagon master and his men thought Woody was dead.

He was safe for a moment, but he had to wait out the storm of death that waited if heard. Slowly the wagon master and his men moved on as Woody could hear the wagon master say, "Next time we'll kill the wagon trail during the day, so we can see everyone." Not only could Woody tell the wagon master was fake because of killing everyone. He now showed to not even know how to follow tracks or Woody would have been caught the moment he'd climbed the tree.

Far away from the wagons, a campfire lit up in the night. Woody climbed down from the tree he'd stayed in all day. Running back to where his life had been turned upside down, he laid on his back pushing at the boards under his family's wagon. The boards began to crack. Woody pushed even harder at the thought of killing the wagon master and his men. Sticking his hands into the broken boards, he pulled out the buffalo rifle and the Colt .44 with its holster as well as a Bowie knife. He also found two boxes of bullets, one for the buffalo rifle and one for the Colt .44 revolver.

Because of the dead bodies lying around, the wagon master and his men camped at a distance as they laughed amongst each other. Loading the Colt .44 revolver first, Woody climbed into his family's wagon. Loading the buffalo rifle which only held one slug at a time, he waited for the dawn's light to appear. Slowly the morning arose as the wagon master and his men mounted their horses. Ready to leave with everyone's money as well as whatever else could be put into a saddle bag.

With the Bowie knife, Woody slit a long cut downwards on his family's wagon's canopy. He stood up with both feet firmly within the wagon. He held the rifle against his right shoulder. Tilting his head so his right eye was looking through the sight, he pulled the trigger. The buffalo rifle knocked him onto the other side of the wagon's canopy. Through the long slit of the torn canopy Woody looked on. He could see the body of one gunman topple over his horse and onto the ground. Quickly standing up he reloaded the buffalo rifle and stood even firmer than the first. He once again pulled the trigger. This time the strength of the kick was less since he was ready for it. Up ahead the second body fell. Specks of blood from the slug exploding the gunman's chest before he fell over, sprinkled onto the wagon master's face. He yelled to his men, "Let's get the hell out of here!"

Woody once again shot into the morning's early hours; another gunman's body fell off his horse onto the ground, dead. Being dragged by his foot, because it was caught in the stirrup. Looking on, Woody vowed to kill every one of them. Not being able to follow was because the wagon master and his men had killed all the horses on the wagon trail.

Sitting down inside his family's wagon, Woody cried once more, for he knew yards from the wagon his father and mother laid dead with everyone else.

Alone, Woody began to bury everyone in shallow graves to save time. The buzzards had already flown in to feast on the dead bodies that laid everywhere. As each night fell, Woody laid under his family's wagon listening to the sounds of distant wolves howling in the darkness of the open country's land. Burying the bodies had taken three days as he camped out under his family's wagon, only one more heartbeat was on the wagon trail. Each night he would leave something to eat under another wagon, for the little pitch black dog which had survived the gunshots of the wagon master and his men. The dog stayed a distance from Woody because it was still in shock of his master being dead.

The dawn's light began to shine over the shallow graves as Woody noticed a horse walking towards him. Another animal that had become a need in Woody's life, stood fully saddled up ready to ride. As he walked up to the horse, a smell overtook him by surprise. The gunman's leg still stuck in the stirrup was the only thing left of the body. Removing the leg, Woody led the horse next to his family's wagon. Bullet holes in the barrels of water, which were mounted on the sides of the wagons, did not keep water from leaking out; there was still water below them. Giving the horse water from a hat that laid close by, Woody looked around the open land. A sparkle in the distance caught his eye, something was moving up ahead. Quickly he crawled under the wagon and kept looking in the direction of whatever had moved. The dog was looking in the same direction as Woody was. As it growled, little sharp teeth could be seen. Up ahead a body tried to stand up, then fell to the ground, A cloud of dust told Woody the gunman he'd first shot was still alive. Mounting the horse, he rode to where the body laid. Next to it, he dismounted the horse and reached out to the gunman, pulling his gun out of its holster.

Woody stuck the gun in the back of his holster and asked the gunman, "What's your name, stranger?"

The gunman with his eyes slightly open as the sun beamed down on him spoke to Woody, "Water, please. Water."

Woody's anger arose, yet he held on because he needed answers. "Okay, I'll give you water." Grabbing the canteen from the horse,

19

Woody wet his fingers first to let the gunman taste it. "What's the point man's name?"

"Water, More water."

Grabbing the gunman's lower jaw, he squeezed it saying, "Tell me the point man's name and I'll give you all the water you want."

In a low weak voice, the gunman spoke again, "More," or was it "Moore?" The gunman's eyes closed letting Woody know he was dead. Had he been asking for more water or was he saying someone's name, Moore?

Woody stood up and out of anger drew his gun and shot the gunman between the eyes over and over again until the gun was out of bullets. The clicks from the hammer continued until Woody heard the dog barking at him. The little dog had followed Woody thinking he was moving on. Waking him from a trance of wanting to kill the wagon master and his men, he reloaded his gun with bullets from the holster's belt. He fell to one knee and looked at the little dog. Slowly wagging its tail, the little dog walked over to Woody. Picking up the little dog, Woody placed it on the front of the saddle's horn and mounted the horse heading back to the wagons.

The remainder of the day, Woody went through the wooden chest in the back of his family's wagon. In a tin can, Woody found his father's tobacco and a box of matches. Sleeping under the wagon again, he knew when the dawn's light came up he would have to move on. He looked at the little pitch black dog lying next to him and said, "I think I'm going to call you, "More." He had named the dog More, so as to not ever forget the gunman's last words.

Frank's clothes were too big for Woody. As the dawn's light began to shine, he went through the other wagons looking for a good set of clothes. A cowboy didn't wear coveralls and that's all he'd ever worn. A good hat along with clothes to wear, even an extra pair rolled up in a bedroll. In addition, the blanket he loved most because his mother Maggie had made it for him years ago, he would move on. However, before he left, he'd taken the gunman's saddle off the horse and dragged his father's saddle from under the wagon. Placing the saddle on the horse, he headed for the mountains' forest. Alone at the age of fifteen, Woody had seen children, women, and men die more than anyone had ever known. Woody at a very young age could claim he'd killed three gunmen, having to boast of killing them, would only stay in his mind.

Felix Flores, Jr.

CHAPTER THREE

The thundering echoes of the buffalo rifle rang through the mountain forest. Seven young Indian warriors followed the tracks of an eight-foot black grizzly bear. The vicious bear had been tormenting the Indian camp each night. It had killed innocent women and children on its rampage of hunger. For days, the tracks were followed and each day they seemed fresh or as if the bear had slowed down a bit. At one point many arrows from the Indian warriors, had pierced the body of the bear. It had tried to drag a body that had become its prey. Now deep into the mountain forest, the bear was trying to escape. It had become prey itself as the Indian warriors risked their lives for their people. All the shots from the wagon master and his gunmen had not been heard, because the Indian warriors had been too far away. Nevertheless, the booms in the early morning hours from the buffalo rifle had sent not only echoes through the forest, but flocks of birds into the sky as well.

Each young warrior looked at each other because they had never heard such a noise in their lives. It had been Woody killing the three gunmen three days ago. Now he made his way through the mountain forest, heading in the direction of the grizzly bear and the young warriors. Using its sense of smell, the bear easily knew how far the warriors were and laid in wait ready to attack once more. Woody moved on deeper into the forest as he ran across a stream of cold river water. Within the forest, a mist of fog danced its way through the trees slowly. As it left the leaves of trees and grass slippery, Woody got off the horse at the edge of the stream trying to fill his canteen.

The little dog, More, growled into the distance because his animal instincts were telling it something of danger laid in wait.

The horse had moved away from Woody and on into the deeper forest. It felt it wasn't safe to stick around as well. Holding the canteen under the running cold water, streaks of sunrays shot into the forest upon Woody's back. He began to pull the canteen from the stream filled with water; a shadow stole the sunlight in front of him. Chills ran through his body, He tried to stand up and turn around at the same time. On two legs the eight-foot black grizzly bear stood directly in front of Woody, It swung its claws across his body. Using the canteen to fend off the ripping swing of the bear, it went flying as the bear roared within the forest. Slipping backwards, he quickly pulled his Colt .44 revolver from his holster. The fear had made him draw the gun lightning fast, the bullets exploded into the bear's lower jaw into its head. Unloading the gun, he fell backwards into the stream of cold running water, which was about a foot and a half deep. Tilting backward then forward, the grizzly bear took a step into the stream, stepping on Woody's ankle that broke from the weight of the bear. It collapsed on top of Woody and was dead from the Colt .44 revolver's bullets in its brain.

Trapped under the bear, Woody held on to his last breath of air. The gunshots rang within the forest. The Indian warriors came into sight of the bear toppling over Woody's body. All seven warriors began to pull the bear off Woody, in a rolling motion with the flowing water. Pulling him upwards from the top of his hair, an Indian warrior stood next to him. For the first time in his life, Woody was now looking into the eyes of a so-called."Red Man," who'd he'd heard so many stories about. Then another and another as they carried him out of the stream. One Indian warrior stood with Woody's horse and another took off the bedroll to cover his body. Woody looked on, each Red Man helped to make Woody comfortable. The broken ankle was now swelling inside his boot.

One of the warriors knew it had to be cut off and a splint made to keep the ankle in place. Next to Woody sat another Red Man with a small bag which contained herbs for the pain he was in. After a moment, the pain subsided and then he began to hallucinate, like having a dream wide-awake. The laughter from the seven Red Men made Woody laugh himself. He fell over on one side out cold. Now the real dreams would take over as reflections of Frank and Maggie danced in his mind. The voice of Maggie as it had been her last word which was, "Run!" echoed in his dream.

As fast as he could, he was running in his dream for the eight-foot grizzly bear was yards behind him roaring. In the distance of a clear beautiful day, a silhouette stood alone. It was of a man on his horse who'd been the point man for the wagon trail.

The dream went pitch black as he slept among the Red Men, who'd he'd heard so many bad stories of and how they killed the white man for no reason.

Waking up, Woody could feel his stomach touching his back because he was very hungry. As he looked on, the Indian people danced around a fire and sang into the sky. Next to him laid smoked meat on rocks with vegetables for him to eat. The sounds of drums sent echoes into the night and far away, the howls of wolves could be heard as well.

More, the little black dog, on the other side of Woody ate peacefully, but kept watch as the dancing continued within the Indian camp. Woody was a hero, but he didn't know it yet, because he'd killed the eight-foot grizzly bear and he would be rewarded with honor. A dry tree limb strong enough to hold Woody up as he walked would become a crutch, for the next three months.

Each day Woody seemed to be learning the Indian people's ways. He sat trying to communicate with them. With drawings on the ground, Woody told his story to the Indian chief. He himself drew a story for Woody to see. He would be safe amongst the Indian people, but a test of bravery had yet to come. His father, Frank, had shared many stories of how the Red Man lived and as Woody sat listening to his father tell stories, it was now he really believed them.

The eyes of the chief to Woody seemed honest as he smiled at him. To honor Woody with his first gift, the Indian who'd cut off his boot, handed him a pair of moccasin boots which were perfect. They fit right below the knees. Another Red Man handed Woody his buffalo rifle. It was inside a beautiful leather scabbard with beads woven in it, along with a thick strap of leather so he could hang over his shoulder. The Indian warrior, who'd first picked Woody out of the stream by his hair, handed him his canteen smiling. Another Red Man stood next to him as he hung on Woody's neck a leather pouch. Looking inside, he found a carved bone smoking pipe, along with the smaller bag he had with his father's tobacco. Remembering the promise he'd given his father not to ever smoke a cigarette. He smiled at the Indian warrior and thanked him with a nod. He would keep his promise not to smoke a cigarette, but would smoke the pipe instead .

The Indian warriors stood aside as Woody looked up ahead. The chief stood holding a black stallion horse to give to Woody. Motioning Woody to come forth, he began walking without the wooden crutch. He limped over to the chief who handed the reins to Woody. Never in his life had anyone given him a gift. Only the Colt .44 revolver, Bowie knife and the buffalo rifle. The only reason he'd gotten them was because his father had told him, in case of an emergency where they had been hidden. Tears rolled from Woody's eyes as the Indian chief put an arm around his shoulders and pointed. As he blinked away the tears, he could see two more Indian warriors holding up a coat made from the grizzly bear he had killed. Wrapping the coat over his shoulder, the black stallion reared in the air and everyone began to laugh.

Out of the teepee next to where Woody had been sleeping, stepped out a beautiful Indian girl about his age. In her hand, she carried a leather necklace that she placed over Woody's head. It was earth tone beads with five claws of the dead grizzly bear. Another five-claw necklace was made so the black stallion could wear it. The chief motioned that the girl was a gift as well.

Woody's father, Frank, had once told a story of his younger days and how he met an Indian tribe. At the time, Frank spoke of his wild adventurous life. Woody never thought the stories were true. But now, as he stood the hero of an Indian tribe, he could only wonder how many more stories his father would have told him if he was still alive. From what he had heard before, the bear claws on the necklace meant strength and bravery. The beads stood for how many Indian people had died in the hands of the bear.

Accepting the Indian girl had been Woody's mistake for now sought to be family of the chief. Woody could no longer leave unless a bigger honor was to be given to him.

The drum beats kept echoing through the night as Woody stood holding hands with the beautiful young Indian girl. Not only had he accepted her as a gift. He would soon marry her without knowing because he knew nothing of how the ceremony took place.

Indian life to Woody seemed so right. He would learn each day how they lived. The hunting started each day before dawn. It always took place away from the Indian camp. The older women would weave blankets and make moccasins while the young ones cooked and tended to the camp.

Upon arriving from the daily hunt, Woody was motioned to enter the chief's teepee. He walked into the chief's huge teepee. The chief sat on his own woven blanket. Another blanket laid open for Woody across from the chief. The young Indian girl sat waiting for Woody smiling. The marriage ceremony was now taking place. He did not know she would be his wife that night. Grabbing each one of their hands, The Indian chief sang in his native tongue and placed their hands upon a piece of spiritual weed that they each had to eat. In moments, the weed would bring visions and sounds of laughter only Woody and the young Indian girl would hear. It would be the spirits that the Indian chief had called upon to come join the lives of two young souls forever.

Stepping out of the teepee, the chief laid down the flap at the entrance, down over the teepee. Woody had never been with a woman before, nor the young Indian girl with a man, but they each now belonged with each other.

As the moon slowly made its dance across the darkness of the sky, Woody would lose himself in a lust of love. He would experience for the first time. In each other's arms, Woody and the young Indian girl had fallen asleep.

Waking up to the sounds of morning drums, Woody sat up as the beam of light from the open space above the teepee, laid across the body of the young Indian girl. Her touch had been so soft and her kisses had left Woody needing more. He leaned over her and kissed her soft cheek.

Opening her eyes, she spoke in her native tongue smiling at Woody. He smiled back and helped her sit up. He told her, "You are the most beautiful woman I've ever seen," even though he knew she would not understand. She placed her head on his shoulder for a moment as the drums continued to beat outside the teepee.

Getting dressed, Woody stood over the blanket and looked at its woven message of a silhouette. It was of a man and woman holding hands with a circle surrounding the two bodies. Looking at the young Indian girl, she spoke again in her native tongue and she pointed at herself, at Woody and back down to the blanket. He knew then the chief had made a marriage. Woody had to honor and realized that to leave another honor would have to be owed to him from the chief.

Woody smiled at the young Indian girl. He was smart enough not to make her cry. Helping her up, she got dressed. Woody said, "I'll be leaving as soon as I can." He kept a smile on his face. He threw the flap over and stepped outside to see the morning drummer look straight into his eyes. He was a much older Indian who looked at Woody with a smile. In his mind, he wondered if the drummer's smile was fake or real, but he returned a smile back at him. He turned around to help the young Indian girl step outside the teepee. Both stood next to each other. The Indian chief pointed across the camp, where other warriors were putting up a teepee for Woody and his wife. The dust from the raging horse's hooves flew into the air. Woody pushed the Indian chief to one side. Falling to the ground, the Indian chief looked in the direction of the running horse. It had been a young Indian warrior who tried to run over the chief because of jealousy. He had thought it wasn't fair that, Woody be honored with the young Indian girl. Standing up the chief looked at Woody with a puzzled expression, which told Woody he could leave if he wanted to. But he walked away with the young Indian girl's hand in his.

Speaking in his native tongue, the chief shouted at the tribe. In moments, other Indian warriors mounted their horses bareback; quickly they would try to catch up to the jealous warrior.

Woody knew if the warriors couldn't catch him, he'd try to come back at night for the young Indian girl and try to kill the chief or even him.

Everyone looked at Woody walk over to where his buffalo rifle had been leaning against another teepee. Checking to see if it was still loaded, he picked up the metal sight to see through. Standing firm on two feet, Woody took aim and pulled the trigger. The booming sound of the buffalo rifle echoed through the Indian camp. The chief looked back at Woody then back at the runaway warrior. Seconds later the horse of the warrior toppled over, sending him shooting forward into the air. Surrounded, the Indian warrior still tried to fight because he knew the chief would kill him himself. All the Indian people looked on, the chief turned to look at Woody and walked over to him and hugged him for more than a moment. The chief knew Woody already realized an honor was owed to him. All he had to do was ask.

Punishing an enemy of the Indian people always took long to put to death, but an enemy of their own would die in an instant. Bringing forth the runaway warrior next to the chief. Another warrior handed him a spear made of a long tree limb with the point of a flint rock, which was very sharp. The chief never hesitated once sending the spear straight through the chest of the warrior. Piercing the heart of the young man who'd tried to kill him with a raging horse. Dragging away the warrior, the chief once again shouted out in his native tongue. The drummer beat the drums as hard as he could and the Indian people began to sing, for it seemed that the death of the warrior was long overdue.

Woody was more than a hero now and everywhere he went the Indian warriors followed, but the test of bravery was still to come.

Felix Flores, Jr.

CHAPTER FOUR

The law of the land to the Indian people was to keep peace until it had no reason for life to continue. As the Indian chief sat among his tribe, his eyes cut across the open land. For today, would be a special day to find out, if Woody could uphold his honors handed down to him. The test of bravery would take place as a circle of warriors stood in their war paint images, which depicted a will to kill. In the middle, Woody stood alone, with only the stories his father had shared with him of how he'd gotten the scars on his body. Closing his eyes, he brought back the moment his mother had told him, "Woody, you need to pay attention where and how far we travel because some day, my son, you may become a great leader yourself." It was then he knew and understood those words. For if he could survive today, tomorrow another journey would await to unfold. Death would bring no promises for anybody, but to have a will to live would at least give him the strength to continue. Opening his eyes, he still stood his ground, but from the inside out, he had become the one who would pay attention and live on to become yet another hero as the scars would tell the story.

To each other's wrist, Woody and a huge warrior were tied to face each other. With a knife in their other hand they would fight until the end. Determined to go forth in life, Woody swung his knife at the warrior first, but missed as he cut across Woody's back when he stumbled to the ground. In an instant, Woody dug his Bowie knife into the ground and pulling it out quickly sent dirt into the warrior's eyes.

With crazy swings, the warrior cut through the air with his knife. Once again, he cut at Woody's chest as he stepped in with the Bowie knife cutting across the warrior's stomach. Reaching from behind, Woody stabbed the warrior again and again until the Bowie knife pierced the warrior's heart. Falling over, the warrior hit the ground face first. Woody stepped to one side. He fell to one knee and cut the leather strap that bound both wrists together. Slowly standing up, he placed his Bowie knife into his moccasin boot and with the same hand reached over his left shoulder pulling the warrior's knife out of his upper back.

Looking at each of the other warriors, Woody walked up to the biggest one, who'd been holding leather straps to tie him up. Once more for his second try, to outwit or die. The eyes of the big warrior hit the ground, Woody stood in front of him ready to go again. Even though he seemed to be bleeding badly, Woody would never think to quit. Pushing aside two warriors, the chief entered the circle of death. He yelled out words in his native tongue, taking Woody by his arm leading him out of the circle of death. The cheers went out into the sky, Woody was again a hero in the Indian people's eyes. He'd not only showed bravery, but the strength to carry on.

Holding Woody by one arm the Indian chief led Woody to his teepee, who was standing dizzy from loss of blood. The chief closed the flap of his teepee. At that moment, Woody began to fall. His Indian wife caught him to break the fall. She laid him down on the woven blanket. Even though he had showed he would carry on into another fight, he would have lost because he would have become too weak to continue.

The drummer gently sang and beat for Woody's return.

The medicine man had stayed within the teepee along with the Indian chief and Woody's wife. Outside the Indian people sat each day, Never had they seen such a young soul, walk out from the circle of death as Woody had done. Now they waited to see if the spirits, would allow him to walk out of the teepee. For three days and three nights only the Indian chief and the medicine man as well as Woody's wife would come in and out from the teepee. Each time the flap opened up, the little black dog, More, would stand up first. He was also waiting on his master to come out.

On the third morning when the flap swung open, Woody's wife came out first holding the woven blanket. They walked to the lake and began to beat it within the lake with rocks. The Indian chief came out and sat next to the fire. It had been kept burning since Woody was last seen. Slowly the old medicine man made his way out of the teepee. He sat next to the Indian chief.

Pointing up into the sky, the Indian chief spoke to his people as an eagle flew past the Indian camp. It was then that everyone stopped what they were doing. Woody was stepping out of the teepee. Standing before everyone, he knelt on one knee to pat his dog, More. He slowly walked to where the Indian Chief was and held his stomach to show he was hungry. Everyone started to laugh because they knew Woody would be okay. They motioned to the food on top of clean warm rocks. He thought he was eating chicken, then remembered the stories his father told of a bird called a grouse, which was a ground-dwelling bird with feathered legs. Its colors could be reddish brown or other pro-tective colors out in the wild. On flat rocks, laid prickly pears from the top of cactus, like his mother would always bring to the table to eat. Berries, carrots and potatoes lay out in the open for Woody to eat as well.

After the good meal, Woody walked slowly to the lake so he could wash up a bit. But, after a while playing in the water, he began to shake and sit on the edge of the grass. He came down with a fever that would cause him to be put into a teepee, with hot steaming rocks from the fire. They would keep the teepee warm so he could sweat out the fever.

Once again, the medicine man stayed with Woody and gave him wild herbs to eat. He would hallucinate then fall into a deep sleep. The sleep had brought images Woody had once lived as a child. In the dream, his father Frank plowed fields all day as his mother baked bread to eat. The images flowed into a path that led to a misty lake. Then gunfire of the wagon master and his men killing everyone and everything as his hopes and dreams had been stolen. Fading away the dream held the scenery of the most important need he wished to know. It was to see the face of the point man, who sat on his horse deep within the mist.

Turning his head from side to side, Woody's fever was beginning to break. Beads of sweat ran down the sides of his face. The medicine man sang out to the spirits to come forth and collect the fever and renew Woody once more. Echoing gentle drum beats outside his teepee would stay to float in his mind. The wild herbs would touch his inner thoughts and put him into a deep, deep sleep. A rest he had needed for a while.

Outside Woody's teepee, deer antlers hung on one side. He would always hang the bear claw necklace he'd gotten for killing the eight-foot grizzly bear. On the other side, hung his bear coat. In front of the teepee limbs of oak trees were dug deep into the ground, a dream catcher swung with the gentle breeze of air blowing through it. Long feathers of eagles on each side was meant the dream caught, would be taken away into another land away from the soul, so it could rest. Colorful beads outlined the circle of the dream catcher. Other feathers danced with the motion of the wind. Surrounded by hot steaming rocks to keep the fever down, Woody laid peacefully asleep in the protection of the medicine man.

Woody's wife would not be allowed inside in fear the fever would pass on to her. Each day, she sat next to the dream catcher singing, while the drummer filled the Indian camp with sounds that touched everyone's soul. Next to her, Woody's dog, More, waited for his master's return once again.

Going into the third day, Woody could now sit up and eat. The dream catcher had filtered all of Woody's dreams and separated the good from the bad. His mind could rest a while. Now began his journey into the life of an Indian tribe. He would learn to survive as well as learn to communicate with words. Each day he would sit with the chief's son who was the youngest. Teaching the young Indian boy the language of the white man would be easily passed over. To learn the language of the native people to Woody seemed so hard. . .

As days mingled together to form months, the months would spring up into years in Woody's life. Hunting would always be necessary as well as to have fun. In the native Indian people's gatherings, a day of horseback riding and fancy tricks on bareback horses was dangerous yet so fun. The sun beamed down with its flashes of heat. The wind blew gently upon the flat land, where the place to be used as a playground laid. Woody on his black stallion, which he'd named Lightning, sat looking at the Indian warriors run past him, Each would do a different trick.

Far in the distant ground, Woody could see dust forming into a huge low cloud. Dismounting his horse, he placed the palm of his hand to the ground, and in an instant, he knew what it meant. From the stories his father shared, it would be a stampede heading in his direction. Quickly mounting his horse, Woody called out to the Indian warriors. The stampede was coming full speed.

The chief's son, Two Feathers, in a quest to try to get out of the way, slipped off his horse on to the ground. Animal instincts told the horse it was dangerous to stick around and fled as fast as it could. Two Feathers stood alone while the others had ridden off, leaving him to stand in the midst of the stampede. Fear and shock overpowered the young Indian boy. He stood still motionless while the chief looked on. Woody watching remembered his father's story of how and when to kill, it would have to become an art, not a pleasure. Now was the time he would prove to be very wise. He pulled out the buffalo rifle from his leather scabbard. Picking up the metal sight and pointing in the direction of Two Feathers. In a low normal voice, he spoke to Lightning to keep the horse still and calm when he pulled the trigger of the buffalo rifle. The echoing boom went into the mountains and the Indian camp while everyone ran for safety. Only two bodies stood still. Two Feathers and the Indian chief who looked at his son, who would soon be stampeded to death. The bullet found its target but the dust had formed all around Two Feathers.

The chief's eyes released tears as he stood alone. He thought Woody had shot Two Feathers, so the young boy would feel no pain from the stampede. Instead, he had shot the lead buffalo, which had toppled over dead only a few yards away from Two Feathers. It had made the buffalo herd stampede divide into a V-shape leaving Two Feathers standing in the midst of the dust.

The chief dropped his head and would not blame Woody for killing Two Feathers, so he wouldn't feel any pain. The buffalo herd thundered by leaving the tribe in shock, the dust began to settle down. In the middle of the stampede tracks, laid the lead buffalo, dead from Woody's buffalo rifle. Yards in front of the dead buffalo, Two Feathers stood in shock and was shaking, but was still alive. To some day share his story with his children. Once again, Woody had displayed to be very wise at his young age. As the Indian chief looked in Woody's direction, he motioned that everything belonged to Woody.

The moon began its journey across the darkness of the sky, Woody sat looking at the dancers for a powwow that would awaken the spirits. To honor Woody once more, the chief stood tall next to Two Feathers. He motioned that his heart overflowed with respect for what and how Woody had saved his son. Walking up to Woody the chief held a beaded leather bag with gold nuggets the size of eyes. Two Feathers walked up and gave Woody a big hug.

He was surrounded by the native people who'd become like his family, but he still felt alone. It was then that he thought to leave and no one would stop him.

Standing for a moment Woody looked up at the moon. He looked back at the Indian chief. He placed his fist against his chest then pointed at the moon, while his hand continued a circle. The Indian chief looked at Woody for a moment. Tears formed at the corners of his eyes. He knew Woody was saying that it was time,, to follow the moon into a new day. Nodding twice the Indian chief spoke to his people. Some walked by hugging Woody for more than a moment. He would leave before sunrise. His wife could only look on and go wait inside the teepee, in hopes he might change his mind. Sitting next to the fire Woody drew a picture, for the chief to read. The picture held the circle of wagons with dots to indicate the wagon master and his men. Woody looked at the Indian chief and back down at the dots then pointed to each one patting his Colt .44 revolver to let him know, he would hunt and kill them all. The drummer stopped beating on the drums, Walked over to Woody handing him a beaded leather strap, which held two arrowhead flint rocks. The drummer rubbed them together; sparks of fire shot into the air. Woody understood he meant they would start a fire for his campfires. He would only need dry grass and beat the arrowhead flint rocks over the grass, like magic the fire would bloom into life.

Woody rode away on his horse Lightning. More the black dog followed behind. Almost four and a half years seemed to pass by as he had been with his Indian family. Now he was free to come and go as he pleased.

The sounds of howling wolves were calling More to come join the pack, but the words he spoke gently at nights comforted the dog. He had grown to like Woody and grown in size as well.

Over the mountains he would travel alone and often promised himself to someday look for the wagon master and his men. But, for now he needed to know if in fact a new world of hopes and dreams was awaiting in the distant land. In the darkness of nights, many times he could feel eyes watching him. But searching he never could see anyone standing anywhere, but still something stood and it WAS all the little hairs on his body. He could still feel the danger that loomed nearby. As the chills ran through his body like the cold wind at nights, the beam of light from Woody's campfire could be seen from far away, but only by wild animals for no human life seemed to be close by. Dozing off into a deep sleep, Woody would always use his saddle for a pillow. He could still hear his father say, "Real cowboys do." At times, the dreams seemed so real.

One night as Woody slept, he awoke to the sounds of growls and barks, More was fighting in the darkened night. Pulling his Colt .44 revolver out ready to shoot, he stood away from the light of the campfire. In the other hand, he held his Bowie knife, the fighting of wolves with More continued. He could not shoot in the direction of the fight, but he would shoot in the air instead to try and scare off the wolves. The silence after the shots told him the pack of wolves was gone. For a moment, he had thought More had followed behind. Waiting in the dark for a while, he stood with his back to a tree. More came into sight limping as if hurt. Calling out to More made the dog stop falling to the ground. He was badly hurt and all Woody could do was wait until daylight.

As the dawn's light began to shine over the mountains, Woody could see his dog was licking his wounds. It told him that his dog would be okay. Lightning had been traumatized by the dogs fighting and still seemed to be afraid. Woody stood next to it speaking to calm it down a bit. On the other side of the campfire laid a wolf, its throat had been torn and was laying open as it lay dead. More had killed the wolf, but had taken a bad beating in doing so. When night fell again, the pack of wolves would come calling again. Woody would have to move on and quickly with More on top of the saddle with him.

Riding all day Woody had come across a stone house, in the middle of nowhere. Trees and bushes hid it from sight. It would do to mend his dog, More, and rest. Also, to give Lightning time to rest as well, The next day's ride would begin early the next day. The stone house was very old with no boards on the windows or even a door. Part of the roof had collapsed into the house. Bushes and tree limbs cast shadows on the walls from the reflection of the moonlight. Starting a campfire Woody could eat and make his coffee from the beans the Indian women had given him. Woody sat alone and opened the leather beaded bag that held the carved bone smoking pipe. The smaller bag inside containing his father's tobacco had lasted him a very long time. For he had not used it but once or twice and in the saddle bag, he carried the tin can that held more tobacco he could use.

The campfire whipped up and down. Woody sat up against the wall in the stone house. Next to him, a small shelf leaned to one side. It seemed to be holding itself up with spider webs and vines from bushes. Tearing away the spider webs, he found three bottles of whiskey still full. Even though he had never drunk, He knew what they were. Sometimes when he was supposed to be asleep, he could hear his mother Maggie, telling Frank not to touch her, if he'd been drinking that stuff. Woody's thoughts went to his father Frank and he remembered him laughing after drinking one too many. A smile formed on Woody's face as he cleaned the bottle and pulled off the cork. Tasting it, he smiled even more. One sip had turned his life into another journey as he was now singing native calls to the spirits. Before the night was over, Woody had danced around the campfire in a powwow of his own. Drinking half a bottle, he walked around too drunk to know what and how to do anything as More looked on.

The morning light came through the roof, Woody sat where it had all started next to the little shelf. He closed his eyes and fell asleep. Out cold, he slept until the next night. The sounds of Lightning's hooves upon the ground awoke him.

Lightning was hungry and needing water as well. An old wooden bowl lay to one side of the shelf and Woody filled it with water from his canteen. The sun beamed through the roof onto the ground and as he gave his horse the water, the sparkle of shining metal caught his attention. Untying Lightning he removed the saddle and Led it outside, so he could eat grass and weeds.

Stepping back inside, Woody picked up the shiny metal. It was a Spanish medallion and as it popped open, the words on each side were, "Por Vida" which meant for life, but he had no clue what those words meant. Woody didn't know how to read Spanish.

In fact, he couldn't read at all. Throwing the medallion into his saddlebag he would keep it for himself.

Cooking a meal for himself and More, Woody remembered his father had once told him…In case of a hangover just drink a little more. Taking one big swig, he would feel better in moments. He would rest for the night to start another journey out onto the other side of the mountain forest.

The new day seemed to come so quickly. Woody stood up and stretched over the dying campfire. Throwing dirt on top of the burning ashes, he walked out and never would return again.

Saddling up Lightning Woody spoke softly, "Sure hope we find a place to get cleaned up." He looked at More saying, "You ready to move on?" More took a few steps and looked at Woody. He petted More on top of his head saying, "I guess that means yes!"

Mounted on his horse Woody looked like a giant of a man.

With the bear coat on and a full beard to match his long shaggy hair. He looked older than his age of nineteen going on twenty, but he was very wise and strong for his age. Under the rugged look, he had been through hell and back. But, life for Woody had just really begun.

CHAPTER FIVE

Slowly riding Lightning through the mountains forest. Woody could see an opening up ahead. Dismounting his horse, Woody led it through the opening as his eyes widened up. Could this be the Promised Land the wagon master and his men spoke about? The open meadow laid for miles with rolling hills and grassy patches of light green and yellow tones of grass. In the midst of the morning low clouds hid down below a town. Woody was now focusing on it.

Trees here and there amongst the buildings that released thin lines of smoke, spoke of life down below. No one would see him approach until he was right under their nose. Wondering if the wagon master and his men might be there, he would have to be very careful. It had been four and a half going on five years since his world had been turned upside down. Now the craving feelings of wanting to kill started to float to the top of Woody's mind.

At Lightning's side More walked as his ears stood straight up and his tail curled up. Once in a while, he looked up at Woody as if the dog was waiting on orders to attack. More had proven to protect Woody against the pack of wolves and now he was ready to protect him against anything or anybody. In the middle of the road that divided the town, he let Lightning set a slow pace.

Young children stopped chasing each other as they looked and pointed at him. From the cracks of the blacksmith shop, he could tell someone was watching him. Stopping for a moment, Woody studied the town. Dismounting his horse he held the reins in the direction of the blacksmith shop. In an instant a Spanish old man hurried to grab the reins and said, "Senor, will you be staying a while?"

Woody never looked at the old man as he spoke, "Yes, it will be a while."

The old man walked away with Lightning and said to himself, "I hope this crazy looking gringo doesn't want horseshoes on his dog?"

Woody acted as if he hadn't heard the old man, then cut a smile and headed for the saloon. More didn't lose a step as he walked next to Woody, "You'll have to wait outside," he told More.

Suddenly the swinging doors hit the side of the walls and Woody quickly reached for his Colt .44 on his hip. Rolling out onto the wooden porch, a cowboy stumbled trying to get up because he was kind of drunk. Two more cowboys flew out as they lost their balance and all three fell off the porch landing in front of Woody.

The swinging doors stood still for only a moment then swung open once more. It was the bartender holding a shotgun in one hand and tossing the three cowboys' hats in the air yelling, "And stay out!" Standing tall, the bartender looked at Woody for the stranger was not about to come in with the dog.

The three drunken cowboys didn't pay attention to the bartender any more. Woody was their main attraction as they stood up, one of them said, "Well, well. Looky here! If it ain't a mountain man!"

Another spoke out loud, "I hope you got some money or I might get a little mad." All three cowboys started to laugh at Woody as the bartender looked on.

Woody took a step closer to them as More growled and said, "I haven't fed my dog in a day. You three just might be what he needs to eat."

Stumbling the cowboys looked at More as he growled at them. The one who'd not spoken yet, looked at Woody saying, "Pay them no mind." And backed up as he whispered, "We'll meet again, Mountain Man."

Woody never let go of his Colt .44 until the three drunken cowboys were out of sight. Before he could say a word, the bartender told him as he walked back into the saloon, "The dog stays outside. "

The doors swung open up again, but this time it was Woody walking in as he spoke to More, "Stay." More sat to one side as Woody disappeared in the saloon.

This was Woody's first time in a saloon, but in his mind, he knew that no one would ever know that. Walking up to the bar, he laid his buffalo rifle against the bar and took off his hat, placing it on the barrel of his rifle.

The bartender held out a hand to Woody and said, "J. D. Freeman."

Woody grabbed the bartender's hand and he could feel the grip; he was checking for strength. Woody held on a moment then looked at JD Freeman saying, "Carlyle Winston Causey, better known as Woody."

JD was every bit six foot two and a barrel of a man, yet it wasn't fat but pure muscle as his weight hit around 245 or just maybe tipping a little over 250. JD's eyes were light blue, but held the seriousness of eye contact that told you not to mistake him as soft. While they were standing on the saloon porch,

JD's boots seemed to Woody to be about 13 or 14 inches. The three drunken cowboys had been lucky they didn't get those boots where the sun don't shine. The thick mustache hid JD's smile. But, Woody could tell by the way JD's sparkling blue eyes lit up, that he was now smiling as he let go of his hand. The only difference in the two was that Woody was slim but very strong. Most of all he was much younger than anyone could tell, because of his long shaggy hair and thick beard hid the real Woody deep inside.

JD looked at Woody once more after a good overall sizing up and said, "That's a buffalo rifle, isn't it?"

Woody took the shot glass from the bar downing it all and blew out air to let JD know the whiskey was strong. He picked up his hat from the barrel laying it on the bar, reached for the buffalo rifle and handed it over the bar.

JD reached for the rifle with both hands to show respect and carefulness of not dropping it. "Now this is a beauty. Where did you get it?"

Woody sat motionless thinking that maybe JD was talking too much to a stranger he just met. "It was a gift." He stood up and asked where he could get a room; JD could sense that the conversation had caught Woody by surprise.

"Don't worry; I don't like anyone in this town." JD whispered to Woody winking. "Sharp keen men seldom ride through this part of the land."

Woody grabbed his buffalo rifle and put on his hat. Looking around he pulled a piece of gold nugget out and said, "This ought to cover everything while I'm in town." He took a few steps saying. "I like breakfast warm."

JD didn't hesitate at all and said, "Yes, sir." putting the gold nugget in his pocket. He reached under the counter and walked around the bar quickly calling out to Woody. "Sir, this is the best whiskey in the world!"

Woody took the bottle by the neck holding it up to the light coming from outside; it was the same kind he found in the stone house. He stood quiet for a moment and looked back at JD. "I'll be back tonight for a room."

JD looked at Woody and again did not hesitate to speak by saying. "Yes, sir."

Stepping outside the door, Woody walked back across to the blacksmith shop with More next to him. Opening the door, the old man, Galindo, stood over the burning kettle where he'd been heating up a pair of horseshoes to fit Lightning. Woody walked over to Lightning and leaned his buffalo rifle against the corral.

He reached for the saddle bags while he spoke to Galindo, "I'd like to leave the dog here with you if it's okay."

"Sure, I don't mind, Senor," Galindo said looking down at More. "In fact, I'll keep him free of charge because he can be a watchdog tonight." Galindo smiled, two capped front teeth sparkled from the burning light inside the shop. He stood five feet four inches and weighed 155. The gold caps on his teeth were real gold as well as, the wire framed spectacles he used when working. The thick black mustache was well kept and seemed to be gray- free for the old man's age.

Opening the saddle bags, Woody placed the bottle of whiskey inside with the other two he had left wrapped in fur so they wouldn't break.

Looking on, Galindo told Woody, "I used to drink that stuff years ago."

Woody turned around asking, "What made you stop?"

Galindo stared into the fire answering, "It's a long story, Senor."

Woody knew he touched the old man's inner thoughts, walked over to him and placed his hand on Galindo's shoulder and said, "I'll be here a while, my friend," looking into the fire. He handed Galindo a piece of gold nugget. Holding it, Galindo didn't think much of it. He'd had his share of such stones and rocks.

Sitting on a tree stump next to the fire, Woody asked Galindo if he could feed the dog while he was gone.

"I'll treat him like my own, Senor."

Something told Woody this man had lost someone he loved because, of how he would seem to be drifting off at times. Woody reached into the other side of his saddlebags and pulled out the silver pendant he'd found in the stone house. Because of the Spanish words, "Por Vida", he thought to give it to the old man because he was Spanish. Holding it out to Galindo made him stop what he was doing and dropped the iron tongs on the ground.

Slowly reaching for the pendant, the old man stared at it and popped it open like knowing that it would. Looking inside, he sat on the ground as Woody looked on. In moments tears formed at the edges of Galindo's eyes and asked, "Senor, where did you find this?"

Woody was puzzled at how the old man was reacting and told him, "I found it in an old stone house in the mountains."

"Senor, it's a small world." Holding the pendant up, he asked Woody if he knew what "Por Vida" meant.

Woody shook his head no and said, "All I know is that my horse dug it up with his hoof one day inside that stone house. I also found three bottles of whiskey."

Galindo closed his eyes and began praying in Spanish. Woody knew it wasn't the right time to ask any more questions. Even to stick around so he slowly walked out of the blacksmith shop.

Walking across the street back to the saloon, Woody sensed someone was looking at him from the windows above. The curtains were moving slowly. The wind couldn't have made them move because the window was closed. Stopping for a moment he looked straight up towards the window, to let whomever it was know he already saw them. The curtains didn't move anymore. Woody was curious as he walked into the saloon. He sat down, JD reached under the counter and brought out a silver platter with a matching silver dome.

It kept the food warm inside. "Mr. Woody, got something for you." JD said, removing the silver dome it revealed a well-done steak with potatoes and a small bowl of gravy on the side of the steak.

"I know you said you liked your breakfast warm," JD said.

Woody smiled looking at all the food, JD reached under the counter and brought out a basket full of fresh warm biscuits the size of a man's fist, "I know it's not breakfast, but I just thought you might enjoy this." he said, placing the basket next to the platter of food. JD walked away so Woody could enjoy his meal.

With the last biscuit, Woody wiped the bowl clean. Then, he filled the shot glass with whiskey, stood up turning towards the stairs, and downed the whiskey. His eyes caught sight of the most beautiful young lady he'd ever seen. As he sat the shot glass on the counter, JD stood on the other side picking up the dirty dishes. Woody whispered, "Who's that?"

JD broke a smile, looked towards the stairs and back at Woody, "That's my daughter, Her name is Jennifer,"

Woody felt embarrassed and asked. "Where's my room?"

JD turned around to face the back wall behind him and stood on a small stool to reach the deer antlers that held keys on wire rings. Slowly, turning towards Woody, JD told him. "That's why I threw the drunken cowboys out earlier." Tossing the key ring to Woody, he noticed the key had a number on it. "Your room is next to hers."

As Woody walked past Jennifer; her eyes never looked at him and he knew exactly why. The big bear coat, long shaggy hair and the beard he had never cut spoke for him. As he walked up the stairs, he remembered his father had caught him shaving with his razor. He stopped and closed his eyes and could still hear his father saying, "Boy, you just awoke the hairs on your face and because of that, you'll have a full beard some day." He opened his eyes and held his beard with both hands; his father had been right because the beard had grown to look like a wild tumbleweed. He broke a smile and continued to find his room. As he unlocked the door, a couple walked past by him. From the corner of his eye, he could tell the woman had put dollar bills in her breasts. Never turning back to look at them, Woody disappeared into his room.

Once inside Woody walked less than ten feet and with one hand pulled the curtain open. Down below, the street that divided the town in half, stood Galindo speaking to a cowboy reaching for his horse. The Cowboy walked under him into the saloon. Woody closed the curtain and turned to one side. A full-length mirror hung on a door that had to be the bathroom. He took a long puzzled look. The reflections on the water were nothing like looking at himself in a mirror. He heard a rapid knock on the door that was kind of soft. Woody opened the door, Jennifer stood outside saying, "Are you ready for your bath water, sir?"

"Sure," He replied walking away.

"Leave the door unlocked. I don't want to keep knocking and don't undress until I'm well out of your way," she said and started to leave. She never noticed he was as young as she was and if he didn't get that shaggy hair and tumble weed off his face, no one else would either.

Jennifer stood at the doorway of Woody's room and yelled, "Mountain man! Mountain man! You better get in there before the water gets cold again." She slammed the door and she was gone.

Woody had laid down fully dressed on the bed and had dozed off into a deep sleep.

The bath water was hot but would cool off. Woody sat in the tub smoking his bone carved pipe and sipping from a whiskey bottle. A knock on the door caught him by surprise. He stepped out of the tub and grabbed his Colt .44. He went to the door, but didn't open it. "Who's there?" He asked.

"Mountain man, when you're finished with the bath water, just pull the plug, the dirty water knows where to go," Jennifer said.

"Sure," Woody said smiling and getting back into the tub washing away weeks of dirt.

Woody had never owned a bed of his own and, in fact, he'd never slept in one. Always having to sleep on the floor or on the open ground, the bed seemed perfect and he didn't want to get up. The knock on the door woke Woody up from dreaming. He sat up in bed reaching for his Colt .44. "Who's there?" He asked.

Jennifer's voice said, "It doesn't matter whose there. Your breakfast awaits you downstairs. Don't keep Pa waiting."

"Sure," Woody said yawning and nodding his head.

It didn't take Woody long to eat and walk across the street to the blacksmith shop. The sounds of the blacksmith shop revealed Galindo was at work in the early morning hours. Woody stood at the entrance of the shop. Galindo stopped at once walking to Woody with open arms and said, "Mountain man, my friend, Please come in, Senor." He turned and pointed to Lightning, "Senor, your horse has shoes now and your dog is well fed." He walked over to More and pet him on the head. "I'm sure glad he likes beans, Senor. I hate to throw them away."

Woody cut a smile, but Galindo couldn't tell because of the tumbleweed beard. He placed his hand on Galindo's shoulder and asked. "My friend, do you know where I can go get my hair cut and a clean shave?"

Galindo looked up at Woody smiling and said, "Are you kidding me, Senor? I happen to be the master of all trades." He walked over to the double doors of the blacksmith shop and closed them both. Once the doors were closed, he locked them with a long four-by-four that fit on the braces on each door and told Woody, "Senor, please come with me." The blacksmith shop was Galindo's home. A door connected both places together. Inside the first room, he noticed hats on the wall and about a dozen pairs of boots on a shelf. To the right of the room a rack of shirts and pants outlined the back wall. Opening another door, Galindo said, "Come in here, Senor." It was the front of another shop he had. The old man was in fact a master of all trades. Now he was cutting Woody's hair and after that would shave the tumbleweed away.

Sitting in the chair, Woody looked out the windows of the barbershop and asked Galindo, "My friend, is the bartender a good man?

In an instant Galindo did not hesitate saying, "Senor, that man is the only man I trust here. Yes, he is a good man."

Woody knew that his buffalo rifle was safe in his room at the saloon.

Galindo stopped cutting Woody's hair and stood in front of him asking, "Why do you ask, Senor?"

Woody looked at Galindo and replied, "I'm thinking of taking him a bowl of beans."

Galindo looked at Woody for a moment and as the laughter of both went outside, the people looked on as Woody sat in the chair.

The word got out that the dirty mountain man who'd rode into town was getting cleaned up. Galindo cut away at Woody's head, he told him about the pendant Woody had given him. It had been 25 years now according to the old man, but it meant more to him than anything in the world. He stopped for a moment to wipe away a tear as he shared more of his life story. An Indian raid had ended the lives of his family.

After the tumbleweed had fallen to the ground piece-by-piece Galindo said, "Senor, I had no idea you were so young." Sweeping the hair into a dustpan, he motioned for Woody to look in the mirror.

Woody was very young and very handsome as the women who stood on the porch told the story itself. From across the street Jennifer looked to see what all the commotion was, but she could not see inside the barbershop because of all the women in front of the windows.

Galindo told Woody, "Senor, I think you need to come with me." Back in the room where the clothes hung on racks, Galindo picked out a black set of clothes with a white long-sleeve shirt. He walked over to the hats and picked one pitch black with a flat brim all around it. Around the hat was a rawhide white band that made the hat stand out.

Standing four or five feet from Woody, Galindo told him, "Senor, you now need a new pair of boots and these I made for my son years ago. You are very welcome to have them, Senor."

Woody sat on a stool and removed his old pair and was about to stick his foot into one, but Galindo told him, "Inside those boots is a pair of spurs to fit perfect. I made them from silver candlesticks that belonged to my wife. Please wear them with honor."

Woody asked Galindo shaking his head, "My friend, why are you doing this?"

Galindo took a step towards a table that had beautiful handkerchiefs folded on top. As he grabbed one he looked at Woody handing it to him saying, "Senor, sometimes the smallest things are the most: important things in this world." He patted the Spanish pendant around his neck. Taking a few steps he opened his arms making motions in the air saying, "Senor, I want you to please come every day in this room and pick something to wear because I'm giving it all to you." Galindo took a step closer to Woody and said, "And a bowl of beans."

Both men stood laughing more than they'd laughed in years and their friendship had just started. Woody started for the door.

Galindo called to him, "My friend, Senor, there's one more thing that goes with all this." He went into his bedroom and came back with a red wine colored cloth. It held a holster and gun that had been made of pure silver and the handles on each side were carved ivory.

Woody walked down the porch along one side of the town; More walked next to him. Everyone in town kept looking at the stranger who had transformed into a handsome young man. Walking back towards the saloon, his eyes locked with the sheriff who introduced himself as Justin Hunt- Shaking his hand, Woody told the sheriff he wasn't planning on staying long. He looked at the sheriff's badge and said. "Carlyle Winston Causey, better known as Woody."

CHAPTER SIX

Jennifer hurried down the steps with the empty buckets she used to fill bathtubs up with hot water. Woody walked slowly towards the first step, then all of the sudden, Jennifer landed on his chest. He caught her midair. Having no idea it was Woody, she said, "Oh. My God! Excuse me, sir."

Woody held on to her and didn't want to let go. He held on for more than a moment and said. "It's okay, Jennifer."

She walked away and stood next to her father. "Who is that?" she asked.

JD smiled because he knew how Jennifer was towards good-looking cowboys and answered. "That's the mountain man,. He got all cleaned up."

Her jaw dropped as Woody disappeared up the steps into his room.

Once inside, Woody walked over to the window, pulled the curtains open and reached for his pipe. Down below, he could see the sheriff walking across the street towards the jail. Woody stood glancing at the women who's still stood speaking to each other and he knew it all might be the daily rumors they shared each day.

Stepping from behind a wagon, the three cowboys JD had kicked out of the saloon approached the sheriff. Without any hesitation, all three opened fire on the sheriff. Justin Hunt in moments laid dead, the three cowboys ran into the blacksmith shop. Galindo would also be caught by surprise and could be easily put to death. Woody quickly put his pipe down which he'd never gotten a chance to light. ? He ran down the steps, JD was walking out of the saloon with his shotgun in his hands. Jennifer yelled at Woody as she went behind the bar, "Woody, please be careful."

In her eyes Woody was no longer the mountain man who'd ridden into town all dirty, she had quickly fallen in love seeing him all cleaned up.

Outside on the street everyone gathered around the sheriff, JD knelt next to him. Woody stooped down at JD's side and put a hand on his shoulder saying, "I'll bring them back dead or alive, but I'll bring them back."

Woody quickly walked across the street as everyone looked on. In moments, he disappeared into the open darkness within the blacksmith shop. The gunfire that followed was coming from more than one gun. As the shots rang out, one cowboy toppled out into the street and crumpled down dead.

More shots rang out inside the blacksmith shop, More could be heard barking. The barks turned into growls as he caught the hand of one of the cowboys. His teeth dug deep into the flesh, the cowboy yelled out. But, in moments, Galindo splattered the cowboy into a wall. His shotgun rang out both barrels at once, ending the life of the second cowboy.

Storming out of the blacksmith shop, Lightning ran out into the street running over the dead cowboy. More shots rang out as the third cowboy was put to death. For a minute or so, it was very quiet. Galindo pulled on the cowboy's leg and drug him out next to the first one in the street.

More slowly walked out backwards as his head looked upwards. It was Woody More was looking at, dragging the third cowboy out by his arm. He stood looking in the direction of JD who was carrying the dead sheriff. Woody turned his gaze to see Jennifer on the saloon porch. His world seemed to be turning around once again. He fell to the ground because he'd taken a slug in his gut. More stood next to his master's side.

Jennifer ran across the street and turned Woody around, and placed his head on her lap whispering, "Please don't, Woody. Please, please don't die."

His eyes held on and could see Jennifer's face so beautiful asking, "Is Galindo okay?"

"Yes, Galindo's okay," she answered as he closed his eyes.

She kissed his cheek saying, "Stay with me, Woody."

He could hear her voice, but his mind was slipping away very fast. Her voice turned into Maggie's voice. He could hear his mother yell, "Run!" His thoughts danced back and forth from the wagon trail to the Indian camp. Woody could not hear nor speak he had passed out.

JD laid the sheriff on the saloon porch then looked for Woody, but he wasn't standing anywhere. He had not seen Woody fall and now he could see Jennifer sitting on the ground with Woody's head on her lap. JD could only imagine if his friend was dead or alive.

In moments, he walked away with Woody in his arms. Jennifer carried Woody's hat a few yards behind. Galindo said to her softly, "He will be all right, Senorita." She wiped away tears from her eyes and couldn't believe how a stranger had caught her heart so fast.

JD walked up the steps to Woody's room and laid him on the bed saying, "Did anyone get the doctor?"

"Forget the doctor. Get me some hot water to clean my hands and the wound," Galindo said from the foot of the bed. "I'll need a bottle of whiskey, too," He said reaching into his pocket for his sharp pocketknife.

Jennifer appeared with the bucket she used for hot water and asked Galindo, "Is there anything else I can do?"

He'd already removed Woody's shirt by now and looked at Jennifer lost in thought. The scars across Woody's chest he'd gotten in the circle of death, at the Indian camp was only a reminder he'd been through hell and back. Galindo cleaned Woody's body, told her, "He's got another scar bigger than that across his back." Jennifer looked at Galindo with puzzled eyes as he spoke softly, "This young man has been through hell Senorita, if he makes it through this, he'll be very lucky." She could tell Galindo meant she was very pretty and Woody would like her as well. He took her hand and walked her out saying, "It's going to get very dirty in here Senorita. Can you please wait outside?"

JD was back from bringing a bottle of whiskey. "I'm staying in here with you," He told Galindo handing him the bottle.

They closed the door behind them and Jennifer went downstairs. Inside the bedroom, Galindo took a big swig from the bottle, then reached for Woody's head. Raising it up slowly, he gave him some whiskey. Galindo knew a thing or two as he'd told Woody, he was a master of all trades. Cleaning his knife with the whiskey, he handed the bottle back to JD. Galindo began to dig out the slug from Woody's gut.

Watching Galindo digging into Woody's gut made JD take a big swig and then placed the bottle down on the corner table.

In minutes the slug hit inside the metal tray. Galindo poured whiskey on his knife. Cutting long strips of cloth to wrap around Woody. First, he wiped Woody's body clean saying, "He'll be okay, lost a lot of blood, but he'll be okay."

JD sat in the chair opposite to the corner table with hot water and the metal tray that held the slug. "He's going to be very hungry when he wakes up," Galindo told JD as he walked out the room with all the bloody rags.

He gently closed the door and went downstairs. Jennifer looked at him with curious eyes. He winked at her to let her know Woody would be okay. She turned around and picked up Woody's hat placing it over her breast, hugging it swaying from side to side with both eyes closed. It seemed she was thankful he would make it. Galindo stopped at the door and called out to her, "Think you can tame a mountain man?" He winked again smiling at her and disappeared out the door.

Jennifer stood looking at everyone coming into the saloon and in a moment's time, every barstool and chair was filled. The daily drunks sat around, some asleep but the recent newcomers were mostly women. Jennifer would have her hands full. The single women sat speaking to each other and just like each day they shared daily rumors, today would be different because Jennifer was going to have some fun. She stood in the middle of the floor as she spoke to all the women, "Listen up! Today is a special day and does anyone know what happens here on special days?"

In the corner of the saloon atop a stool, an old drunk stood as he tried to keep his balance and not fall. "I know." Jennifer smiled because she already knew he would answer correct because she had already put him up to it. He said, "Free drinks.''

Jennifer clapped her hands and said, "That's right." She asked, "What else?"

The town drunk still standing on the stool answered, "Drink or get out."

Jennifer clapped once more saying, "That's right." She started passing out bottles of whiskey along with clean shot glasses to drink from.

Not long into the night all the women began to feel a little tipsy as they loosened their hair and removed garments to shake off the night's heat. What Jennifer had hoped for would soon take place. The women began to point at each other rolling their eyes. Telling each other they could lie better or whatever they were listening to was a lie. Then it all began as one loud slap took place, then another. In minutes the hair pulling and clothes tearing started, some of the women laid their heads on the tables out cold.

The town drunk's job that night was to cut off anyone's hair if they passed out. He cut away with a sharp knife and at times got so close to the scalp, he had to stop and start again. Jennifer laughed her heart out as she pushed her way through the crowd refilling empty shot glasses. In her mind she knew when Woody's health got better, the bald-headed women would be nowhere in sight, until their hair grew back out.

JD looked on as Jennifer was having her way. Rubbing the back of his neck, he was too tired to go downstairs and yelled, "Jennifer, the party's over!" Then he headed to his room. Jennifer smiled and began telling everyone to leave, even pushed a few out the doors.

Galindo sat in his barbershop looking across towards the saloon and polished the silver pendant. Woody would be okay, he just needed rest and a good meal whenever he got up. The night was very quiet as the moon sent a glow over the town. Slowly a lone rider rode his horse down the street and out of Galindo's view. For a moment, he stood outside the barbershop porch as he searched for the lone rider. The rider's horse stood next to the blacksmith shop, Galindo made his way to the horse and could hear someone inside. The lone rider had made his way inside because Galindo hadn't closed the doors, due to the beautiful night. Calling out into the darkness of the night, Galindo took a few steps inside the doors and said. "Who's there? May I help you?"

Everything went pitch black as he dropped to the ground. The lone rider had knocked Galindo out cold.

After dragging Galindo deep inside, the lone rider came out into the glow of the night. Standing for only a moment, the Lone rider took his horse inside the blacksmith shop and slowly closed the doors behind him.

Nothing had ever scared More than the night everyone had been killed on the wagon trail and even though it been about four and a half years ago. The dog could still remember the silhouette of the point man. More laid quietly in the blacksmith shop in fear of death. For an animal to be afraid of the point man meant the man held a presence of death.

Inside the blacksmith shop, Galindo awoke tied to a chair with his hands behind him and each leg tied to the chair. Across his eyes, a bandana kept him from seeing the point man. Slowly Galindo could feel the point man running a sharp knife across his throat and said, "You will only get one chance to live, so do not try anything," Stars danced in Galindo's head. The point man hit him with the butt of the shotgun, he found inside the room. Then the butt of the gun found Galindo's side. For a moment, he listened as he tried to spit the blood from his mouth but the cloth stuck in his mouth would not allow him to. Wondering if the point man was still in the room, Galindo lowered his head in hopes to listen for a clue.

Then the boot across his chest sent him flying backwards still tied to the chair, lying on the floor the point man's footsteps slowly walked over to him and said. "I told you only had one chance to live and that was it. The next time I sense something, you're dead on the spot." The point man was very keen and had sensed Galindo trying to listen for him. Grabbing Galindo's hair from the top of his head, the point man picked him back up saying,

"I've been on a long ride and need to get cleaned up a bit."

Galindo could hear the point man as he rummaged through the drawers of his room. The squeaks of the water pump inside the blacksmith shop, told Galindo the point man was getting water to bath. After a while, he could hear the point man's footsteps approaching. He went airborne still tied to the chair. He was very strong carrying Galindo into the bath area and placing him inside the tub of water. He could hear the chuckle from the point man as the water was soaking his clothes. It was quiet for a while. Galindo toppled backwards into the water unable to help himself. Holding his breath, he held on as much as he could. Raising back up from his hair being pulled upwards, he took in more air. The point man was now playing with his life; whispering in his ear. The point man spoke very clear that he would soon return and left Galindo still tied to the chair. As he sat in the chair, he could feel the rope loosening up from the water. He knew he'd have to get free because if he didn't, the point man would kill him when he returned. Pulling his hands free, he took off the bandana from his eyes and pulled out the cloth from his mouth. Reaching in the water, he untied the rope that bound his legs to the chair. He was free and would have to hurry and find his shotgun. Looking everywhere, he could not find it. He ran to the doors of the blacksmith shop that still swung open. The point man had taken the shotgun with him.

Stepping out into the street, Galindo noticed More was in a state of shock; fear had overtaken the dog. Whoever the point man was had more than the presence of death with him. He had Galindo's shotgun that would stand out and come daylight it would give him up because it was made of pure silver. Galindo had handcrafted it himself.

Galindo quickly walked across the street to the saloon.

He banged on the doors behind the swinging doors hoping he would wake up JD. In moments JD opened the doors and held his shotgun straight towards Galindo's body, "It's me Senor, Galindo from the blacksmith shop." He was bleeding from his mouth and soaked in water.

Letting Galindo in, JD called out to Jennifer, "Turn all the lanterns on; we need light in here." He could tell something strange had happened and the lights would help scare off whoever it was.

The dawn's light was beginning to show as the town sat open prey to the coming of the wagon master and his men; saddled straight up in their saddles. The wagon master rode between two riders and the others rode in fours and fives next to each other. Their presence spelled nothing but trouble and no one was about to try to stop them. Dismounting their horses, the wagon master introduced himself, "Jerry Wheat" while reaching out to shake JD's hand. He asked for rooms for himself and his men while walking inside the saloon. Once inside, the wagon master spoke to JD as he downed a shot of whiskey, "What's the sheriff's name?" JD looked at the wagon master and explained that the sheriff had been ambushed by three cowboys but that his name had been Justin Hunt.

The wagon master took another shot glass and held it up to the morning light coming into the saloon. "I think I knew him."

JD could tell the wagon master was lying and had said he'd known him because he was dead.

The wagon master spoke again and walked to the double swinging doors, laying a hand on top of each, "I'm taking people across the mountains to a better place if anyone wants to go. I'll be leaving in a week." He turned around and asked JD, "Want to go?"

JD smiled at him and quickly said, "No thanks, I'm fine right here."

The rugged men started coming inside after dusting themselves off. From the building across the street, the single women all wore some type of hat so no one could tell what had happened to them the night before. Smiling and waving at the cowboys, they would sign up to ride the wagon master's offer.

Each day that passed more people from outside the county line, were showing up with every cent they'd saved to join the wagon trail, Wagons outlined the street waited on the week to pass.

Upstairs Woody looked on as the wagon master and his men stood along the sides of wagons which made his blood begin to boil with anger. The gun shot was still painful but he could walk slowly, Making his way downstairs. He wanted to shoot the wagon master on the spot. Instead, he just walked across the street to Galindo's blacksmith shop. Woody told him to close the doors behind him as More growled at the cowboys. He looked at More and could tell the dog was afraid, but growled to let Woody know danger loomed yards away. Walking over to More' Woody turned around and yelled at his dog, "More" to quiet him down. Woody had sat on the stool inside the blacksmith shop, The crowd of cowboys was right in his path of view, Hearing the word "More "a cowboy in the crowd slowly turned to see who had called him. The doors to the blacksmith shop slowly closed, Woody could still see in his mind four and a half years ago. The cowboy on the ground he'd shot with the buffalo rifle saying, "More." Woody now knew who he was and how he looked, His gut still hurt so bad.

Helpless Woody wanted to kill them all, but would have to wait out the storm in his mind. As well as the gut shot he'd now held on to.

Galindo knelt next to Woody asking, "What's on your mind Senor? Do you know those men?"

Woody nodded answering. "Yes I do. They all are no good,"

Galindo helped Woody stand up as they looked through the cracks, of the wooden slabs of the blacksmith shop. He whispered, "One of them almost killed me last week. He left me for dead, Senor." He told Woody he had been the first one in town.

Woody didn't need any more information about who did it, because the point man was always ahead of them all. Woody looked at Galindo saying, "The one who did it was Moore; he's the point man for the wagon master." He walked over to his horse, Lightning, and said. "We'll be following them shortly." Galindo stood next to Woody and said, "Senor; you're in no condition to ride anything right now,"

"Well then; hook me up a wagon so I can follow them. I'll tie my horse to it."

"I got a buggy out back, not a wagon," Galindo said, pointing to the back door.

"Then I'll ride out of here in a buggy," Woody said smiling.

Galindo said to himself. "You gringos are crazy people."

Then he turned to Woody saying. "I'll go with you, Senor. You will need some help." He did need help and Galindo would have to do.

The next day the wagon train would be leaving. Woody would have to spend one more night at the saloon before he'd have to leave. Speaking to JD about what had happened years ago.

Jennifer listened from the crack of her opened door.

They spoke in the hallway upstairs looking at the wagon master and his men.

As the night rolled around, Woody sat in his room alone, thinking of how to bring down the wagon master and his men. Then a knock on his door awoke Woody, from being lost in thought of killing them all. As he opened the door, Jennifer stood wanting to come in. He looked at her knowing it would be the last time he'd see her. Stepping aside, he let her come in. From the moment he had set eyes on her, he'd liked her. Now, behind closed doors, the wound would not stop him from making love to her. Jennifer was much more than his Indian wife and she seemed to care even more as she lost herself making love to Woody. The night seemed so short as the knock at Woody's door awoke him up. Jennifer was still asleep as he opened the door to see it was JD. He looked at JD then dropped his eyes. JD said.

"Son, at least it's you and not those rugged cowboys," He handed Woody a basket of food asking. "All I need to know will you ever come back here if everything turns out right?"

Woody nodded his head saying "I promise to come back some day." Taking the basket of food in one hand and shaking JD's hand with the other, they each left it at that.

Closing the door, Jennifer opened her eyes asking. "Who was that?"

"It was your father," Woody said setting the basket of food on the corner table. He bent over to kiss her saying. "I promised him I'd be back again." She smiled kissing Woody once again.

Riding away the wagon master and his men led the wagon train away from the town towards the mountains. Woody counted a total of eighteen wagons that had become scattered out in the open land. Following the wagon train Woody stayed far behind. He rode in the little black buggy. Galindo would not be with him and when he woke up from the headache, that put him to sleep from Woody's gun to the back of his head. Woody would be long gone, He had decided to go alone.

CHAPTER SEVEN

Following the snake like trails through the bottom of the valleys, would at times bring pain to Woody's gut wound. More sat next to him on the little buggy seat. He looked around with his ears pointing straight up. In the distance up ahead; dust flew from the wagon train. Woody was in no condition to follow.

The concern he had for the people on the wagon train was and would be more than anyone could ever imagine. In about a week or two on the trail. The wagon master and his men would choose a spot somewhere, to slaughter everyone including the horses. Woody could still hear in his mind the wagon master saying. "Next time we'll kill the next wagon train during the day, so we can see everyone." He'd sat above them in the tree he'd climbed to escape deaths. On the last wagon train nearly five years ago. Making camp for the night, Woody's fire would have to be behind some huge boulders, so that he could not be seen from far away. The circle of wagons would be safe at night. But any day as the dawn's light shined upon the country's land, everyone could be killed because the wagon master would keep his word. To slaughter everyone in daylight for fear someone getting away, as Woody once did.

In the back of the buggy laid a potato sack with food Galindo had thought to eat, when he would be coming with Woody.

As Woody looked inside, he found bread, cheese, a bottle of whiskey, dry beef jerky and a box of matches. JD had given him a basket of food for the journey as well. Inside the saddlebags, the three bottles of whiskey still remained unopened. He smiled as he slowly walked over to Lightning, giving it rope to move around and graze on the grass. He poured water out of a barrel into a tin bowl Galindo had placed in the buggy. Turning around looking at More, he said. "Well my friend, we can eat now." Woody knew his dog was hungry and that More would help him if danger came his way.

Resting after the meal, Woody couldn't sleep. The pain seemed to be getting worse each hour that passed. Sipping whiskey, he looked into the fire. Remembering Maggie next to the campfire right before the wagon master and his men had killed everyone.

How she had yelled, "Run!" Now on the trail of the wagon train.

He would not run but face them with the wisdom; he'd learned listening to Frank's stories. Also the wisdom he had learned from his Indian friends.

Looking around the night darkened into a pitch black. The thick clouds danced above him. Then the wind began to pick up as it got cooler. Far away lightning flashes whipped across the sky. A storm was on its way. In moments, the sprinkles of raindrops landed all around Woody. The lightning was now shooting right beyond Woody's camp. The roar of thunder that followed seemed to make the clouds release more rain. In a very short time; sheets of rain poured over his campfire and over his body as well, The cold wind sent chills into his body, as sharp pains made him twitch, Covering up with his bear coat, he drank big drinks of whiskey in hopes to get warm. The cold wet rain had soaked far into his life. Trembling Woody was getting very weak and by

74

morning, he had gotten a fever which had turned into pneumonia. It left him lying on the muddy ground passed out. For hours he laid out in the open valley's dangerous darkness. Next to him, More sat looking for any danger to come his way.

Slowly the dawn's light blue sky started to spread over the valley and on to the mountains at the right side of Woody's path. The storm had passed, but Woody still laid out cold because he drank more than he should have, Waking up to the sound of More's barking, Woody could only open his eyes, because he was too weak to sit up. As the chills would come and go leaving his gunshot wound, with sharp flashing pains going through his body. More jumped over Woody's body without a sound. Then In the distance, he could hear More growling at something.

Trying to sit up Woody would slip back down. The pain and chills would take control. Someone was behind him for now whoever it was, was removing the soaked bear coat off Woody's body. He could hear a low cold voice speaking to someone else, "Start the fire again, we got a sick cowboy on our hands."

In the background, Woody could hear someone breaking twigs. The one who'd spoken was now kneeling right in front of him.

An old man of about 55 or 60 smiled at Woody as he rubbed his bushy gray beard. "Son, how long you been here alone?"

Woody closed his eyes too weak to speak and passed out once more. It had been hours before he opened his eyes again. The old man had made himself a good place to roll out his bedroll. While looking at Woody, he sat down to speak. He removed a weather beaten hat, which seemed to have a bullet hole going through the torn brim.

"Seen you a ways up yesterday." The old man adjusted his hat again and rubbed his bushy gray beard. He handed Woody the saddle bags he'd gotten from the back of the wagon. "These here bottles of whiskey for a special occasion, son?"

Woody shook his head no, then slowly began to sit up but was very weak and dropped back down. He told the old man, "Drink all you want."

Licking his lips, the old man opened the bottle and took a big swig. "Name's Joe Riggins," he said setting down the bottle next to his bedroll. Pointing behind Woody, to the fire that now whipped flames of heat towards Woody's body, Riggins said. "That there's my grandson." As he looked towards the mountains, he took a deep breath of air. "His folks now lay side by side up there in them mountains." Taking another big swig, he continued, "Wagon rolled off a cliff and killed them both." Standing up, Riggins told Woody, "Me and my grandson Henry buried them and decided to turn back."

Woody knew how hard at times the mountains were to climb, even find a way where a path could be used. Henry walked around where Woody could see him. A thin redhead freckled kid about ten years old stood bowlegged in front of Woody wearing a straw hat and packed a gun inside his britches. Smiling Henry reached out to shake Woody's hand. Woody shook the kid's hand and noticed his grip was somewhat strong for such a young age. "Glad to meet you Henry; Woody said. Pointing to the buggy, he told them, "There's food in the back. You're welcome to it."

In moments, both Riggins and Henry enjoyed their meal. Riggins handed Woody some food and told him, "You're weak because you need to eat son. What's your name anyways?"

Woody took a bite of food and after chewing it, he swallowed it then took a good look at Riggins saying, "Name's Carlyle Winston Causey, better known as Woody."

Riggins looked at Woody for a minute then said, "I once knew a Woody back in the day. Man saved my life in a bar fight." He rubbed his bushy gray beard and continued, "It's been so long ago, but as I recall, Woody was about to get married to some gal named Maggie." Woody knew then it was Frank and Maggie the old man was speaking about. He went on to say, "On the other side of those mountains is where a small town lays alone in the open country."

Woody pointed at the whiskey bottle. After taking a big swig, he told Riggins, "Then folks you're talking about were my Ma and Pa."

Puzzled, Riggins looked at Woody and asked, "What you mean, were your folks?"

Woody took a bigger swig then handed the bottle back to Riggins. "They died on a wagon train." Riggins handed the bottle of whiskey to Henry and he took a small quick sip and smiled at Woody. He returned the smile and went on to say, "The wagon master and his men slaughtered everyone."

Riggins stood up and moved closer to Woody kneeling next to him asking, "You on that wagon train, son?"

Woody nodded his head saying, "I was the only one to live through it."

Riggins dropped his eyes as he spoke to Woody, "Sorry to hear about your folks, but glad you made it through. About four days ago up in those smaller mountains, we ran across a Marshall. Said he was looking for a wagon master named Jerry Wheat and a point man by the name of Danny Moore." Riggins wiped his bushy gray beard and went on, "Marshall's name was, let's see now…something like Jake Malone. Anyways, he had a posse of about twenty men. "

Woody wondered how the Marshall had heard or knew the ways of the wagon master and the point man and asked, "Did the Marshall say how long he'd been looking for the wagon master?"

He couldn't remember but asked Henry, "Do you remember how long the Marshall said?"

Henry walked a bit closer then said, "About ten years now."

Woody knew now the wagon master and his men had slaughtered more than one wagon train and any day now was to slaughter the one Woody was following.

As the night's moon appeared in the sky; the stars blinked in the distant darkness. Another night in the lonely valley because Woody lay too weak to travel. Riggins was on watch as Henry laid to rest. More laid close to Woody as his eyes glowed in the moonlight. Woody would be safe from danger and could rest well. Into the night dreams of his past life danced in his head. The drum beats of the drummer was something that lasted forever in his mind, the dreams drifted off into a misty horizon, a man's silhouette stood all alone in his dream. That man was Woody's most wanted and now the silhouette had a face as well as a name. But, in the dreams Woody would always get close yet so far away, always unable to catch Danny Moore. Tossing his head from side to side. Riggins could tell Woody was having a nightmare and could hurt himself moving with the open wound on his side.

Waking Woody up, Riggins told him, "That wound needs to be cleaned and a new patch will help out a lot."

Woody looked at Riggins saying, "I'd like to thank you very much, sir."

Riggins cut away the old patch of cloth and dug into his saddlebags he'd been carrying since he didn't have a horse. He and Henry had been walking for days and had refused to tag along with the Marshall and his posse.

"You seem to know a lot about wounds, sir," Woody said.

"Out here it goes with the territory Woody," The old man said smiling. He had the new patch comfortably wrapped around Woody's body as he knelt whispering, "Please call me Riggins, not sir, okay son?"

Woody smiled holding out a hand for Riggins to help him up.

"I'll call you Riggins if you call me Woody please, okay?"

Riggins' habit of rubbing his bushy gray beard would always take place before he spoke, "Okay, we got a deal Woody; besides, I like you. You seem like an honest young man."

Woody sat up against a rock, he looked into the fire, "The fire's got plenty of wood to burn a while. I'll sit and watch so you can get some shut eye."

Riggins wondered just how smart Woody was, at such a young age as he kept looking at him. "You sure are something else; Carlyle Winston Causey and I am indeed honored to have you as a friend."

Woody winked at him pointing to the whiskey bottle. The whiskey would help keep him warm inside and kill some of the pain as well.

Across the sky, a falling star shot through the darkness of the night. Woody closed his eyes praying to someday catch up with the wagon master and his men. Opening his eyes, he spoke softly, "And that goes for Danny Moore," meaning the point man. Woody could rest now because More sat next to him and no one could get to him before he would bark.

CHAPTER EIGHT

Another night had slipped away from Woody's life, he slowly walked around getting ready to ride out. Riggins looked on as Henry stood next to him. "You should wait out at least a few more nights. You're an awfully sick young man," He told Woody handing him his saddlebags.

"Keep the food in the sack," Woody said, pointing to the buggy. "I'll do just fine. When you get to town, deliver the buggy and horse to the blacksmith shop." He put his hand out to shake his farewell, then mounted Lightning. Pulling at the reins to turn his horse around facing Riggins and Henry he told them,

"The owner of the blacksmith shop is an old Spanish man named Galindo." He winced as a sharp pain shot through his gut pressing the wound with his hand. "Tell Galindo I said thanks and if you can remember, tell him I said that Por Vida, he's my friend."

Riggins rubbed at his bushy gray beard looking down at Henry, "This here boy will remember every word you said and I promise your friend will get your message."

Woody kicked at the sides of Lightning gently, "Let's go." Then he yelled at More, "Come on boy."

More took off ahead of Woody. Lightning made his way around the rocks that provided shelter for the night. They followed the dry ruts from the wagon trail on the ground; he could tell how Jerry Wheat and his men rode along the left side of the wagons. Back in town, he counted ten men including the point man. Now the clues on the ground and three burnt out small campfires. Told him more men had been waiting to join them. The circle of tracks further down the rolling hills, in the valley showed where camp for the wagon trail, had been.

Dismounting Lightning Woody walked around noticing more tracks. Riders from the mountain side had joined and followed the wagon trail. He then remembered Riggins saying a Marshall and about twenty men were looking for the wagon master and the point man. He stood looking in all directions taking out a bottle of whiskey. After taking a swig, he bent over picking up dry grass and twigs to make a campfire. Striking the two flint rocks together over the dry grass ignited a spark and a fire began to burn.

Woody unsaddled Lightning letting him roam free.

He was now quite used to his companionship and wouldn't leave. Unrolling his bedroll, he spoke to Lightning and More, "From now on, we're making camp during the day until we get closer to the wagon train at nights." He was smart not to follow in the daylight for fear of someone spotting him a mile away.

In one side of the saddlebag was the other bottle of whiskey. In the other side, Riggins had rolled up some bread and cheese in a shirt and pants. As he sat eating, he glanced at the opening of the saddlebag and hanging out from inside a silver chain dangled loosely. Pulling on the chain, Woody was now looking at a pocket watch. He wondered if Galindo had put it in there or had it been JD? The click of Woody opening the watch gently broke the silence. He sat staring at the name engraved on the inside cover. "Riggins," He spoke to himself. He saw that it was 4:35 in the afternoon. He could rest before nightfall and hoped to follow the wagon trail without knowing or seeing the tracks.

The moon's soft glow held a peaceful light over Woody's camp. He slept with mere worries for the people on the wagon train. Saddling up ready to ride out, he looked up into the mountains. Here and there like glitter shining on a Christmas tree, small sparks showed campfires. Mounting Lightning he thought about his Indian friends. They used to hold powwows to celebrate special occasions. He had learned so much while living in the midst of the native people and would have stayed longer.

Craving to know if in fact a promised land awaited to unfold lingered in his mind. Leaving had only brought more grief and pain as he crouched over the saddle from the sharp pains shooting in his gut. Letting Lightning set the pace, he would be able to spot someone or something.

As the dawn's light came over the mountains, the whiskey would help keep Woody's bones warm and reduced a little pain.

But it seemed that he had a need to drink because he took bigger swigs, each time a bottle ended up in his hands. Stopping for a moment Woody listened to the echoes from the mountain beyond. Lowering his head and closing his eyes, he listened to the echoing drum beats in the distant mountains. Sounds of the same Indian tribe who'd become his friends. Opening his eyes he looked up at the blinking stars as tears rolled down his cheeks. He could hear his mother telling him, "Woody, you need to pay attention where and how far we travel because one day, my son, you may become a great leader yourself." He wiped away the tears as Lightning slowly moved through the night.

Tipping the whiskey bottle up holding it against his lips, Woody waited for the last drop to run down into his mouth. But no matter how good he ever felt, it seemed he would never stop thinking. He let the bottle drop off to one side of Lightning, and smiled in the dark night as he patted his saddlebag knowing another bottle awaited him.

Deep into the night's journey, Lightning stopped moving as More growled at something up ahead. As he dismounted Lightning he rubbed his neck to keep still. In a low tone, Woody called out to More,. "It's okay boy. It's okay," He scratched the top of More's head. Scattered camp fires down below the steep cliff made Lightning refuse to walk down and now came into a clearer focus. Kneeling next to More, he held Lightning's reins. It was time to back up quietly, not to be seen or heard. Woody was not looking at the Marshall or his men because the men down below were pushing and pulling at someone. Listening carefully, he could hear the cries of a woman in need of help. Not understanding he still made his way down the cliff. More walked quietly beside him.

Three campfires lit up the area below, Woody counted a total of six men. Two pushed and pulled at the woman who cried out for help, four others layed out on their bed rolls laughing. They seemed to be waiting their turn. Woody got as close as he could and called out, "Nobody moves, nobody gets hurt." Only one was too drunk to call his bluff and moved towards his guns. Woody's Bowie knife cut through the night's glow and found its target within the body of the drunken cowboy. "Who's next?" He asked, walking into the glow of the fires while More growled at the five remaining cowboys.

The fear and cowardice of one of them made him speak up, "Mister, I don't want any trouble." Stepping closer to him with his gun in his hand, Woody knocked the cowboy smooth out. Another one tried to move, but More was already tearing him apart.

Pointing his gun in the face of another, Woody spoke in a low voice, "You the leader?"

Trembling, the cowboy said, "No, sir," falling to his knees holding up his hands. Woody kicked the cowboy under the jaw with his boot tossing him backwards.

"Anyone want to try their luck tonight?" Woody asked looking at the rest of them. "Over here ma'am," He said, pointing to the woman. She ran to his side as tears rolled down her face. "It's okay now," He whispered.

He gathered all the cowboys together saying, "Please don't make me kill you." He was lucky not to have shot anyone. Someone would have heard the gun shots if he had to.

Sitting around until the dawn's light came, Woody kept a close watch focusing on the looks of the cowboys. There was no doubt they had once belonged to the wagon master's outfit, because of Woody's keen memory. He could still see each one as they appeared five and a half going on six years when they slaughtered the wagon train that left Frank and Maggie dead.

The dawn's light showered the area where Woody's captives begged for mercy. He put out the campfires with dirt kicking a pile on each one until nothing showed. The five men would have to die. They were too far gone in their minds to let go. From the same reins of the cowboy's horses, Woody cut enough to tie two to each other's wrist and let them go at it until one would either live or die. He looked at them. "Only one will live through this battle." As the fight for survival took its toll, he kept watching while he pointed his gun at the others.

"Why are you making them kill each other and not just shoot them?" the lady next to him asked.

"One shot and everyone in this territory will come running," He told her smiling and then said, "I told them that only one lives through this battle. What's your name anyways?" Woody asked.

Throwing her hair back with one hand, she answered, "My name is Margie."

"Margie, these men are all going to die no matter who wins this battle." He got up to tie another to the first survivor, then another until only one stood his ground. Still tied to each other, only one remained alive. Woody walked over to him whispering something Margie could not hear, "Bullets sure cost a lot." He then drove his Bowie knife straight into the cowboy's heart.

Turning around to look at Margie, Woody dropped his head and said, "These men and their friends killed a wagon train years ago. My mother, Maggie, and my father, Frank, died back then."

Margie walked over to Woody and after a moment, she said, "I was on the wagon train with those men, but a fight broke out on account of who'd get me. Those six men stole me at night and rode away until you found their camp." She wiped away tears from her eyes. "No telling what they would have done to me after they had their fun."

Woody could tell she was still scared and handed her the whiskey bottle, "This here cures almost anything."

He was surprised to hear her say, "That's bad for your health."

He could sense the innocence in her concern, but took a big swig anyways. "That's my dog, More' and that's my horse Lightning." He took a step closer and said, "My name is Carlyle Winston Causey, better known as Woody." He walked over to the other horses asking, "Which one would you like to ride out on?"

She stood still answering, "None of them."

"Why not?" he asked smiling.

She pointed behind him and as he turned to face the valley, farther down below a bunch of riders cut across the trail onto the tracks of the wagon train. He quickly gathered the horses pulling them behind some bushes not to be seen. "I believe they might be a posse, but we have to be careful out here," He whispered to Margie. He could feel her behind him as her warm breath touched the back of his neck. She held on to his shoulder as she tiptoed trying to see the riders. Her breasts now pressed against his back and both of them were lost in the moment for a while.

As the riders faded in the distance, Woody slowly turned around and Margie was frozen in the same spot. "How many family members you got on the wagon train?" he asked.

She didn't move and said, "I came alone. That's why they all wanted to fight for me."

"I'll take you with me because you're not safe out here alone," Woody told her taking her by the hand leading her away from the rocky ground.

An hour passed before Woody decided it was safe to ride out. Slowly following the tracks of the posse and wagon train, he could see some sets of horse hoof prints heading away. He saw another set of prints to the other side. Dismounting Lightning, he helped Margie down. "I need you to stay as low to the ground as you can." He pulled out his buffalo rifle from its leather scabbard holding it up into the sky. The booming sound echoed into the mountains and in moments clouds of dust headed towards Woody's intended sound. Mounting Lightning, he would meet the riders head on.

As Margie looked on, she could sense a sign of bravery she had never seen in a man. But the man she was looking at was still young, yet he seemed so mature. He had a way of carrying himself that spoke of a respect he earned just being the way he was. He had saved her life. Now he was trying to do more than that. He rode on to meet the marshal and his posse. More walked next to Lightning and Woody told him, "Stay with me boy." He reached behind him and took the last swig from the whiskey bottle. The circle of men in the valley's rolling hills surrounded Woody as Margie looked on. It seemed like he had taken over as he pointed to the mountains and to the other parts of the valley.

Marshall Malone stuck out his hand. Woody shook it and pointed to where Margie was lying low. Two riders rode up to her helping her back to where Woody and the marshal sat on their horses. They spoke of how to capture the wagon master and his men. Jerry Wheat was a dangerous man according to Marshal Malone. But the one who'd always stayed ahead was the brains of them all, Danny Moore always rode ahead and would be very hard to catch.

Marshal Malone spoke in a low voice looking at Woody with cold steel blue eyes. His wrinkled face held a wisdom only time could give a man. His three-piece suit, pants, top coat, and vest were as dark as the night with a white long-sleeve shirt. As the top coat hung on either side of his legs, the bulges from the double holsters; each held Colt .44s he played no games. Every rider in the posse now surrounded Woody, protecting Margie as well. He had just saved them all. As he spoke to Marshal Malone, Margie sat on her horse amazed at how much wisdom he displayed. He pointed to unseen tracks on the ground. He then showed them more on the other side of the trail. Jerry Wheat and his men had already made plans to ambush the marshal and his men as riders laid in wait to kill them all.

Not only had Woody saved Margie, but he had saved Marshal Malone and the posse as well. The booming sound of the buffalo rifle had spoken its tune to Jerry Wheat and his men. In about half an hour, the wagon train stood still and no dust was kicking from the wheels. Slowly Marshal Malone and his men rode along each side of the wagons. Woody and Margie rode slowly at the rear. In the distant valley where it divides into the desert, Jerry Wheat and his men rode away as fast as they could. Woody had saved the wagon trail. Marshal Malone with his posse would have to stay alongside it until everyone made it to the nearest town. The cloud of dust in the distance told many riders high tailing it out of the country as fast as they could.

Felix Flores, Jr.

CHAPTER NINE

Daylight was fading away as the moon made its dance across the sky. The stars blinking once again in a peaceful moment seemed like magic was taking place. The circle of wagons formed the place camp would be for the night. Everyone was safe and now Margie could claim her wagon back as she rode it to a stop. She stood up looking out the side smiling, in search of her hero Woody. She motioned for him to come over to her wagon. He rode along side of Marshal Malone. Campfires lit up the night as Woody kept seeing children running and playing. The women began to cook for the night's meal. The men stood or sat in crowds of their own.

Woody was motionless as a woman looked at him. For a moment, she seemed so much like his mother Maggie. As the woman looked at him one last time, he saw a young boy under a wagon sitting alone. Woody went off into another world of thoughts that made him think of himself, the night his world had been turned upside down. Then the voice of Margie woke him up. "Woody, Woody, would you please come here?"

He blinked away tears as he walked over to Margie. "May I help you?"

She could tell he was lost in thoughts and seemed to be cast out. Reaching her hand out, she said, "You're welcome to stay in this wagon with me tonight."

After thinking about it for a minute, he answered, "I think that sounds okay." He dismounted Lightning and said, "But there's something I've got to do first."

She kept her eyes on him because he was very different. In all ways than any man on the wagon train. In fact, he was very different than any man she had ever met. He quietly spoke to Lightning removing the saddle. He walked across to the other side of the circle of wagons. He bent down pushing his saddle and bed roll under the wagon, where he'd seen the young boy sitting alone. "Here's my bed roll and my saddle so you can use it for a pillow, because that's what real cowboys do." The young boy's smile revealed a missing tooth, but he was the happiest young boy in the whole camp. Woody called out for More and the dog ran up to him. He asked the boy, "What's your name, son?"

"My name is Jason Brooks, but they call me Jay."

Woody shook his hand and asked, "How'd you like to earn some money, Jay?"

"Yes sir," He quickly answered. Woody opened the small cloth pouch from around his neck, which hung down inside his shirt. Pulling out an eye size piece of gold, Jay's eyes widened. "Gee, thanks mister!" He responded.

Woody stood up and could tell More knew to watch over Jay for the night. He laid under the wagon staring into the night. He took one step to turn around and could feel someone behind him. As he turned to see who it was, a big bellied man without a shirt stood starring at him.

"That's my boy," he said. "Don't you think that's too much money to watch a dog for the night?"

Woody noticed the man's body was covered with hair. He put out his hand and the man shook it. His grip was very strong. "That will help you when you get to the next town," He said walking away. He had the feeling the boy's folks were poor and most likely had spent their last cent on the wagon train.

Walking away Woody could hear the fat bellied man say, softly, "Thanks mister."

Knocking on the tailgate of Margie's wagon, Woody asked, "Am I still welcome?"

She appeared in the moonlight tossing her wavy black hair over her shoulder, holding a sheet that dropped over her body with her other hand. "You think you can handle the heat in here, cowboy?" she asked dropping the sheet to her side.

The moon gave enough light to see and he said, "The heat's okay. It's the fire that counts."

Inside the wagon, Woody and Margie got lost in making love to one another. Being strangers didn't seem to come between either of them. Because it seemed they each needed to be with one another no matter the price.

The night rolled on into the dawn's morning light. Marshall Malone and his men put out the camp fires making sure everyone was ready to roll out. Calling for More to come to him, Woody told Margie, "You know this is where we part."

She sat on the front seat of the wagon never looking at him and said, "Isn't that the way it goes out here?"

He mounted Lightning and pulled the reins to turn his horse around and said, "Last night didn't seem to be your first rodeo."

He wasn't trying to be mean. He only did it so she would think he really didn't care.

Even though it had only been one night at Woody's side, Margie said, "Hope someday we'll meet again, cowboy."

Riding Lightning with More next to him, Woody spoke to Marshal Malone a while and rode off into the way Jerry Wheat and his men had gone. Danny Moore had been long gone up ahead of everyone, but now the wagon master had been stripped of a wagon train he would have enjoyed killing.

As he rode away, he could hear Marshal Malone yell. "Roll 'em out!"

He turned to see the wagons slowly rolling and could hear Jay Brooks yelling at the top of his lungs, "Roll 'em out!"

From other wagons, Woody heard the words, "Roll 'em out!" kept echoing down the line, frozen in thought of the first day he was on the wagon train many years before. The barks of More in the distance told him it wasn't a dream. Lightning began moving in the direction of the runaway cowards, Jerry Wheat and his men. The day had almost come to an end as he stood up in the stirrups to see what lay ahead. In the distance, the cloud of dust he'd been following had come to an end. The closer he got he could not believe his eyes. Tied to each other a herd of mules were entangled with ropes. Each had been dragging weeds or broken limbs from trees and bushes. Nowhere could he see any cowboys. It was then that Woody realized he'd been tricked. Jerry Wheat and his men were still on the wagon train and would in fact, soon ambush Marshal Malone and his men. It had taken all day to get where he was now loosing the mules and it meant that the wagon train would be twice as far. There was no way he could catch up to warn the marshal and his men. Stopping for only a moment at night to give Lightning and Moore rest, He could only wonder if anyone would live or was still alive.

Danny Moore and Jerry Wheat had proven to be wise because they had hidden inside the wagons and kept everyone at gunpoint.

Marshal Malone and his men could not tell. As the sun rose once again, he rode on in a pace. He could no longer stop until he'd seen or found the wagon train as he had done for two nights. He would have to wait out a storm in his mind that he'd already figured out, what Jerry Wheat and Danny Moore along with their men had done.

The answer came as the next day's dawn came with the sun's beaming light, empty horses stood saddled up that had belonged to the marshal and his men. Bodies of ambushed men outlined the ground. Wagons without hitched horses were left scattered out. Children's bodies laid hanging over still-smoking wagon parts. Women's bodies also laid dead as if they'd last reached for their child. The men of the wagon train all seemed to have been lined up and shot in a row; all laid dead on the ground. Jerry Wheat and Danny Moore had used their own horses to pull the wagons making their getaway. Into the mountains they had escaped again outwitting Woody. They even had outsmarted the Marshal and his men, making everyone keep quiet while they planned it all.

Riding Lightning, Woody looked inside Margie's wagon, but it was empty. Searching for her body he never could find it. Only two things could have happened. Either she'd gotten away or had been taken along with them. He rode along side each wagon as bodies laid here and there. As he dismounted Lightning to see whose feet stuck out of the wagon across from Margie's, a small young boy laid dead with his fist closed tight. It was Jason Brooks who'd told Woody they called him Jay. Woody reached under the wagon and closed Jay's eyelids. Kneeling next to Jay's body he opened the young boy's hand. He still held the gold nugget the size of an eye. He stood up throwing the nugget as far as he could shouting into the mountains, "Run! Run as fast as you can because I'm coming after all of you!"

Woody slowly walked around looking in the wagons, for a shovel to bury the bodies as he'd done before. But this time, although there were 18 wagons instead of 24 the first time, Several more bodies laid around belonging to Marshal Jake Malone and his men. Before he buried the bodies, he rolled all the wagons into a circle with the help of Lightning. Inside the circle of wagons, the bodies would dwell forever. This would be Woody's second circle of death and each grave would have to be shallow to save time.

Since the wagon master and his men along with his point man had ridden out so quickly after killing everyone, the food and water had been left untouched. He made camp away from the circle that had taken him three and a half days to finish. Now he needed to rest and get his thoughts together. More sat watching into the darkness and the sound of wolves sent chills through Woody's body. The flames of fire leaping inside the circle of rocks he had made brought memories to his mind. He thought of the night the flames of fire slapped inside the stone house, where he'd found the three bottles of whiskey. A drink of whiskey would do him some good to ease his mind and come morning he would search the wagons for food, finding a bottle of whiskey or two would be nice.

Closing his eyes, Woody drifted into a deep sleep he'd needed for a while. But the dreams would always seem to find their way into the edges of his mind. In the moon's glowing light, he could see a dark silhouette of Danny Moore on top of his horse and the dream seemed so real. Woody opened his eyes and the flames slowly continued waving into the night, Moore laid looking straight at Woody.

Felix Flores, Jr.

CHAPTER TEN

The cool morning wind blew. Woody rolled up his bedroll and put out the dying fire. More, full of energy, jumped up and down Woody's sides, holding on to him a while and let him go he'd take a few steps to do it all over again. Taking off the wrap from around his waist, Woody threw it to one side.

He put on a new shirt he'd found inside a wagon. He opened a wooden chest, his dream came true as the bottles of whiskey stood straight up in padded dividers. Opening one, he sat on the wagons' seat looking into the mountains. Moore barked at Woody to let him know a storm was on its way.

Gathering food and water, Woody packed Margie's wagon ready to ride out. Jake Malone's and his posse's horses would pull the wagon. The wooden chest of whiskey was a must. He smiled making room for it. He refilled the water barrels on the sides of the wagon.

Woody tied Lightning to the back of the wagon, the clouds began to darken. Lightning bolts whipped the sky in the distance.

Echoes of thunder roared above Woody. Unsaddling Lightning would at least keep him more comfortable. The saddle could ride in the back of the wagon to keep it from getting wet. Inside the walls of the wagon, he had tied four lanterns to use as light, but only for emergencies.

Woody's saddlebags held Marshal Jake Malone's guns and badge.

Woody had planned to turn in if he were to make it into a town. Slowly the wagon wheels rolled through the muddy path on the ground. He gently whipped the reins on the horses' backs. Sipping on a whiskey bottle the rain beat against the canopy. He rode on in hopes to catch up with Jerry Wheat and his men. By now they would be deep into the forest, where Woody had lived with the Indian people who'd become his friends. Staring into the darkness of the clouds, he began to think of Margie and why she had not been killed. Why had she been taken from the wagon train by the six men he had left lying dead. Now she was the only one who'd been taken away. Trying to make sense of it all, he took a big swig from the whiskey bottle that seemed to become more of a need in his life.

Slowly the clouds began to part as beams of sunlight shot through the sky above. The storm had lasted a good six or seven hours straight and the ground would be muddy for a few days.

Woody had shown to be smart once again since he took Margie's wagon. Camping out in the open, Woody ate dry beef jerky and drank warm water from the barrels. More sat right alongside of Woody inside the wagon as he dug into Margie's belongings. The brown suitcase with fancy designs on it spoke for itself. The owner was wealthy to posses such a handcrafted suitcase just to travel. Large fancy letters on top of the suitcase read, "Blaylock." Unfastening the snaps on each side, He smiled because he knew he was being nosy. Once opened, he held up a silky bra while his smile widened. The matching silky panties were the next thing he held in the air. He dug everything out, pants, shirts, socks, gloves, scarves, brushes, and combs. Then wrapped around a cloth, he found all the secrets Margie had about herself in a Diary. Everything she loved as well as hated.

As the day's light began to fade, Woody lit a lantern with matches he'd found in a box In another wagon he nosed around in. The warm light sent out a dim glow within the canopy, as he sat with his back against the seat reading and drinking whiskey. The first page was the introduction with Margie's name, age, height, weight, eye and hair color, and on and on as women write about themselves. But skipping chapters to almost the last few pages, Margie had written all the answers Woody had wondered about Jerry Wheat and Danny Moore. Of how they had been hired by her father Judge Robert Blaylock. To carry out the people of each wagon train into the open country, to slaughter each and every one of them.

Woody couldn't believe his eyes as he kept on reading of how Margie was told to leave on the next wagon train, and go start a new life of her own. She had written about every wagon train, her father had ordered to be put to death. The list was long of many people dying but not one name was written. Only where and when the wagon trains had taken place. Woody's eyes watered as he read of the wagon train that left for a promised land exactly five and a half years ago from the town of Lubbock. It was when he had gotten away. Slamming the book shut, Woody tossed it inside his saddlebags.

Judge Robert Blaylock was someone Woody knew. But no one had ever gotten away as Woody had. Margie's diary was enough to hang Blaylock. Woody would have to be very careful. If anyone on the Judge's side of corruption were to find out he had this type of information, he would be hunted down until he was dead.

Woody began thinking of Marshall Jake Malone and how his posse had been looking for Jerry Wheat and Danny Moore. He sat inside the wagon wondering if he should go after the wagon master and his point man or head into Lubbock in search of Judge Robert Blaylock.

It had been well into the night when Woody had fallen asleep. To only dream of some past moments in his life. Like always the moments of rest would come so quick to an end. Daylight meant it was time to move on as Woody rode away in Margie's wagon. Following Jerry Wheat and Danny Malone would do no good. The real problem now was Judge Robert Blaylock. Now Woody had proof of how the wagon trains always ended up dead. The Judge could not be working alone. If Woody were to talk about it with someone on the Judge's side, he would end up somewhere else pushing up daisies.

As for Margie, she would be okay even in the hands of Jerry Wheat. After killing the six men who'd kidnapped her from the wagon train and being back in the hands of the wagon master would take a more careful watch of her.

Woody would head to Lubbock and seek out the Judge, or better yet, just kill him. He pulled at the reins thinking for a moment. Bringing the wagon to a stop, he jumped off with a bottle of whiskey in one hand and food in the other. Puzzled, he scratched his head throwing his hat in the back of the wagon. The words his mother once told him seemed to echo in his mind, "Woody, you need to pay attention where and how far we travel because some day, my son, you may become a great leader yourself." Standing in the direction of the mountains, the town of Lubbock would be on the other side of them going south. He remembered asking his father, which way were the mountains leaving

Lubbock. Frank had told him northwest.

Not understanding why Margie was on her way back to Lubbock, Woody had read in her diary that her father had sent her away to start a new life. Digging out the diary, he jumped back on the wagon after a meal and watering Moore and the horses. Margie's diary would explain everything, or at least he hoped it did. As the wagon moved slowly along, he read the diary again. This time he would not skip chapters. Her life story was revealed as far back as she could remember. Of how the Judge had gained his power by letting evil men go and using them for dirty deeds. How her own father abused her and used her as he pleased any time he felt like it. He began to read why her father had cast her away. The smudges among the words she wrote appeared as if from her tears. Woody read of her father's wishes for her to marry the banker's son. She wrote of how her father plotted the banker's death leaving everything to his son. After one year of marriage, the son's plot of death would occur. Margie would be the sole survivor of all deeds and currencies of the bank. The Judge thought of no one but himself. The smudges continued through the pages she wrote of how she thought, it wasn't right that her own father had cast her away. Reading on, Woody found out why she was headed back to Lubbock. The reason was to kill her own father, then herself.

Closing the diary, Woody sat for a moment staring into the snow-capped mountains, wiping away tears rolling down his face.

It was hard to understand how a judge could do such things and get away with it for so long. The only person with power in town would be the banker, but would he be fit enough to fight along Woody's side was another question.

If Woody was right, Jerry Wheat and Danny Moore would not cut over the mountain, but would only ride beside it. After a few days riding, he had come across some tracks of more than a dozen riders. He was half right, some would follow the bottom of the mountain and the other half would cut across the top. The riders at the bottom would most likely keep Margie and Jerry Wheat would be in command of them all. The other half would cut over the mountain and report to the Judge, picking up another wagon train they would slaughter them all somewhere. Danny Moore would take a week to gather more wagons. That would give Jerry Wheat time to arrive in town to guide it out, Danny Moore would leave ahead of them again. The town would once again be filled with ruthless killers. Woody once thought they were good men. This time he knew who the main problem was and he had to be stopped. Killing Judge Robert Blaylock would be the only way anyone could be safe in town.

Riding hard for two more days, Woody came to a stop along a river. The wagon would not make it across. The roaring water would wash away the wagon and most likely topple it to one side. Woody would lose everything. The river was rushing downwards quickly, pushing everything loose until it broke or stuck between the rocks. As the wagon sat still, Woody untied the horses from the wagon. Using the cloth from the canopy he would use it to make hanging bags, to haul the wooden chest of whiskey bottles and Margie's belongings. Another horse would haul food and water for the journey into Lubbock. Leaving the wagon was a must because it would only slow him down.

Woody decided he would cut over the mountains to save time. Finding a place to cross the river would be easier once he was up in the mountain. More's growls told him that something or someone was up ahead. Dismounting Lightning, it reared up as if it were afraid of something within the trees. Catching a glance of something moving in the bushes, he stood still. He quickly pulled his Colt .44 revolver out of its holster. With the other hand, he tied the horses to the small tree limbs, pulling out his Bowie knife out of its leather scabbard. Slowly crawling, he could hear odd birdcalls. He smiled sending out a birdcall himself. Yards away his painted Indian friends had been following him all day. They stood up to greet him once again as a friend he truly was. The son of the Chief, Tow Feathers, stood up from behind a bush. His smile spoke for itself. The Indian boy who Woody had saved was now 12 years of age. Woody had only been 15 when he had killed the eight-foot grizzly bear. Five years had passed but he was still remembered. The bear coat hung over one of the horses. He still wore the bear claw necklace he'd been given as a sign of strength and bravery.

Hugging each and every one of his friends, Woody pointed to the pack horse with the wooden chest containing the whiskey bottles.

In moments, the firewater would heat up inside their bodies and all hell would break loose against Danny Moore and his men.

Woody drew on the ground speaking to Two Feathers. He spoke a few words he still remembered. Two Feathers spoke to the other Indians. They quickly lit up a fire using the wagons' canopy to send out smoke signals to the rest of the tribe. Woody wondered how they could speak to each other with clouds of smoke, but he was very glad to have someone on his side.

More could feel the Indians were his friends and wagged his tail among them. He had been a little puppy when he first came to the

105

Indian camp. Now More stood huge and would attack anyone who might be a threat to Woody.

Motioning Woody to sit down, he could feel a hunt was already taking place for Danny Moore and the dozen who rode with him. The moon took its place as the young braves danced around the campfire.

Some fell to the ground from the fire water running through their bodies. The laughter continued to rise as Woody unrolled his bedroll for the night. He laid tired looking up at the stars and he slowly drifted into a deep sleep. In the distance, past the sound of the howling wolves, Woody could hear the faint sounds of drums echoing softly through the mountains.

CHAPTER ELEVEN

A misty fog danced through the forest as Woody laid still. Listening to the morning birds, he could see only about a foot of bushes clearly, the fog hid everything above that point.

The grass and weeds laid flat where the braves had been sleeping, but not one of them was in sight. Woody sat up slow as More quietly slept. Lightning's legs were coming into view as he shifted his weight and grazed on fresh grass.

The campfire slowly sent the last of its heat up into the trees, that rocked with the wind. In the misty forest down below the braves moved quickly in the direction of Danny Moore and the dozen men with him. In the open country, they could easily pick apart the braves with their rifles. Within the forest, the odds were against anyone with guns. The braves knew how to use the forest better than anyone. The arrows silently killing them one by one would quickly come to an end. If anyone escaped, it was because they'd been high tailing it the moment they hit the trees. Knowing the point man like Woody did, he'd already left his men to die.

Woody moved slow and quiet putting out the fire with Lightning and Moore by his side. The Colt .44 revolver ready in his hand with the hammer pulled back, the slightest touch of the trigger would cause the gun to blast away. The remaining two horses moved on slow but only one was carrying the food and water along with Margie's suitcase.

Hours had passed, Woody now stood still. He could sense someone or something was watching him. Stopping in his tracks only made Moore growl at whatever was out there. Standing next to a giant tree, Woody didn't move an inch because his gut feeling only grew. The passing wind touched his face. An arrow dug deep into the tree. Turning his head to one side, Two Feathers smiled at him from inside some bushes. Woody smiled back at him turning around to kiss the arrow. Two Feathers looked away laughing at the other braves. Quickly Woody threw his Bowie knife in the direction of Two Feathers. It passed above his head and into the bushes behind him. He looked at Woody for a moment and at the other braves. Standing up he began to laugh, His friends joined in. They thought Woody had lost the Bowie knife. More's growls slowly drowned out the laughter. The bushes behind Two Feathers opened. A gunman stepped out with death's grip on his face. The Bowie knife had found a resting place straight into his heart. Woody could claim another soul and had saved Two Feathers for the second time. As the gunman collapsed to the ground, Woody sent out birdcalls speaking easily to every brave within reach. Playtime was over meaning more gunmen most likely had separated into the bushes.

Silently creeping deep into the forest, Woody followed his Indian friends. Each of them had found a soul to claim. They possessed skills to bring a quiet death only the Indian people could master. Woody had learned from them how to hunt or seek someone out.

The morning fog had lifted and the forest began to warm a little. Sounds of bows releasing arrows quietly sent out a message that someone had been found. Woody looked to his left, a gunman stood up straight against a tree, four to five arrows pierced his body. He died in an instant with his eyes still opened.

The sound of another gunman yelling before he fell to the ground dead, let the other gunmen know Indians were behind them. Stopping the chase of the hunt, the gunmen let out scattered shots of bullets into the forest behind them. Mounting their horses, riding deeper into a place they would all soon die. The forest was no place to be caught at night and it was too late to turn back now. Woody would be waiting as his Indian friends crawled slowly, with only one thing on their minds. Another yell gave another message of death. Woody mounted Lightning riding into an opening in the forest that had been made from an avalanche of rocks many years ago; smaller trees grew here and there.

The steep clearing revealed two riders on horseback storming downward hoping to escape death; arrows swam in the air next to them. Dismounting Lightning, Woody pulled out the buffalo rifle from the leather scabbard on his horse's side. Kneeling on one knee, he broke two healthy branches to use as a rifle stand. He pulled the hammer back aiming at the two riders. Trees ahead of them told Woody only one could be killed or caught, the other would vanish into the shadows of the forest below. Carefully aiming, he set the sight on the rider's back. He began to squeeze the trigger. He noticed the long hair waving in the wind. It was a woman and it could only be Margie. Dropping the sight lower he aimed at the horse's hindquarters, he pulled the trigger. The booming sound woke up everything and everyone in the forest.

The horse toppled over, the body went shooting forward.

In moments, Margie was fighting to stay alive. The braves held onto her. Terrified she began to yell in fear of the red men all around her. Danny Moore rode away never even thinking to help. Woody could have killed him first, but then Margie would have been lost alone in the forest. Not knowing who had shot, she would not have waited to find out who or why someone was after them. Kicking and scratching, she fought for her life as the braves held her arms and legs.

Mounting Lightning Woody headed down towards Margie. Without a sound, she froze as he approached his friends. She had no idea he knew them. Woody dismounted Lightning, speaking a few words to Two Feathers, Margie was released. Running quickly to Woody's side, she asked him, "Where did you learn to do that?"

He smiled motioning for his friends not to follow Danny Moore, and told her, "If you kiss me, they won't kill you."

She instantly hugged him; the braves looked on with smiles on their faces. The bodies of the dead gunmen would soon be eaten by buzzards and ants and would leave nothing but bones. The guns and rifles now belonged to the Indian people. Some of the braves kept the hats, which would soon have feathers in them. Margie looked at the Indian braves asking Woody, "How long have you known them?"

After thinking a moment, he answered. "Since they saved my life when a bear fell dead over my body under water."

Puzzled, Margie didn't understand what he had said or what he meant to say, but it would do for now. He looked in all directions and pointed to a huge rock with smaller rocks around it.

It would come in handy to form a ring and start a camp fire. Leading the way, he told her, "We're camping out here for the night."

Margie stood still then realized she'd just been saved and was grateful to be by Woody's side. "Only if we sleep together."

Woody's smile and his glittering eyes spoke for him as he nodded. "It'll be a cold night out here. Sure could use some body heat." He whispered to her.

"You got it cowboy," she said, pinching his side.

The campfire sent a yellowish orange glow with blue tipped flames dancing up and down. Woody spoke to Margie holding her suitcase in one hand and a bottle of whiskey in the other. The Indian braves sat skinning a wild hog cutting big chunks to cook over the fire. On one of the packhorses, he had brought bread wrapped in a clean cloth. It laid within the saddlebags to keep fresh. Setting the suitcase down next to Margie, she looked at Woody asking, "Have you looked inside?"

He looked into her eyes saying, "If I tell you no, I'd be lying and if I say yes, then you'll ask me if I read your diary."

Standing straight up, she looked at him right in his eyes. "Well did you?" she asked taking a step closer.

"Did I look or did I read your diary?" he asked smiling, taking a step closer to her. Before she could answer, Woody pulled Margie against his chest hugging her tight, kissing her for a moment. Trying to fight him away with a push that really said it was okay, she slowly gave herself away placing both arms around his neck.

The Indian braves began to sing in their native tongue.

Woody and Margie took a step away from each other; they watched the braves dancing around the fire.

Woody called Moore to come to him. Petting the top of his head, he asked, "You hungry boy?" More wagged his tail and waited for Woody to cut off a piece of raw meat from the wild hog.

After a good meal, everyone sat around the fire enjoying the peaceful night. "Guess you had every right to read my diary," Margie told Woody as she kept her eyes on the flames.

"Margie, you don't have to kill your father and most of all, you should never think to kill yourself," He told her moving closer to her.

She took a deep breath saying, "Nobody ever spoke to me the way you do."

Woody could tell she meant every word. Even though they were really strangers, it seemed like they'd known each other for years. Curious Woody said, "All those years I've lived in Lubbock and I never got to see you. Where were you?"

Margie wiped away a tear that slowly rolled down her cheek and looked at Woody saying, "My father gained his power killing innocent people for their money and I grew up in a room as his prisoner."

Woody put a finger to Margie's lips saying, "It's okay. You don't have to say any more." He wiped the tears away and held her close to him. "We'll go at this together, but we must be very careful, okay?" he whispered letting her know he really cared.

"Thank you, Carlyle Winston Causey," she said, nodding.

He took a big swig of whiskey handing Margie the bottle and saying, "This will warm your body up a little."

"A little, but it's not body heat," she said smiling.

Woody kissed Margie for a long needed kiss. Then they both went to his bedroll for the night. Lost in each others' arms, they made love.

The morning breeze quickly crept up with the light of dawn coming over the trees, to start their journey back into Lubbock, Texas. Standing next to Two Feathers, Woody gave him a hug handing him a bottle of whiskey. It was time to depart once again, but the friendship would always be there, no matter what. Two Feathers wiped away the tears from his eyes as he took a step closer to Margie smiling at her. No words were needed; she took a step over to him hugging him real tight. Trying to speak to him, she looked at Woody. He told her, "Just nod your head and put your hand over your heart. They will all know what you mean."

Riding away was the hardest thing to do for Woody because, it would be the second time he'd ride away from them. The ride back to Lubbock would give Woody enough time, to make a plan that would keep Margie from getting hurt. Riding next to each other had given them enough time to really get to know each other. They shared their dreams of how a better future could unfold if their plans would work.

In the forest, it would stay cool and the heat wouldn't be so bad. Once out of the forest, the sun would bake an egg on the rocks in less than two minutes. Each night they made camp, Margie was surprised at how much Woody knew about cooking outdoors. He also knew a lot about where to find the right vegetables roots to make soups. Also cooking chili and beans like Maggie used to cook for him. Pointing in a deeper wooded area, he told Margie, "We'll go this way and I'll show you where I first met my Indian Friends."

After a few hours of cutting through the forest, he pointed to his right. "Over there is where I met my red man friends."

The cold river water cut through the ground as it cleaned itself ready to drink. He pointed over at the bear bones. A skull lay on top of rocks where his Indian friends had skinned it.

Broken arrows laid scattered out that had once pierced the body of the bear.

Margie looked at Woody asking, "Why did the bear need killing?"

"The bear had been tormenting the Indian camp while the men hunted. It would take women and children and eat them," he answered dismounting Lightning. Margie jumped off her horse as fast as she could running to Woody's side, "Are there anymore out there?"

He knew what she meant, but to make her relax, he answered,

"Are there anymore out there? Do you want to eat women and children, too?" She hit him on his arm like his mother used to hit his father. He could only look at Margie because he knew what that gentle punch meant.

"Not women and children, but bears," she asked.

"You want to eat a bear?" He answered, keeping the humor up.

"Carlyle Winston Causey, you're asking for it," she said.

He stood next to the stream of water and spoke, "Well, I guess you're sleeping alone out here in this dark bear country tonight."

She pushed him into the cold river and began laughing aloud. "And you'll sleep alone in the water."

He made his way over to the edge of the stream reaching out his hand, hoping she would help him out. Still laughing, she reached out to help. Woody pulled her hand making her fall into the cold water.

In moments, both undressed then wrapped the bedrolls around them to keep warm. Putting on more clothes, they sat next to the campfire for the night. Enjoying another meal, they sipped on a bottle of whiskey. Another night came across the sky. Woody asked Margie, "You sleeping alone tonight?"

She smiled at him moving closer to him, giving him a warm, sweet kiss saying, "It's up to you, cowboy."

He stood up holding Margie's hand, helping her up. Tossing more wood on the fire, Woody made one bed roll for both of them. Soon they laid beside each other under warm blankets.

Looking at the stars, Woody asked Margie, "You ever thought about starting a family?"

She gazed up at the stars for a moment, then answered, "Every woman's dream is to marry and have children." She was quiet for a moment then said, "Unless something or someone takes that dream away."

Woody knew that she meant her father Judge Robert Blaylock had taken away all her dreams. Woody held Margie in his arms kissing her on the cheek and soon she was sound asleep.

Woody closed his eyes, reached out of the bedroll feeling for Moore. He laid next to him like so many times before. He thought of the day the wagon train first took him away. Frank and Maggie's face held a smile he'd never forget. But somehow a dark silhouette stood alone as Woody slowly faded into a deep sleep. The silhouette was no longer the point man, but of a man at the edge of town. Waving good-bye, Woody could see the Judge standing as the wagons rolled by. Years ago, Woody never thought a judge could be so cold. But as the picture unfolded, the Judge had been the cause of it all.

Opening his eyes, Woody could only see the darkness of night as the stars glittered in the distance. Holding Margie close to him, he honestly didn't know how to bring down a Judge. No telling how many more men with power knew of his dirty deeds. But one thing for sure was, that the banker and his son had no idea how Judge Robert Blaylock had been planning the deaths of the wagon train. Also planned on killing both of them as well.

Woody could only recall moments in town and rarely got out to meeting everyone, being a poor man's son, he only worked and was taught at home. Maggie and Frank had never taught their son how to read and write very well. Out in the open wild country Woody had learned from his Indian friends and on his own.

The night had passed as the cool misty breeze woke Woody up, to find Margie gone. Sitting straight up, he felt under his saddle for his gun. He pulled it out of the holster, More barked at the edge of the stream.

Margie was splashing water at More as she laughed at him. He noticed how the two had become friends very quickly. Woody sat looking at the dying campfire. He knew it was time to head for Lubbock, Texas.

Felix Flores, Jr.

CHAPTER TWELVE

Riding out of the mountains' forest the clear sky seemed, like an ocean at its gentlest moments of the year. The green grassy rolling hills held the beauty of what a promised land should be like. The trees shadowed areas where Woody and Margie would camp each night. Next to each other on horseback, Woody asked Margie, "What do you think your father will say when he sees you?"

"I really don't care what he thinks," she said looking ahead. "I only want to put an end to him killing the wagon trains."

Woody pulled on the reins to bring Lightning to a stop. He took a long look at Margie, then said, "Your diary is enough to hang him." He looked away asking, "Is that what you really want?"

She pulled the reins on her horse, removing her hat and placing it on the saddle horn, she tied her hair in a ponytail and asked, "Is that the only way or do we kill him?"

Woody could tell she was serious asking, "We? Well, you're not killing your own father and We sure as hell aren't either."

Margie could feel Woody's concern towards her, but it didn't really matter to her anymore, how her father would be brought down even be killed, she looked at Woody saying, "Do you have a plan, cowboy?"

He smiled at her kicking Lightning softly on his sides to move on.

"Yes, I think I do."

"Well, can you let me in on it?" she asked, catching up beside him.

"See those trees up ahead on the second hill?" Woody asked, pointing.

"Yes, I do. Why?" Margie answered.

He smiled and let her know it would be the camp for the night. However, the only way he'd let her in on the plan was if she could beat him to the trees. She agreed but Woody would have to tighten her saddle. As he got off Lightning and took a step, Margie said, "See you at the trees, cowboy," kicking her horse's sides.

Margie's horse had a long head start. Woody jumped on Lightning telling him, "Let's go get her, boy." He dug the silver spurs Galindo had given him as a token of their friendship. Lightning dug his hooves into the grassy field. With each step, he got faster. The black stallion was too much for Margie's horse as he passed her in no time. "Cheaters never win!" he yelled back at her.

Woody sat at the trees with his whiskey in one hand and a canteen of water for Margie in the other. "That horse is fast," she said, dismounting her horse.

"An Indian chief gave him to me as a gift," He told her handing her the canteen. Taking another sip of whiskey, he looked away as memories shot through his mind of how his life had turned upside down.

"You're one hell of a man, Carlyle Winston Causey," she replied as she sat beside him.

"Guess you're going to try and trick me into telling you the plan, right?" he asked, taking a big swig of whiskey.

Hitting his left arm, she asked, "How did you learn all this?"

He wandered off into a moment of his own before answering. Standing up, he said, "My father Frank used to tell me many stories and at the time, I used to think nothing could have happened the way he explained it." Wiping a tear from his eyes, he continued, "Now I believe every word he said to me because it's all unfolding right before my eyes."

"I'll be around as long as you'll have me," she said holding his hand. She could tell he'd been through hell.

Taking another swallow of whiskey, Woody pointed to change the subject. "That dog seems to amaze me," He said laughing.

More walked in their direction with the reins of the other packhorse in his mouth, leading the horse to Woody's side. Margie couldn't believe her eyes at how smart More was to bring the horse to them. "I suppose you taught him how to do that?" she asked.

He took the reins from More's mouth as he petted him on the head. "Good boy." They started unpacking for the night.

Margie sat beside the fire after eating. Looking at Woody, she could tell he kept sipping on the whiskey bottle until it was almost empty. "Carlyse Winston Causey, you're so young to be drinking like that. Are you trying to wash away memories or you just don't care about your life?"

He took the last drop from the bottle and tossed it into the fire. He spoke softly, looking at Margie, "Young! Well maybe I am, but you said you'll be around as long as I'll have you." Spreading out his bedroll, he spoke again without looking at her, "I'll have you as long as you take me the way I am, no changes." He had no intentions of quitting his drinking for anyone.

The night was warm and the moon glowed over the country's silent magical moment; displaying blinking stars above. Woody and Margie lay next to each other; something had suddenly come between them. Margie was quiet thinking that her concern for his drinking had bothered him. Woody was pondering if he'd answered her too strongly. Out in the open country in the middle of nowhere, they were falling in love with one another. Love had a way of coming into someone's life at any given moment. Staring into the stars Woody and Margie had fallen asleep. Their dreams took each of them away into past memories still floating in their minds.

The dawn's slow moving light caught More's attention as an eagle soared through the sky. Its morning screeches echoed into the mountain forest. Woody opened his eyes just barely catching the last glimpse of the eagle. It disappeared over the towering treetops. It would be a beautiful day and cutting across the mountain shoulders, had given Woody enough time to catch a glimpse of Jerry Wheat and his men. They had disappeared down below the rolling hills heading towards Lubbock. It would be okay knowing the wagon master and his men would be waiting for him when he got there. As for Danny Moore, he'd be waiting for Jerry Wheat somewhere on the trail. But he'd be alone since Woody and the Indian braves had killed the men who were with him.

The ride into Lubbock from that point below the mountain would take at least three weeks with wagons. But on horseback they could cut it down to two weeks. Woody would not be in a hurry because he already knew another wagon train was planned. Margie's diary set the pattern Woody used to know, how long it would take to set up a wagon train. But since the wagon master and his point man had run into trouble. It would take a while to gather more men and to explain to Judge Robert Blaylock, how they killed Marshal Jake Malone and his posse. What would be harder to explain was how a bunch of Indians had killed so many men and had taken his daughter.

Around the mountains, going southeast would be where the circle of death laid. Woody had buried his mother and father almost six years ago. The "circle of death", was what Woody had named the shallow graves he'd left behind when his world had been turned upside down. But the rewards of still being alive stood next to him. "What's wrong, Woody?" Margie asked.

Woody blinked away tears forming in his eyes as he said, "Just thought I'd heard something."

"Listen close and you can hear it." Margie said, holding on to Woody's arm. "It sounds as if drums are beating in the distance." She didn't know it, but she was right. The mountain forest people better known as the redman sang and danced to the sounds of the drummer each day and night. The mountain was alive and the heartbeat was the drumming that kept the mountain alive forever.

"Hells going to break loose once we get to Lubbock," Woody told Margie softly.

Felix Flores, Jr.

"Once I tell my father I'll marry the banker's son, he will do anything I say."Taking a step away from him without looking back, she continued, "I'll keep my father busy for a while to give you time to let the banker and his son know what my father's plan will be for both of them if I marry him." She began gathering food from the saddlebags for breakfast.

Thinking for a moment, Woody called out for More. Saddling up Lightning, he told Margie, "Start breakfast. I'll be back in a while." He rode off slow around large boulders that outlined the rolling hills. Once out of Margie's sight, Woody dug his heels into Lightning's sides. The silver spurs set a fast pace in the direction Jerry Wheat and his men were last seen.

Up ahead, Woody had a clear view of the riders at the edge of a lake. The lake, as he studied it, was where the wagon train would be next to, or what was left of it. Frank and Maggie's graves lay down below and everyone else, he had buried in shallow graves as well. The wagon master seemed to not be in any rush to leave, He sat once again in the same area he'd sat before killing the wagon train almost six years ago. As Woody looked on, his mind went wandering off into another world that brought the memories much closer to him. Thoughts that fit the scenery he was now watching. The wagon master, Jerry Wheat, once again sat close to the edge of the lake pulling up his left pants leg. He unwrapped a cloth four or five inches wide and pulled his fake leg off. He began to pull out rolls of money from inside it.

Counting the men, Woody could easily see nine, including Jerry Wheat; Danny Moore was nowhere in sight. Almost six years ago, Woody could still see in his mind all 30 men who'd taken the wagon train. He'd escaped from them then and now followed the remaining nine cold blooded killers.

For some reason Jerry Wheat would live today, but Woody would kill as many as he could. Dismounting Lightning he removed his buffalo rifle from its leather scabbard, breaking it down then loading it. Snapping it in place, he laid the barrel on a rock about knee-high as he knelt on one knee. He took a good aim at the back of one of the men's heads. The thundering boom echoed throughout the open country and the mountain forest waking up every living thing around. The nine men turned to see where or maybe who had shot. As the bullet entered the back of one of the gunmen's head, it blew out half his brain as it exploded through his face.

Reloading the buffalo rifle quickly, Woody took aim again. Because they ran for cover, he took a better aim at a much bigger target. He set his sights on a gunman's back. The second boom echoed even louder than the first as it left another gunman dead.

By the edge of the lake, one rider raced away as his horse jumped over the first dead man's body thinking he got away. Woody aimed right under his arm pit. In seconds, after another boom, the rider flew off his horse. He was dead before he hit the ground.

Woody stood on top of the biggest boulders he could find yelling," Run!" at Jerry Wheat and the remaining five men. He jumped off the rock and mounted Lightning. More had been standing on a rock himself looking down at the wagon master, growling while the hair on his back, from his neck to his tail stood straight up. One order from Woody and More would have taken off in the direction of the gunmen down below. Digging the spurs into Lightning, Woody rode back at a fast pace as More ran next to him. He looked down and could tell More had been his only true friend. "Come on boy. Let's go eat breakfast."

Margie stood by the side of the campfire with a Winchester .44-40 ready to use. Woody jumped off Lightning, and told her, "Everything's okay. Jerry Wheat and his men are now making space between us." He took a step closer kissing her on her cheek. "I'd like you to get real close to More, He really is a good dog and a great friend to have."

She smiled at him and could tell he was up to something as she knelt next to More, "He's already my friend." She hugged him with both arms as he wagged his tail from side to side. Standing up she walked around the fire calling for More to come to her. "Here you go boy." She handed him some dry beef jerky from a pouch on the saddle horn. Woody didn't know that she had been tossing More beef jerky for a while since they'd been riding through the mountain forest.

Margie kept looking at Woody for a while before she asked, "How many men have you killed, Carlyle Winston Causey?"

He smiled at her remembering his father Frank had told him once, to never tell on himself no matter what. "Just for the record, I'd like to plead the fifth on that, if you don't mind."

Margie could tell he wasn't about to give her a number and it really didn't matter anymore to her. Picking up a stick, she hit the top of a rock like a gavel hitting its block saying, "OK, court's adjourned."

They both broke out in laughter and studied one another for a while.

Their eyes held on to each other like never before.

Love had eased its way into the two young souls' lives. They sat staring at each other without making a sound, but the feeling going through them spoke a thousand words.

"Do you think you could really love the daughter of a Judge who had your family killed?" she said breaking the silence.

Woody never took his eyes off Margie as he crawled closer to her, kissing her gently on her cheek. "What happened was never your fault. And yes I could and do love you."

Margie closed her eyes to save the moment in her mind, feeling Woody beside her. "Carlyle Winston Causey, I will never betray you."

He stood up gathering the dirty plates. "I'll put them in the saddle bags and we'll head down below. There's a lake where we can get cleaned up at." Margie started helping gather up all their belongings as Woody told her, "I'd like to show you the place I named the circle of death. That's where my parents died one night in the hands of the wagon master and his men."

Felix Flores, Jr.

CHAPTER THIRTEEN

Three dead gunmen lay face down in the knee-high grass beside the lake. Buzzards circled above ready to feast on them. Woody and Margie rode past them on to the other side of the lake's better view of the mountain forest behind them. Six or seven thin smoky lines beyond the towering trees, told Woody his friends were at their homes, most likely having a powwow. To the rocky side of the lake the six-year-old wagon train still stood.

Only a few wagons had broken wheels and leaned to one side. Inside the circle of the 24 wagons laid the shallow graves of rocks Woody had made. Studying them he stood looking in the direction Frank and Maggie laid to rest. His light blue eyes began to sparkle as tears rolled down his face.

Margie, now standing next to him she could tell she needed to say something. "Let's clean the graves and find some flowers for them," she said softly. She took his hand in hers and walked inside the circle of death.

Once inside the circle of wagons, Woody stood motionless. Flashbacks of the night's unforgettable moments went through his mind. Echoes of Maggie's voice rang in his ears as he could hear the word, "Run!" over and over again.

"Woody, Woody," Margie called out bringing him back from the dreadful moment that seemed like forever.

"I'll be okay, thanks," he told her. They removed tumbleweeds away from the graves, moving them outside the circle of wagons. They blew away onto the drier side of the open country toward Lubbock.It appeared that no one had ever stopped at the circle of death and more than likely no one ever would. But to Woody, this place would always stand out.

Every grave had been cleaned. Finding nails in the back of one wagon made Woody search until he found a hammer. Removing a few boards from each wagon, they made small crosses for each shallow grave.

A few days had passed and Woody really wasn't in a hurry to get to Lubbock. Camping out beside the lake made him feel better and having Margie with him made him wish each moment would last forever. Cooking fish and frying beaver tail cactus with potatoes had been their main dish each day.

On the third day, they rode away from the circle of death. A lone rider rode by at a distance. Woody could tell the rider was not trying to hide as he followed them slowly off to the side.

Pointing to the rider, Woody told Maggie, "We got company to our left and he's not shy."

She pulled the reins of her horse to come to a stop. "Maybe he's one of my father's men."

"If shooting starts, ride as fast as you can to Lubbock," Woody told Margie as he turned Lightning toward the rider. "I'll catch up later."

In moments, Lightning and the lone rider's horse were head to head. Woody talked to the rider. Slowly the horses were side by side. Woody and the lone rider shook hands heading to where Margie and Moore waited. Off his horse, the lone rider stood 6 foot 2 inches and had dark black hair. Margie could see him now since he'd taken off his hat when he said, "Nice to meet you, ma'am." As he put his hat back on, thin wrinkles ran across his forehead, his black eyebrows rose when he said, "Name's Matt Bryan." He'd already told Woody, but now he was telling Margie.

"I think I've seen you somewhere," Margie said after studying the stranger for a while.

He kept looking at Margie for a minute Then a thin smile appeared on his face, his thick mustache widened. "Well, I'll be damned. Are you Margie Blaylock, the Judge's daughter?"

She leaped into the air into Matt Bryan's arms saying, "It's been a long time ago."

"My little baby girl," he called Margie spinning her around. She wasn't his little girl, but he had been around her long enough to have raised her himself. He was Margie's mother's only living brother

The odds were way much better now for Woody as he smiled at both of them. The sparkling double holsters with silver guns and shining engravings told Woody that Matt wasn't just an ordinary cowboys. Thin strips of leather tied just above his knees held his holsters from moving, meant Matt could be a good gun slinger. Black leather gloves with the fingers cut down to the first knuckle, gave him the look of either a hell-raising fighter or a gun fighter himself.

"Margie pointed at him saying, "You promised to come back and you told me you'd bring me a surprise.

He looked at Margie for a while and took in the beauty of the snow-capped mountains behind her saying, "Yes, you're right. I did say I'd be back and I sure do remember the surprise I promised you."

Her eyes glowed with a smile on her face as she wondered what surprise her uncle would give her. "I suppose the surprise is in those saddle bags of yours?" she asked him with a puzzled look.

He shook his head saying. "You're smarter than I thought, but like they say, looks are deceiving."

She hit his arm saying, "All you men are alike, promises, promises." She walked over to Woody asking, "What's your promise, Carlyle Winston Causey?"

He looked straight into her eyes speaking loud enough so her uncle could hear, "I promise to stop the killings of wagon trains and if you'll have me as I am, I'll promise to take care of you the rest of my life."

Margie tiptoed and kissed Woody on the cheek saying, "You got it, cowboy. Now let's find some food." A white-tailed rabbit ran from behind a rock as Margie pointed, "That would be a nice meal with potatoes and carrots."

"Yeah, but if I shoot it with my buffalo rifle, nothing will be left," Woody said laughing.

Matt Bryan stepped in front of Margie and Woody. As fast as a blink of an eye, he pulled out his right side gun from its holster and back into it. The sound of the shot seemed slower than the entire draw. His voice cut through the air at Margie, "That's one surprise for today. Now go get lunch."

The rabbit was lying on its back, with a bullet through the side of its head. Margie looked at the rabbit, then at her uncle saying, "Wow, that was fast!"

Matt smiled and told Woody, "I promise to stop the killing of wagon trains myself if it's okay with both of y'all?"

Woody held out his hand to seal the promise, but he had to let them know something, "I'm not fast like that at all and I'm glad you're on our side, sir."

Matt unsaddled his horse as Margie went to pick up the rabbit. "Where's the potatoes and carrots or do we have to find some?" he asked.

Woody let him know that more food was on the packhorse along with cooking pans.

"What the hell are both of you doing way out here?" Matt asked with a puzzled look.

Woody sighed as he looked at Margie. "I'll let her explain everything to you," he told Matt.

The fire didn't take long to get ready while they spread out the bed rolls. Woody had cleaned the rabbit while Margie cooked the meal. Matt seemed to be in a daze scanning the area.

"It sure is beautiful here," he said as if he were thinking out loud. "I could build a cabin and stay here forever." He looked at Woody and Margie, "I came back to see you Margie and also see my sister Kathy like I promised many years ago. But I was held up longer than I wanted." Margie dropped her head closing her eyes for a moment. As she opened them again, Matt put his hand on her shoulder, "Where's Kathy, baby girl? Is she sick?"

Tears began to roll down Margie's face like rain drops flowing down a window. More tears followed as Matt knelt beside her, "It's okay, baby girl. Let it all out."

Woody already knew what had happened to Kathy since he'd read Margie's diary and the real reason she was headed back to Lubbock. Standing up he made his way to her belongings looking for her diary. Holding it in one hand and a canteen of water in his other, he knelt beside her saying, "Margie, you mean the world to me and we have to let your Uncle Matt know everything, because he's the only one on our side right now."

Margie took the canteen and took a few drinks. Handed it back to Woody, She reached for her diary. It revealed every dirty deed her father Judge Robert Blaylock had committed, including the dates of all the wagon trains.

Woody and Margie slept peacefully while Matt sat next to the fire, reading the diary she'd written while he'd been away. He cut his eyes across the fire and Moore stood on the other side with glowing eyes. However, he wagged his tail as he looked at Matt staring back. Quietly he put down the diary calling out to More "Come here boy. Come on, it's okay." He crept around the campfire next to Matt, he scratched More's back. In the middle of the pitch-black night, he told Moore,

"It's going to be a bloody day in Lubbock pretty soon."

Tossing the diary in the fire, Matt didn't want the Judge, who was his brother in law, to face a trial. Plus Margie would have to testify to the facts. No diary, no witnesses, no trial. Only a bullet between the Judge's eyes would be fair enough for Matt Bryan. Reaching into his saddlebags, he pulled out a badge.

With the yellowish orange glow of the fire, the badge read "U. S. Marshal" which meant not many people would ask questions as to why he had to kill a judge. However, he would have to make his first move and Matt was probably the only man alive who'd have the biggest reason to make him react.

Lying on his back looking up at the stars, Matt remembered why he'd left Lubbock when Margie was about eight or nine. It was to try his best to be the fastest gunmen anyone had ever seen.

But, becoming a U. S. Marshal was something special that had happened along his journey. Now what he'd hoped for was no longer there. His hopes were to show his lovely sister how quick he was with guns and to let her know he'd made U. S. Marshal. But she was dead by the hands of someone many people thought, was a good man. The Judge Robert Blaylock himself. Nothing could save the Judge in his eyes and somehow he'd have to talk with the banker and his son before killing the judge.

Slipping away into a deep sleep, the sounds of a little girl laughing echoed in Matt's mind. The dream started trying to find answers to his present day questions. Margie, so young, giggled as she ran around him. He'd blindfolded himself betting her he could find her in minutes.

Grabbing at the sounds of laughter, he'd reach out picking her up swinging her around in circles.

That would make her laugh even more. The dream would shift into scenes of Kathy laughing with them. Being Matt's only sister set deep in his heart.

Suddenly cries for help leaped from the darkness of his mind. He sat straight up breathing heavily with his hand on the butt of his gun. Kathy had been calling in his dreams for a while now. In fact, the dreams were what made him come back home. But it was not what he thought it would be. More walked up to him,, licked his hand and sat down beside him as a sign of caring. Even a dog could tell when people were having bad dreams. Matt laid back down dozing off while Moore slept beside him.

While the fire slowly burned down, Woody had been staring towards the dim glow. He could hear his mother yelling, "Run!" Watching Matt react to his dreams made him wonder where he'd been for so long. He'd seen the glow of the U. S. Marshal badge and he could tell he was a good man in more ways than one. Woody wondered where or how a man could learn to draw a gun, as fast as Matt had done when he'd killed the rabbit. He kept looking at the dying fire imagining how many men Matt may have killed, face to face or any at all. He tried to remember how many he'd killed. His count was much higher with the buffalo rifle than with a pistol.

Only once had he killed a red man with a knife, while being tied wrist to wrist with him. His count increased when he thought of men he'd like to kill. Danny Moore and Jerry Wheat were the main two he wished to kill, since they were the ones who'd killed his parents on the wagon train. Finding out about the Judge only rose the count to three besides anyone around them. In his mind, he knew he would have to speak with the banker and his son. But no matter how hard he tried to remember, the people of the small town of Lubbock, He could never recall anyone. Growing up, he was only allowed to work the fields all day. While others went to school, he was taught at home. That was a one-room, wooden shack outside the town's back buildings. There other weathered out old one room shacks stood ready to fall at any time. But, he had learned a lot from Frank and Maggie that soon could help.

Turning his head to one side, Woody could see Margie's face by the glow of the fire as she slept peacefully. Reaching out he touched her cheek softly, promising himself to take good care of her. She smiled in her sleep reaching to hug Woody, which seemed to be an act of love taking place out in the open country.

All three slept soundly as the moon slowly made its journey across the night sky. More slept lightly, often opening his eyes searching the flat land. In the distant darkness, the sound of howling wolves filled the air. No one could come close to the campfire, before More could spot them. But from a distance, a fire could be seen. Only an Indian would have a good chance to sneak up on a dog like More. But any noise would wake him up and hell would break loose. More had grown to be a big stocky dog and he would obey any command Woody would say.

Felix Flores, Jr.

CHAPTER FOURTEEN

A few weeks of camping out at nights and riding slowly on their horses had brought their journey within sight of Lubbock. Grassy meadows to one side joined together with patches of dry flat land, Tumbleweeds rolled away with the motion of the wind. Woody, Margie, and Matt all were in need of a hot cooked meal and a warm bath to wash away days of piled up dirt on their bodies.

Dismounting their horses, Matt spoke first, "We'll stick around here until night fall. Then we'll ride into town in different ways."

Woody stood at the edge of some rocks motioning Margie to come his way. "I think it's a good idea to wait until dark, but should we send Margie in alone?" he asked Matt.

Matt put a wad of chewing tobacco in his mouth. Adjusting it to one side, he said, "I'll be keeping an eye on her." He spit at a scorpion beside Woody's boot and told him, "As well as on you."

Margie was to go straight to her father's home which was the biggest two-story house before the town. Smaller buildings were connected with a wooden porch and a roof to keep the sun and rain away from the people. Woody was to go around the back, to the one room wooden shacks that outlined the fields . Matt planned on going to the banker's house. It set deep to the back of Lubbock surrounded by large oak trees, with a nice white picket fence. But no one was to say the others were in town until it was time to bring down the Judge and his men.

As the sun lowered on the horizon, the sky turned a myriad of colors; indigo and purple mixing in an ocean of bluish tones. The pastels caressed the sun's sinking deep orange. Disappearing motions dipped gently each passing minute. Matt, who looked so rugged, was on his knees praying, which seemed to catch Margie by surprise. She remembered her Uncle Matt to drink and curse from sun up to sun down. Wherever Matt had gone had an effect on him. It seemed for the better as he continued praying. Standing up he put his hat on pulling it down tight on his head. "I'll ride in first, then Margie, you ride in right after me." Mounting his horse, he rode next to Woody saying, "That's one hell of a dog you got there, son." Shaking his hand, he told him, "Pretty soon I'll clear this mess up, so you two can start your life together." Pulling the reins of his horse, he disappeared into the night.

Margie turned around facing the town. Lanterns in some buildings lit up here and there. Woody walked over to her placing an arm around her. He could feel her body shake in fear. "It's going to be okay." Moving in front of her, he held her shoulders with both hands. "Your Uncle Matt is a hell of a man and I don't doubt his words to stop your father."

Hugging in the glow of the moonlight, they locked in each others' arms as Margie spoke softly, "Please be careful Woody, because I don't know what I'd do without you."

He gave her a long tender kiss and wiped away the sparkling tears from her eyes. "It will all be over soon And we can start a family."

Margie smiled asking for help mounting her horse, then disappeared into the darkness of the night. Woody stood alone for the first time in many, many nights.

As Woody looked into the sky, More began growling at something or someone coming from behind them. He waited behind the rocks, sitting as he held on to Lightning and told More to be quiet. Two riders on horseback were coming into town, most likely some more men joining in with the Judge. With the dim glow of the moon, Woody stood motionless trying to see who it was. Right in front of him rode Jerry Wheat and Danny Moore.

Without thinking Woody quickly pulled out the buffalo rifle, pointing it straight at the wagon master's head. The need to kill both of them left no time to think, only react as the thundering boom echoed into the night. Jerry Wheat's head exploded off his shoulders. Woody tried to reload his rifle, Danny Moore took off into the pitch black night. The wagon master was now dead. Woody stood motionless once again. His mind raced in hopes to see Danny Moore's horse run away. But it was too late for he'd fled away once again from the grip of death.

People of the town began turning on more and more lanterns because of the booming sound of the buffalo rifle. Standing on the front porch of her father's house, Margie looked back to see what had happened. She had already knocked on the door. Because of the booming noise and the knock at his door, Judge Robert Blaylock held a shotgun in his hand. "Who's there?"

Margie quickly said, "It's me Daddy, Margie."

Opening the door, the Judge wore undergarments and a long stocking cap. His round short fat body jiggled from side to side trying to see past Margie. "Is anyone with you and what the hell was that noise?"

Margie knew who'd shot the buffalo rifle, but acted as if she didn't know. Besides, it was too late to turn back now. She had to say something to her father, so he wouldn't think she was any part of the booming sound. "I came back to do anything you wish of me Daddy."

Not even a heartbeat later, her father could only see dollar signs and now the only thing on his mind was making her marry the banker's son. Then have the banker and his son killed to keep their land and money. "My precious baby girl, please do come in," smiling he continued.

"I been missing you." Judge Robert Blaylock was a dirty, money hungry, cold-blooded killer and thought no more of the booming sound he'd heard before. Taking her by the hand, he led her down the hall stopping at her room. "This is still your room honey."

He smiled at her saying, "I'll see you in the morning okay, baby girl?"

As she went in her room, she listened to hear anything she could. Within minutes, her father's voice was clearly heard echoing through the vents that joined every room in the house. "She's back and this time she'll do as I say, or I'll take her life myself and bury her next to her mother."

Margie didn't know who her father was speaking with, but it was a woman for sure. Her voice in the background saying, "Be careful, she maybe up to something. You know how you Blaylocks can be." Then she laughed aloud.

Turning the lanterns off, everyone at the Judge's house went to sleep, except for Margie. She looked out the window from her darkened room.

Outside on the street people gathered around to see the rider with his head blown off. Woody rode into town alone, no one could see him since he rode in the back way, where he used to live in the one room shacks.

Matt Bryan knocked on the door of the banker's house. In a few seconds a voice spoke out, "Who's there and what's your business?"

"I'm U. S. Marshall Matt Bryan," He said in a low tone of voice.

The door opened slowly as the thin old man who'd been the banker, for many years stood looking at Matt. "Well, well, if it ain't Kathy's brother and you say you're a what? U. S. Marshal?"

He said adjusting his spectacles.

While Matt waited for the banker to stop talking, he noticed someone else in the house. "Is your son here?"

"Pointing a gun right at your gut," the banker said.

"I need to speak to both of y'all and it can't wait another minute," Matt said stepping into their living room.

Bryan, the banker and his son spoke as they sipped on some hot black coffee. J. W. Travis and his son J. W. Travis Jr. had known Matt all their lives and knew when he spoke, you could bank on his words. Leaving and coming back a U. S. Marshal only made it more interesting to listen. He told them about how Judge Robert Blaylock intended on killing each one of them after Margie married J. W. Jr. They both showed signs of hate and anger that told Matt that they would help bring down the Judge.

Woody stood in the rutted road in front of the one room wooden shacks. His thoughts began to settle back at when he once lived in the small shacks. Then a voice in the night spoke, in a low cold voice, "Mister we folks in these shacks don't have much and I won't hesitate to shoot if you're here to rob us."

Woody raised his hands in the air answering, "I'm not here to harm anyone. I just need to speak to y'all."

After a moment standing in the dark, a match lit up and an old man with a long gray bushy beard held a shotgun under his left arm and a lantern in his hand. Lighting the lantern he said, "There's no doubt in my mind you shot that buffalo rifle a few minutes ago."

"Yes, sir. That was me." He said slowly lowering his hands. "And I shot down a man who's been killing wagon trains. His name was Jerry Wheat."

The old man chuckled, "I told everyone that man was no good before and all his men seemed kinda crazy to me for some reason."

Woody pulled Lightning's reins to move closer to him. He called out to More. "Come on boy. Let's find a place for the night."

The old man let out another chuckle, "Tie the horse out behind this shack. Come on in so we can talk more in private."

It didn't take long for Woody to tie Lightning to a tree and tell More to wait outside. Entering the shack, he had to stoop a little to clear the doorway. Inside the one room shack, an old lady sat up from a squeaky cot. She reached for her glasses on a small wooden tree stump. "Howdy there young'un. You need something to eat?"

Woody cut his eyes to one side to see a kettle of beans and chili still a bit warm that kept the inside of the shack warm as well. "Sure wouldn't turn down beans and chili. Grew up on it."

The old lady stood up next to the old man and was about a foot taller than him. "What's your name son?"

"Name's Carlyle Winston Causey, better known as Woody," he said sitting in a rocking chair.

Turning around the old lady dropped a tin plate as it rattled on the floor. "Frank and Maggie's son." She pointed to him as she looked at her husband.

"Yes ma'am," Woody told her picking up the tin plate.

The old man shook Woody's hand saying, "I'll be damn, you're a big boy now. Where's your folks at son?"

"They're both dead," He answered lowering his head. "It's been about six years now."

As the old man's wife sat back down on the squeaky cot, the old man told Woody, "I knew them very well. Ol' Frank used to bring us small bags of coffee and beans once a week when I got hurt. See, I fell off a wagon bed on my back."

The old lady pointed at her husband saying, "That boy don't care to here none of that," she told Woody, "Pay him no mind son. Now take this here wooden spoon and get all the beans and chili you need."

As Woody ate, the old man whispered, "If my back didn't hurt like it did. I'd tell her what was on my mind." Then he winked at Woody.

After a few hours, all three laid asleep until the light of dawn began to seep into the cracks of the wooden shack. The old lady woke up first and her voice filled the one room shack, "You two go out back to wash up while I start breakfast."

Making their way out of the shack, Woody caught a glimpse of the old lady reaching for the smoking pipe that laid on the tree stump. He smiled to himself and reached for his Colt .44 revolver, to see if it was loaded. The old man was to speak in his behalf to the other men, to help stop the Judge and his men.

Matt Bryan, J. W. and his son walked out of the bank onto the street. While Margie and the Judge walked beside each other. About eight or nine rugged-looking men walked as if trouble was about to come down. Some of them had .44-40 rifles under their arms. During the night, the Judge had called his men to stay close by since he didn't trust Margie one bit. Plus, Jerry Wheat's head had been blown off the night before. The Judge looked like he wasn't packing, but inside his vest pocket he always kept a small double barrel 38 Dillinger.

Walking through the sides of some buildings, Woody made his way to the streets of Lubbock facing the bank. Noticing Matt, the banker and his son, Woody spotted J. W. Jr.. They smiled at each other because growing up they'd become friends. Woody was never allowed to go into town, but J. W. Jr. always loved to play in the fields tnat belonged to his father. They shook hands and he told Woody, "That's a mighty hand shake my friend."

His grip spoke for itself and the flow in his eyes as well.

J.W. Jr. was glad to see someone he truly knew for so many years and said, "Let's bring down these low lifes and make them eat lead."

"If anyone marries Margie, it's you and not me," J.W. Jr. told Woody. He released his grip adjusting his guns saying, "I learned how to use these two at the same time."

"I may not be as fast my friend, but you can count on a good aim to the heart," Woody said holding the butt of his .44 revolver.

"The Judge and the four to his left are mine," Matt told them.

The banker spoke up, "That there four boys are a rowdy bunch and pretty quick with them guns."

"Like I said, their mine and the rest belong to y'all," Matt said spitting a wad of chewing tobacco.

Five more men walked to the right of the Judge. Margie

ran from the shove her father gave her. In seconds ten men stood in the middle of the streets of Lubbock to face only four.

"I'm the Judge of this town and my name is Robert Blaylock, I'm ordering you cow hands to turn in your guns."

Matt had been lowering the brim of his hat by keeping his head down, but he raised his head saying, "Name's Matt Bryan,

U. S. Marshal, Kathy's brother and you can go straight to hell."

The judge's eyes looked like they'd seen a ghost. Before he could blink, Matt had sent two shots of lead into his heart.

Matt broke down two more men before they knew what had happened. The other two brothers quickly raised their hands begging for mercy. But Matt was in no mood for buying hogs that day. Just as fast as the others had died,the remaining two brothers dropped to the ground dead. Matt was faster than anyone had ever seen.

To the right side of the dead Judge, the other five gunmen had gone for their guns. The banker cut one in half with his

shotgun. His son's draw was almost even with Matt's, He cut

down two of them with no problem. Woody's slower draw took aim at one man and pierced his heart. More had been running towards the last one and a shot rang out. A yipping sound echoed in the streets of Lubbock, then died down as More fell to the ground dead.

Watching his best friend die, Woody unloaded his gun going ' into a trance. He pulled the trigger while his gun clicked over and over. Matt moved past him giving him a push to awaken him. They walked to the men lying on the ground and if one moved,

Matt shot straight into the heart. Ten men had died in a matter of seconds.

As the dust began to settle, people from their room started appearing.

Coming from the Judge's house in the distance, a window breaking caught everyone's attention. Then the sound from the rifle pointing out the window went off. Margie stood looking at Woody holding onto her gut. Holding herself up with one hand against the building, she cried for help. Catching her before she fell, Woody heard her say, "I love you." Then she closed her eyes and was also dead.

Woody's voice cried out, "Nooo!" Matt stood next to him.

Felix Flores, Jr.

CHAPTER FIFTEEN

Margie's body laid in Woody's arms, dead from the rifle shot to her gut. He carried her towards her father's house. Up ahead Matt kept his eyes fixed up, to the window where the shot came from. As the people followed behind J. W. and his son, a shotgun blast broke the silence, shattering the rest of the window, the body of a woman still holding a rifle tumbled out. She most likely had been the one with the Judge the night before, who was laughing behind closed doors.

As everyone stood in the streets of Lubbock, an old man made his way closer to the busted window. He waved at Matt shouting, "That's the last of them all."

Inside the house, Woody laid Margie's body on top of a huge table, after Matt shoved everything on it onto the floor. Woody placed both hands atop the table standing for a moment. Tears ran down his face as he turned around saying, "We need to bury her next to her mother."

Placing his hand on Woody's shoulder, Matt said, I'll see to it that she gets cleaned up and ready for the funeral. You need to go wash up, son."

Tears flowed steadily as Woody nodded slowly making his way out the door. J. W. and J. W. Jr. stood on each side of the door. He made his way to the street where everyone else was. Without saying a word he kept walking back to where the ten dead men lay. Looking at the dead bodies, he mumbled to himself, "Danny Moore, you're next to die."

Woody took a few steps towards More, reaching down to pick him up. "I'll take care of the dog for you," He heard a voice speak in a low tone.

Woody dropped to his knees. His vision blurred out. Another voice yelled out, "He's been shot, get the doctor." Everyone had thought all the blood on him had been from Margie's body, Woody had caught a slug to in his side before falling to the ground. Woody passed out from loss of blood, too weak to stay awake.

A few days had passed and the sound of someone moving about in the room awake Woody. Still weak he tried to focus on who it was, but the voice was blurry. "You'll be fine, son. I'm right here with you." His vision got clear as Matt stood next to the bed holding a plate of food. Trying to sit up, his body fell back onto the bed and he asked, "How long have I been passed out?"

"Only two days and you have got to get some food inside you son," Matt said holding up two fingers.

Woody turned his head looking at the bottle of whiskey, on the nightstand by the bed. Reaching for the bottle, Matt knew why handing him the bottle.

Moments later Woody sat up with Matt's help. Leaning back on the headboard of the bed, he asked, "Who shot the woman who tumbled out the window?"

The room was quiet for a moment, then footsteps on the wooden floor slowly got louder. An old man stood to Woody's left side saying in a cackling voice, "I did sonny. She was a saloon girl who looked much older than she really was." He looked at the empty whiskey bottle asking, "Need another bottle sir?"

Woody couldn't tell if the old man needed a drink himself, or if he just wanted to know if he really needed another drink. But He nodded and said, "Sure could use it and please don't call me sir, okay?"

The old man started walking away then told Matt, "I'm glad you're back sir, I think I'm going to like that young man."

Matt smiled because he'd known the old man since he was young. "Can't break old habits," He told Woody. "He's been using the word sir, since he started taking care of the Judge and Kathy." Woody tried to get out of bed holding onto his side, but he was too weak. "When you get the strength to move around, we'll go put some flowers on Kathy's and Margie's graves," Matt said standing by the window. From where he was standing, he could see the gates of the graveyard opened up again. Someone else was being laid to rest.

Gunfights happened each day in the town of Lubbock, the Sheriff watched. It was time someone spoke to him or put him out.

Tying down the holsters to his legs, Matt walked out of the room and told Woody, "Need to adjust the Sheriff of this town a bit. I'll be right back."

Knocking on the Sheriff's door, Matt spoke, up, "I know you're in there. Come out and smell the roses."

In moments, the Sheriff stood at the door and held on to the top edge keeping his balance. He was too drunk to stand on his own. "What the hell do you want?" He asked Matt.

Matt's right fist sent the Sheriff's body stumbling backwards and answered, "U. S. Marshal, Matt Bryan." He smiled to himself closing the door behind him. Walking over to the sheriff's body, he took out his gun with one hand and drug him into the cell with his other hand. Locking the cell door, Matt sat at the desk looking for paperwork. When he ran across what he'd been looking for, he stuck the papers in his shirt pocket. He stood up and saw J. W. Jr. walking across the street. Pulling a coin out of his pocket, Matt knocked on the window.

He turned to see Matt inside the sheriff's office and headed to the door. He looked into the cell at the Sheriff shifting to one side. "What the hell happened to him?" He asked with a puzzled look on his face.

Matt pointed at the coffee pot asking, "How'd you like a sip of coffee son?"

"No thanks," he quickly said. "You okay?" he asked the Sheriff walking to the cell door. "What happened?"

"Get me the hell out of here!" he said slowly standing up.

"You're staying in there till you get your head clear and you're not the Sheriff anymore," Matt told him.

"You can't take my badge, mister!" he told Matt at the cell door.

Tossing the badge on the table, Matt told him, "I already did cause you haven't tried to stop any fights with or without guns." He watched two cowboys facing each other on the street. Opening the door, he shouted, "Hey! Whoever wins is going to jail. The other is buzzard food cause I ain't got time to bury you. "

Both cowboys looked at each other smiling as Matt made his way onto the porch. J.W. Jr. stood beside him with his hand on the butt of his guns.

The gunfighters both studied Matt and J. W. Jr. "I know you, you're the banker's son and I ain't got no beef with you."

"That's right, J. W. Jr," the other one said with his hands up. "We ain't got no beef with you."

Matt tossed a coin in the air, caught it and slapped it on his other hand. "Heads or tails boys?" he asked stepping into the street.

"Heads or tails for what?" one asked.

He walked between them saying in a low tone, "So the beef can be all mine."

"Who are you, mister?" the cowboy on his left asked.

"Matt Bryan, U. S. Marshal."

The other one said, "Matt Bryan, the fastest lawman with two pistols. He dropped to his knees, "I ain't got no beef with you either sir."

Shaking like a leaf, the one on Matt's left knelt down saying, "Spare me, Marshal. I didn't mean to upset anyone sir."

Matt looked at the coin and told them, "This is your lucky day. It's a tucked tail. Now get out of my sight and leave those guns where you stand."

Not hesitating, the two cowboys dropped their guns and sped away as quickly as they could. Matt picked up the guns and told J. W. Jr., "I need you as Sheriff.

"That's my future job when Dad passes it to me or dies," he said pointing to the bank laughing aloud.

"I saw the look on those two fellows when they seen you," Matt said walking next to him. "However you got that respect wasn't being a daddy's boy. Besides you being Sheriff will keep anyone from your father."

Looking at the Sheriff's office he said, "Hell, I've got two guns that I polish each day. Don't need a badge to keep shiny."

Matt smiled as they walked into the Sheriff's office, "I'll send someone over here each day to polish the badge and clean up your office." Pointing to the Sheriff he said, "I'll let you keep that as your deputy if you like."

Matt looked out the window towards the Judge's house.

Someone had been pointing a very long barrel out one of the windows. Then he put it together noticing the length of the barrel. Matt thought it was Woody backing up his play outside with the cowboys. But it was the old man, the Butler, ready to shoot one down for Matt.

He tossed the badge at J. W. Jr., "Just till I find a good man like you."

"Ain't nobody good as me," he said pinning the badge on.

"That's right," Matt said smiling. "So you'll be Sheriff awhile."

Looking him in the eyes Matt said, "This is your town now. Get it cleaned up. If you need me, I'll be at my new house." He winked at J. W. Jr. and walked down the street real slow so everyone could get a good look at him.

A few women watched how he handled the two cowboys. One of them said, "Good morning, Marshal."

"Good morning ladies," he said nodding holding his hat with two fingers.

They smiled at each other as more people came outside the long porch that outlined the buildings.

J. W. Jr. stood outside the Sheriff's office; everyone whispered pointing his way. The two women made their way by the Sheriff's office. J. W. Jr. stepped out into the street.

The sun hit the badge making it shine, one woman asked, "J. W. Jr., you're our Sheriff now?"

"Sure am and I'm having a town meeting next Friday at our house," he told them. "Sort of like a big picnic," He thought maybe he could push off the badge to a chosen one. "Spread the word for me ladies, Friday afternoon." They walked away and the gossip started as he smiled at his plan.

Opening the door, Matt noticed the Butler coming down the steps and asked him, "How's Woody doing?"

"He's drinking a lot sir," the Butler whispered. "Asked for another bottle sir," holding an empty bottle.

Matt smiled telling him, "It's okay, let him drink. He's trying to forget something." In the back of his mind, Matt knew Woody had been through hell to be so young.

Matt sat in the Judge's desk in the study pulling the papers out of his shirt. He read the message that U. S. Marshal Jake Malone and his posse were to meet U. S. Marshal Matt Bryan in Lubbock. When he'd met Woody and Margie, Matt had been on his way to Lubbock. But they never said a word to him about Marshall Malone.

"This for you, if you care for it," the Butler said, entering the study with some food and a bottle of whiskey.

Matt was hungry and could use a drink to ease his mind. "Sure, bring it in, please."

The Butler sat the tray down on the desk cutting his eyes to the papers, then at Matt who was looking straight into his eyes. "Oh my God. Excuse me sir. I didn't mean to be nosy," the Butler said backing up with his hands behind his back.

"I know the Judge was a crooked person, but Kathy spoke highly of you," Matt said, pushing the papers to the edge of the desk.

The Butler smiled, relieved to hear Matt say those words.

"Mrs. Kathy Blaylock was a splendid lady and we used to speak a lot sir," he said leaning closer to the desk.

"Know that name?" Matt asked pointing at the papers reaching for the tray of food.

"Sometimes I get too nosy sir," the Butler said after he read the papers.

Matt couldn't understand and asked, "What do you mean?"

"I'll be right back sir," he said putting the papers back on the desk.

Matt started enjoying his meal and the Butler came back in the room after a few minutes. Matt looked up to see the Butler with saddle bags in his hands. "What you got in those bags and whose are they?"

The Butler put them on the desk and turned around to shut the door. "These belong to your friend Woody. Please look inside sir."

Matt pulled out a holster with the gun still in it. Unwrapping the belt, a badge fell onto the desk. He picked it up reading it out loud, "U. S. Marshal Jake Malone."

Grabbing the holster and gun, Matt stormed upstairs. "Carlyle Winston Causey, where in the hell did you get this at?" He held up the holster with the gun still in it and the badge in his other hand.

"Jerry Wheat and Danny Moore along with their men ambushed the Marshal and his men on the wagon train coming this way," Woody explained pulling himself up.

"Why didn't you tell me earlier?" Matt asked walking to the window.

"It wouldn't matter. He's dead anyways." Woody always spoke his mind and never lied just to please anyone.

"Maybe you had your reasons son, but you can count on me," Matt told him. He liked Woody the day he met him and today wouldn't be any different.

Before the day was over, Matt and the Butler knew all about how U. S. Marshal Jake Malone and his posse died in an ambush.

For the next few days, Matt wasn't the same. Deep inside he needed to know the whereabouts of Danny Moore.

Woody kept getting stronger and Matt let him know when he was better, they would go look for the point man. Each day Matt would show Woody in the backyard, how to draw his gun to become fast someday.

J. W. Jr. stood at the back gate of his family's house.

Friday morning had brought the town's people together. His plan to elect a Sheriff was working. But as he stood there, only the old folks made their way to the meeting. He had told the women it would be like a picnic. Tables with white sheets held drinks and food as some children ran in the yard playing.

Hours later the younger couples headed in wearing their Sunday best. J. W. Jr. looked on to see who would or could fit into a Sheriff's mold. Only a few packed pistols and were known to use them. But to be able to clean up a town known for trouble, would take someone with a unique style. At least brave enough to sound important and let the badge stick out in view hoping fools would think twice.

The Butler walked along side Woody as Matt kept a few feet behind them. J. W. Jr. stuck out his hand to shake Woody's, "Sure am glad to see you Woody. How you feeling?"

"Feels like a mule's kick," he said, stopping at the gate and holding his hand to his side. "Which way's the drinks?"

The new Sheriff pointed, Woody and the Butler walked past him. Matt told him, "Nice way to hunt a new Sheriff son. But it takes time." He smiled saying, "Hell it took you five minutes to pick me."

"Yeah, but I've known you all my life," he said studying the crowd. "Let me know first who you plan on picking okay?"

J. W. Jr. may have been fast with guns, but to outwit a man like Matt Bryan, would take many more years of wisdom to even get close. He hit the nail on the head and knew J. W. Jr.'s plan from the start, but his eyes studied the crowd of men to see if anyone of them was Sheriff material.

The sounds of music echoed in Lubbock as an old man played fiddle and another played flute. The rattles of the washboard added even more tunes. The people kicked up dust as they danced.

Matt studied the dust passing the far side of the house. It told him it could be one of two things. Either a stage coach had pulled up in Lubbock or a bunch of riders had just ridden into town. Matt strolled slowly towards the front of the house. As he looked on, he couldn't believe what he saw.

Felix Flores, Jr.

CHAPTER SIXTEEN

The dust settled past the banker's house where everyone was having a good time. The eight Mexican riders dismounted their horses outside the saloon. They were all hungry for a meal as well as a drink, but not a drink of water. Swatting away dust from their clothes, one at a time each followed into the saloon. At least half wore big sombreros with strings through them tied at their chins. The others had gotten regular cowboy hats but the leader stood out the most. He wore a grayish white straight brimmed hat, with a dusty black bandana around his neck.

Matt Bryan studied each one making their way in the saloon. Opening the swinging doors, he stood facing the men alone, they all turned to see who the leader was speaking to. "Well, well, if it ain't the man of the hour, or should I say in his last hour."Laughter echoed in the saloon as the Mexican riders thought, Matt was just an ordinary cowhand looking for a drink. The laughter subsided as his eyes spoke for themselves. "So, what do you have to say for yourself gringo?" the leader asked with his hands at the sides of his buletos across his chest. They all laughed again while drinking their whiskey. One had slapped the bartender as he went behind the bar.

Matt spoke and they all got quiet. Looking at each other, they laughed harder than before. Whatever he told them didn't to fit in their ears. "Speak up gringo. I have dust in my ears," the leader told him.

They kept laughing as Matt took a few steps inside, with his hands on the butts of his guns. His voice broke the silence, "Each and every one of you can drink all you want, but I'll take those guns while you do."

All eight Mexican riders looked at one another. One spit out his whiskey across the room and started to laugh. Throwing a bottle against the back wall of the bar shattering the mirror, the leader stepped out in front of Matt asking, "What did you say, gringo?"

"Put your guns on the counter and I'll put them in a safe place for you," Matt answered.

"What if I don't gringo?" the leader asked.

"I'm going to shoot you between the eyes twice if you don't put them guns on that counter," Matt told him loud enough for everyone to hear.

The leader started to laugh and quickly went for his guns. Matt's lightning speed thundered as his guns went off and putting them back in the holsters in one swift move. The Mexican leader never got his guns out of his holster. He only grabbed the butts of them. His body flew backward onto the bar then tumbled to the floor. Matt's quick draw surprised the rest of them. One of the Mexican riders knelt next to their leader. "Gringo, you told him you would shoot him twice between the eyes, but he's got one bullet hole. Is it because only one gun works or you missed?"

"Turn his body over and look at the back of his head." Matt Bryan was so fast only one shot was heard. He had pulled both triggers at the same time.

Still on his knees, the Mexican rider rolled the body over for everyone to see, two bullet holes had exited his head. Chills shot through the rider's body, Matt had taken a few steps his way. He stood saying, "We'll pay for our drinks and the mirror too." He walked up to the bar placing his guns on the counter holding his hands in the air.

The others followed suit as J. W. Jr. busted through the doors, "What's going on, Matt?"

"Get the guns. I got your back," Matt said standing still. "And that bartender is a friend of mine. Don't touch him."

Walking to the sheriff's office, Matt asked J. W. Jr., "Did you find anyone who might want to be sheriff?"

"You're one hell of a man Matt Bryan," he answered smiling.

"It comes with the territory son," he said in a low voice so no one could hear him. After a few steps, he slowed down and told J. W. Jr., "Take the guns to your office, Sheriff. I'll be there shortly."

J.W. Jr. liked the sound of how Matt called him Sheriff. He smiled and said, "Yes sir," winking at Matt, he knew something was in the air.

J. W. Jr. entered his office; Matt had slipped into the blacksmith shop, stepping back into the shadowed area within. The thuds on the ground told him more riders were, on their way into town. Making sure both guns were loaded, he moved to the opened door. Sure enough, six more Mexican riders rode together in a wild bunch. Each was dressed almost like the other eight, these were older than the first bunch already in the saloon getting drunk. Dismounting their horses, one stayed outside while the others went in the saloon.

In moments, one flew out the swinging doors and tumbled to the ground holding his mouth. Then another and another until all seven stood looking at each other.

The swinging doors opened with a Mexican rider holding each side, and two carried the body of the leader Matt had killed.

They threw him over his horse and yelled at the seven riders to mount their horses. The other six stood talking to each other. Woody made his way down the street, with his hand on his side. That alone made Matt step out into the street himself.

The six older riders made their way to Matt. He stood slightly open legged holding the butts of his guns. "Are you the one that shot one of my men?" One of them asked.

Matt always played his cards as fair as he could, until he had no choice in the matter. That would only make him draw his guns, in a thundering speed never missing his targets. "That was me," Matt told him looking in his eyes.

Spreading his hands out, the others moved away from him as if he was going to draw against Matt by himself. "Watch out for that gringo. He's real damn fast," said one of the riders who'd seen Matt shoot his leader in the saloon.

The older Mexican standing in the middle of the street spoke to Matt, "Before I kill you gringo, tell me your name."

"My name is Matt Bryan, U. S. Marshal." He took two steps closer studying the crowd of men on the street, and the ones on their horses, He didn't really worry about them because their guns were in the sheriff's office.

"Matt Bryan?" the older Mexican said loudly. Throwing his hands in the air he said, "U. S. Marshal?" They all looked at each other because they had never seen their real boss back down from anyone. He was the oldest, but he was slim and was known to draw a pistol lightning fast, but today he held his hands high in the air as Matt walked closer. Woody stopped at the side of the first building. Matt kept moving closer to the leader.

A big smile broke out on the Mexican man's face, still holding his hands in the air. Hearing Matt's full name had rung a bell inside his head. Down in Mexico every older man including the women knew of the gringo called Matt Bryan and how fast he was. But he knew Matt and said, "Mijo, where in the hell have you been?"

No one had ever known looking at Matt Bryan or Kathy that they were both half breed until that day."Well I'll be damn Pops. What the hell are you doing with this bunch of nothings?" Matt said laughing out loud.

The older Mexican man put his hands down, spoke a few words in Spanish making the other riders cool down a bit. Matt Bryan's father was half breed himself since his father had married a Mexican woman in Mexico. The last name Bryan was known in most small towns and in Mexico because of the size of ranch the Bryans owned. If you messed around with a Bryan, hell would break loose.

Matt looked at his father asking, "What brings you out here?"

Carlos Bryan touched his thin mustache a few times, then said, "Came down here to see my baby girl Kathy and my grand-baby Margie." He walked over to Matt giving him a hug. "Last time I seen you boy, you only packed one pistol. Why now two?"

Matt held his father's shoulders with both hands as he began telling him about Kathy and Margie's death and how crooked Judge Robert Blaylock turned out to be.

Carlos held on to Matt's arms and felt weak from the news and said, "I got here too damn late."

"What do you mean too late?" he asked looking at his father curiously.

Carlos spoke words to his men and every one of them rode off out of town. Matt needed answers why his father had said too late, also why he rode with a bunch of men into town. However, he didn't have to ask because his father Carlos Bryan had the wits of an otter.

He could tell Matt wanted to know, "I got a letter from Kathy saying she needed help and brought her some cattle sitting right outside of town." He stood still for a while, then looked up at the sky, "Dark clouds from the north are headed this way. We got to put the cattle somewhere safe."

"I took over the Judge's house. He's dead as well by me," Matt said pointing towards the Judge's home. Then Matt called Woody over.

"With this weather coming son, you shouldn't be walking around with a wound like that," Carlos said. He'd shown concern the moment he'd seen Woody holding his side. Woody nodded taking in the scenery up above, that promised one hell of a storm.

The cattle, that earlier sat only a few miles right outside of town, had all been brought to the Judge's fenced off land.

Half of the Mexican riders stayed there and the rest at the banker's home.

Dark clouds hovered over Lubbock as lightning flashes in the distance, shot through the darkened sky above. The thunder took its toll barking amidst the silence of the night. Winds began whipping the falling rain as it beat upon the windows.

Flashes of light shot into the bedroom where Matt laid. He thought about his father and he could not remember why he left when he'd been so young. It seemed his father hadn't changed, only his hair had turned gray. But now, Matt was a man and at the moment the only friend Woody could depend on. To pass on the talent of using guns, was only one of many Woody would learn from Matt.

But each lesson had a price money could not buy the price of loyalty, bravery, and will power to succeed all laid within his heart. It would all burst out completely and would become a leader himself.

For now, Woody laid in a bed only a few rooms from Matt. His wound sent flashes of pain within his body. He not only drank to kill the pain, but to help forget the past he'd lived.

The storm continued through the night and half the next day. But to keep a man out of a saloon would take much more than raindrops. All the Mexican outfit hung around to hear the piano player and Dusty Winters sing in her high pitched tone. Her voice made the Mexican riders yell at the top of their lungs. For years Dusty had been the only one to sit on top of the piano. Also, a hat turned upside down so anyone with a heart, could drop a coin or two for her and the piano player. Dusty stood four foot eleven and was round as was tall. However, she sang her little fat butt off for the cowboys in town. Getting on and off the top of the piano took at least two men. That night the drunken Mexican riders tossed coins in her hat as they sang along beside her.

The swinging doors flew open as three rough looking men stepped inside, all soaked in rainwater. Each walked up to the bar, taking off their ankle length black silk coats. Tossing them over the backs of chairs, they turned to watch Dusty sing her song. She set her eyes on the three men and could tell they were not just any cowhands looking for drinks. Each one packed double holsters tied right above the knees. The saloon in moments got quiet, then one of them said, "I don't care who the hell does it, but get up and go get Matt Bryan. We already know he's here in Lubbock."

In the corner of the saloon Carlos Bryan studied the three men standing up saying, "You boys won't see the sun come up tomorrow and you sure won't get to see Matt Bryan."

"Look old man, I don't want to hurt you, but you're asking for it," one said.

"All three of you are still wet behind your ears and it ain't from the rain," Carlos replied.

Not wasting any more time, one of them drew his guns out at Carlos. But he was way much quicker as he sent the gunman's body past the other two with a bullet in each eye, "That was pretty damn fast old man," one of them said.

"Now stick those back in your holsters and try me."

"Both of you will have to draw because I'm shooting to kill each one of you," He said as he spun his .44's on his fingers dropping them back inside his holsters.

One of the young gun-ho men spoke up to try to confuse him. "We're looking for Matt Bryan." But he tried to sneak in a quick draw, Carlos again with lightning speed ended the lives of both men as the thunder rocked the sky outside.

Matt Bryan tossed and turned in his bed. He could tell the sounds of thunder and guns in Lubbock didn't ever sound the same to him. When would the killings or at least the shootings stop in Lubbock went through Matt's mind, staying in bed until he went to sleep.

Throwing the bodies out the back door of the saloon, an old man dug through their pockets in the rain. He took off their holsters, pocket watches, hats, boots and anything he could get to sell and feed his family. The back door opened again as the bartender tossed the three black coats out, "Keep everything you find. But come morning, bury them somewhere away from town okay?"

"Yes sir. Just keep tossing them out here. I'll take care of the rest," the old man answered.

"There's three horses out front. Take them, too," the bartender said.

More men had been killed in Lubbock and more would meet their maker. Now two Bryans were in town and both were lightning fast with pistols.

Inside the saloon, Dusty began to sing as the piano player played through the night. Carlos and his men sat drinking whiskey.

The saloon girls one by one took men to their rooms.

CHAPTER SEVENTEEN

The lone spire of a yucca plant, better known to most as "God's Candle", stood straight up in the white sands. Ricochets of heat waves shot into Woody's face. He wiped away sweat pouring down his face. The paint he was riding was another gift from Matt Bryan's father Carlos. Lightning was too old for the journey into Mexico. The last known place Danny Moore had been seen, was at a ranch in the far eastern mountains, in the most dangerous territory in Mexico. To most Mexicans a white man was known as "gringo" and to make it through, the gringo would have to know his stuff. Speaking a few words in Spanish would help and Carlos had shared plenty. He also showed him how to treat a senorita with words of charm and respect. He had learned a lot from Matt and Carlos Bryan during the five years he'd been with them in Lubbock. But he now followed the map in his head Carlos had given him along with the privilege of being called his friend.

Friendship in a land of the unknown only went so far. Money and gold would do the trick to find out information. Once his back was turned, his survival depended on how he'd hide his tracks, or kept looking over his shoulder ever so often.

Woody's .44 pistol sparkled as he sat on his paint checking to see if it was loaded, thinking something was up ahead. His lightning speed draw Matt and Carlos had spent time perfecting, was one quick motion, combined with placing it back in his holster would come in handy. Many times he would be tested by more than one at a time. Another spare gun, tucked away in the back of his belt, had a hair trigger. He still carried his Bowie knife on his left side. His buffalo rifle was in the leather scabbard to one side. He'd used it many times and would use again.

On the other side was a regular .44-40 Winchester loaded and ready to use. Still mounted on his paint, Woody could have been gunned down easily. He'd been spotted miles away, the ten to twelve Mexicans now pointed their rifles at him. A voice echoed through the mountains, "Gringo, slowly dismount your donkey, put all your guns on the ground, then step away from them." He had said "donkey" but was far from right. The paint was beautiful and he'd said "donkey" to show humor to the others listening.

Doing exactly as he was told, Woody slowly dismounted the paint. He stood outnumbered and quite unarmed. "What brings you here gringo?" one Mexican asked for all the rest.

"I'm a friend of Carlos Bryan and I'm looking for Danny Moore," Woody answered with his hands up high.

"Senor Carlos Bryan. Yes, of course we know him, he's a good man," the Mexican man replied motioning to the others to put away their guns and rifles. "This gringo you say you're looking for Danny Moore, is he a friend of yours as well?" he asked stepping closer looking Woody in the eyes. Before Woody could answer, the Mexican man shouted, "We do not like that name here!"

"I'm here to kill him," Woody responded with his hands still in the air.

A big smile broke out on the Mexican man's face while the others began laughing out loud. Woody smiled back lowering his hands. "Mijo, you need an army to get at him," the Mexican man warned. "That man is the worst outlaw any man will ever get to know and you alone will not do it."

"He belongs to me and I will kill him along with anyone else who steps in the way," Woody said walking to his guns.

"If they ride up on you like we did, you will have no chance," said the Mexican.

Woody had already known this bunch was friendly by what Carlos had said, but played it off anyways. According to Carlos, the deeper into Mexico, the more dangerous it would be. As the night took its toll, He was told he could stay at the small village, where music continued through the night. He tied his paint next to a broken down wagon after feeding and watering it. He took his saddle under the wagon where he laid to sleep. As his dreams began to unfold, He could feel the hypnotic beat of the drumming. Like he knew from the Indian tribe he knew so well. But flashes of silhouettes danced in his mind. The need to kill Danny Moore was the only thing he wanted in real life and even in his dreams.

Eleven years had passed since he had lost his parents to the hands of the wagon master and his men, including Danny Moore. Not one shot was fired by the point man to the wagon train. Just leading the way was enough for Woody to want to kill him.

As the sun made its way over the mountains, Woody was standing holding the reins of the paint ready to ride out. The laughter of the children running outside houses made of clay, sand and water caught his attention. They looked so happy and near them stood the most beautifulest Mexican woman Woody had ever set his eyes on. She looked his way, he held his hat with two fingers at the brim nodding as he said, "Good morning Senorita."

She stopped and smiled at him because she had never seen a gringo so young, that held the presence of a well-educated man.

"Good morning Senor," she replied holding the hands of two small children smiling warmly.

Carlos had told Woody many women would always pay more attention to a respectful man than a fool. Mounting his horse, he rode behind the children. In a corral with hay bales for seats, the children waited for the young Mexican woman. As she closed the gate, Woody stopped to take a good look at her. When their eyes met, time froze for a moment. " Es usted la maestra?" Woody asked.[*"Are you the teacher?"*]

"Si, yo soy. Le gustaria venir a la escuela y escucharme algun dia?" she said with a smile. [*"Yes, I am. Would you like to come to the school and hear me one day?"*]

"Alugn dia. Le prometo gue lo hare," he answered swallowing the beef jerky he'd been chewing on. [*"One day. I promise I will."*] " Si vengo en un dia, estar bien?" he asked after dismounting his paint walking up to the gate. [*"If I come one day, is it okay?"*]

"My name is Ruthy Cantu and you may visit any time you wish Senor," She said taking a step forward. He studied her eyes for a while and could feel she meant every word. She had been able to speak

English with Woody, but she wanted to see how much he actually knew.

Carlos had taken his time teaching Woody quite well, "I'm going into the mountains for a while, but I'll be back by here soon," Woody told her.

"Last night I heard my father tell my mother that a gringo is here looking for Danny Moore to kill him." She took a step closer speaking very low, "That man is a very bad man and from what I hear, he has killed many men before."

Woody stood motionless seeing Danny Moore in his mind; that image, along with what Ruthy told him, would not be enough to stop the hunt of death he needed to finish. "I always keep my promises," he said nodding once. As he mounted his paint, he looked back at Ruthy. Knowing they liked each other the moment their eyes met.

Woody rode freely past the men behind the rocks since he'd told them he was there to kill Danny Moore. At least that was what he thought. But the real reason was that he'd said Carlos Bryan was a friend of his.

The ride further into Mexico would become quite dangerous.

Carlos had painted a picture with words that made the danger so vivid in Woody's mind. As if the nightmare came true only miles down a sloppy path, bullets raced by his head. To stay alive he had to dive off the paint. Throwing himself to the ground only made him tumble down the path, the paint nearly stumbled over his body while running and sliding. Outlaw territory was a dog eat dog world and only the smartest or fastest with guns would survive. The bottom of the path opened up and a cliff loomed downward into a wide rushing river. Grabbing the paint and jumping into the cold river, may have been why he remained alive. Down below he swam to the edge quickly making his way into the darkness of the forest, Gunshots towards him echoed in the air.

Never getting to see whom or knowing why he could now understand what Carlos meant by sleeping with one eye open. Falling asleep on the paint was how he almost lost his life. Now he would have to find a good place to rest up for the next day's ride. Within the forest, he would have to stay a while. Thinking of how to kill several men one at a time. For the ones who'd shot at him once would come calling again. To them it was a game to kill the gringo on the paint. But to Woody it was and would be survival and to go on with his plans to kill Danny Moore.

Unsaddling the paint, Woody had picked a spot with only one way in and out. If they wanted him, the outlaws would have to enter that way. He left them no choice. He broke twigs five or six inches long on the ground scattering them along the entrance. If a horse stepped on them, he would know someone was on their way for him.

The night was quiet as the moon sent a dim glow but misty from the river close by. It would be cool and he would have to pull out his bear coat to keep him warm. A campfire would only pinpoint his spot.

The dawn's early light was the only thing that made the owl stop hooting, it flew over the paint causing it to flinch. The sudden rustle in the bushes the paint was tied to, made him draw his pistol lightning fast. Standing to see the owl disappear into another part of the forest, he saddled the paint. Walking towards the entrance, he could hear twigs breaking. Whoever it was didn't care about being heard and was getting closer and closer. Mounting the paint, he held onto the reins with one hand and his pistol in the other.

Digging his spurs into the sides of his paint, Woody rode towards the breaking twigs as fast as he could, knowing exactly what was up ahead. The sound of hooves stomping on the ground as twigs snapped in pieces, made the brown bear rise on two legs as Woody stormed past it.

Cutting to one side of the river, Woody's paint had covered ground, but the gunshots started as before. This time he only ducked down on the paint, He raced away out of sight into more trees. For the moment, he was safe, allowing the paint to rest in case they had to run again. "Gringo you have nowhere to hide," a voiced echoed through the trees, breaking the silence. "Come out and meet your maker."

Woody knew he was being tested and once they knew where he was, he would be shot down like a dog, so he remained quiet.

Tying his horse to some bushes, Woody pulled out his moccasin boots. Dashing into the trees with his Bowie knife in his hand, he could see through the trees and bushes up ahead. The five men who awaited him to make any sound. Woody threw a rock into the trees over their heads. The five outlaws dismounted their horses. Pointing to the sound, one of them seemed to be in control of the rest.

That one was to die first, the others might choose to ride on if he could sell his hog right. In no time, he stood behind the leader. As he turned looking at Woody in the eyes, The butt of Woody's gun smacked down on the man's head knocking him out cold. Carlos had told him that if you taunt with a man's life, you might as well kill him or he'll come back someday for your life. The cut from the Bowie knife was thin but deep ending the man's life on the spot.

Backing up into the trees, Woody waited for the others to find their leader. Sure enough, as soon as they spotted him, they all hurried to their horses. They walked backwards looking to see if Woody was after them. In minutes, each one had disappeared into another part of the forest.

A few days had passed as Woody had been riding along the river that seemed endless. Each time he saw a certain type of flat rock, he would dismount the paint and put them into the pouch he carried the gold nuggets in.

While he made camp, he kept his thoughts together by chipping away at the flint rocks, shaping them into arrowheads. White smoke drifted sideways up ahead. Woody followed it until the forest opened up. The stream slowed down weaving into beautiful meadows displaying flowers and trees. Up ahead stood the most well built cabin Woody had ever seen. Many horses running wild and eight to ten cows grazing on the grassy fields.

An old gray haired Mexican man stood beside the cabin, Woody made his way closer. The shotgun was in plain sight and he knew the old man would protect himself and his land as well. "Estoy muy consado y necesito descansar y comer algo, Pagare con dinero o con oro," Woody told him with his hands in the air. [*I'm very tired and I need to rest and eat something. I'll pay with money or with gold."*]

"You gringos learn to speak Spanish and you think you can buy the world," the old Mexican man said smiling at Woody.

"Thank God you can speak English." Woody said.

"Let the paint ride out in the pasture with my horses, then come on in and we'll talk about your gold and money," He said with a wink. He made his way inside talking with someone else.

Woody placed his saddle on the wooden fence that outlined one side of the old man's land. He was still wearing his moccasins and held his boots in one hand. As he knocked on the door, it opened and he stepped inside. "Close the door it gets cold at night and we have to save the heat," said an old white lady standing over to one side.

He closed the door and was told to have a seat. After a good meal and a few hours rest, He got up and went outside to walk around the cabin. He saw the old Mexican man and his wife looking east to the mountains. "I pray he rots in hell," he heard the old lady say. He stood still wondering what she meant. They turned around seeing Woody only a few steps away.

"Sorry you had to hear that son," the old Mexican man told Woody holding his wife's hand. "She was talking about that son of a bitch Danny Moore."

"I'm looking for a man by that name," Woody told them more confused than ever. "Do y'all know how far east I got to go?"

"Sonny, he's six feet under us and about fifty miles into those mountains dead," the old lady said laughing.

"I don't understand what you mean," said Woody.

The old man spoke softly as he began telling the story of Danny

Moore's evil acts. He killed him after he'd killed his father-in-law, many years ago for his money. His death had haunted him and his wife and each day they stood looking into the mountains cursing the name of the dead man, Danny Moore.

Woody took off his hat putting the story together and told them both all about the wagon master and his men and how he'd killed them all. Except for the point man, whose name was also Danny Moore.

"Danny Moore raped me and when I had his child, he took him with him," the old white lady said.

"That's when I went into those mountains and killed him myself. But never knew what happened to the child. I used to work for my wife's father and after Danny Moore killed him, we got together and we've been here all these years," the old man said wiping tears from his eyes."Many years ago, a man came by and told us a story of a man whose name was Danny Moore Jr. That's when we found out where he was and that he was more evil than his father used to be."

"I've got to be leaving now," Woody said putting on his hat. "I want to thank you folks for the food and rest," he told them handing the old man a gold nugget and some paper money. "Danny Moore killed my mother and father and I won't stop until I kill him," Woody said.

Woody rode away toward the eastern mountains with a rage instilled inside his heart knowing Danny Moore Jr. and to die as soon as possible.

CHAPTER EIGHTEEN

Carlos Bryan's ranch, which had been said to be the largest in all of Mexico, lay opposite the direction Woody was heading.

The idea of going there someday set in his mind. For now, he rode away from the small cabin with the information he'd gotten about the point man. Danny Moore being a Jr. only made Woody want to kill even more for the bloodline of Moores seemed to have a way of taking many lives for the love of money and gold.

In the brisk morning open flat land, anyone could easily lose their life to the band of outlaw Mexicans. They laid in wait to kill anyone. They nested next to narrow trails going into the mountains. Being a gringo, Woody would be killed on the spot and left for the buzzards to feast upon.

The glorious desert held its beauty as the many scattered Joshua trees, "Yucca brevifollas" stood their ground. Patches of burnt tones on the grassy weeds seemed to call for water as they held on for life. Woody took the last drink from his canteen while his paint rode on its own. Letting the reins loose would allow his horse to seek out water. Where there was water would be other types of life gathering as well.

Falling asleep the paint made its way around big boulders, Woody dreamed on of past events. The silhouette of a lone rider seemed to always find its way into his mind, setting a scar within his soul.

The night had begun as the wind turned into a bitter cold.

Opening his eyes, Woody looked on at the sparkling water hole up ahead. The paint had done well and only it could drink the water. Woody would have to boil his drinking water. The two flat arrow shaped flint rocks his Indian friends had given him, still hung around his neck on a leather strap, Dismounting the paint, Woody gathered dry weeds, starting a fire tapping the flint rocks which hung from his neck everywhere he went. In moments, dark clouds hid the moon from view. Woody sat eating pieces of rattlesnake he'd cooked. The clouds began rolling even quicker by the minute, telling Woody a storm would soon hit. Sounds of thunder following flashes of light echoed through the desert. It was good for rain to fall upon the dry land.

What wasn't good was the hard blow that knocked Woody out cold. It had been the end of a butt of a rifle. Three Mexican outlaws stood over his body. Laughing at the gringo on the ground, they tied him up throwing him over the paint.

Mounting their horses, they rode away with a treasure they should have killed on the spot. If he had the chance, each one would die very quick. After riding a mile, they laughed speaking of how they would punish their captive gringo.

A small shack had been built many years ago it squeaked with the motion of the wind and could fall any minute. The falling rain had awakened Woody. The three Mexican outlaws tied him up from all four of his limbs between two of the Joshua trees that seemed to live in the desert forever. He would spend the night out in the cold. The storm took its toll. Laughing, one of the Mexican outlaws told him, "You will enjoy the water; it will be your last bath before you die, pincha gringo."

The other two were inside with everything he owned, while the third one tied the horses up to more trees. Before he went inside, he walked up to Woody making sure the ropes were tight, then backhanded him as he passed out once more.

The thunder roared the desert's open range, flashes of lightning appeared closer and closer. Inside the shack, the three Mexican outlaws turned on a lantern and were surprised at how much money and gold nuggets Woody had been carrying. Drinking whiskey straight out of the bottle with no hesitation, they each danced around the shack with their share of gold and money.

Outside the storm danced over the small shack, lightning pounded the ground within inches of Woody. Soaked with the falling rain, he would die if hit by lightning. But that night Woody was once again awakened by a flash of lightning inches away from his left arm. Sending the Joshua tree splintering into pieces, Woody's arm had been freed and it was then that the flint rocks around his neck would come in handy. Quickly cutting away at the ropes, he was free. In seconds, he stood outside the door of the shack. Through a knothole in one of the wooden boards, he looked to see where his guns laid. He would have to be very fast kicking in the door. Like the strike of a rattlesnake, Woody kicked the door in, knocking one Mexican off his feet as he dove inside. Lightning fast Woody grabbed his pistol rolling to one side, bullets from the other two pierced the wood floor. Woody didn't miss like they did, which had caused the two still standing to fall dead. Woody now stood over the one who'd gotten hit by the door, a smile overtook him and kicked at the Mexican's face.

"Get up and go outside to enjoy your last bath," Woody said.

"Senor Gringo, please forgive me," the Mexican outlaw began pleading for his life.

"Does that mean you have enjoyed your bath?" Woody asked still holding his smile. As flashes of lightning brought thunder, sounds of Woody's gun echoed as well. Three more men had died taunting with Woody's life.

Gathering only the items belonging to him, Woody waited out the storm until the morning dawn's light. Mounting the paint, he rode on once more into the desert. Pulling the leather strap from under his shirt, he kissed his arrowheads. Without them, he would probably be dead. At times, the shadow of a bald eagle would pass Woody's path and he could feel his life was under the watchful eyes of his Indian friends. Only a white man who had lived with the red man would know how the spirits stayed in one's life.

Many times in the hands of death. Woody had been able to escape and luck would have little to do with surviving as he had done. Closing his eyes while on his paint he could hear sounds of the Indian drummer within his mind. The chants of the medicine man were also heard as they remained in his life forever. The need to kill Danny Moore had grown even more. Woody thought of how many more people would die, if another wagon train took place.

The desert edge of the mountains started with large boulders that seemed to have crumbled down in the years past. Small trails led Woody into a narrow pathway between two mountains. He walked next to his paint saying, "The pathway in between the two mountains, will lead you straight through a valley that sets deep inside." The words Carlos Bryan had told Woody remained as if Carlos was the one speaking.

Once inside the valley Woody would have to travel at night very carefully. Only a wise man would not become a sitting duck, to the eyes of the many outlaws roaming from the law.

The gushing sound of the waterfall was where Woody would have to swim into. As the water fell into the lake, it seemed to not go anywhere. Swimming through the falling water would take him to the other side of the valley. There streams flowed from the lake. Three streams would come together at one point and it was there he was told all hell would break loose. Echoes of wild men known to the law as wanted dead or alive sat around playing cards. Some cleaned their guns and some slept. Woody quietly moved through the night, the camp fires let him see about 30 men scattered out. He knew only what Carlos had told him of these men and how they'd killed many people for the love of money and gold. Strapping on his moccasins Woody would leave a message, making them think a traitor among them had killed one of their own.

Woody moved through the night stealthily as if he were hunting an animal. As the outlaws slept, Woody cut across their throats.

Whatever dreams the outlaws were having would be their last. Crawling into the silent darkness of the night, he checked to see which one carried a knife. Pulling the knife out of its sheath, he used it to cut the closest to him, then placing the knife beside another who slept. The outlaws would awaken thinking the one with the bloody knife had killed the rest. Carlos was right hell could and did break loose. Woody crept on next to a stream by the glow of the moon.

After about an hour, Woody was far enough to stop to take a good rest. The next morning, the valley at dawn was just as Carlos had told him and its beauty would remain in his mind. Going back through the same way would not be safe and making it looking for Danny Moore was not safe at all. The paint had made the trip well enough. Woody sat up straight in the saddle. The open land up ahead was another memory, that would stay within Woody's mind forever. The three streams came together as Carlos had said and the most beautiful meadows He'd seen left him motionless. This had to be the Promised Land that no wagon train would ever see, but all were told of.

In the distance up ahead surrounded by a small white fence, lay a graveyard where Woody would go first. Looking at the largest tombstone, he read the name carved in it to himself, "Here lies Danny Moore Sr." The name was of the father whose son Woody had been hunting for many years.

Riding on Woody could see a big ranch where the point man would most likely be hiding out. Scattered cattle grazed on the meadows as wild horses roamed the land. Woody stood motionless counting the men moving about. It would be very hard to get to Danny Moore alone, but there was no turning back.

For two days, Woody camped out alone in the unknown land. Just when he'd finished making dozens of arrows' out of the white boards of the graveyard fence. He was about to add a flint rock arrow head to each one. To his left around a bend, a stampede of wild horses rushed into the meadow up ahead. Many more cowboys were to be added to the count with the others. It would be even harder to kill that many and not be noticed. So a better plan had to be taken, Once Danny Moore was dead, it would all be over. To kill one would be easy, but to kill so many would be tough for one man. He sat wondering as he mixed powders together with water from his canteen.

As the night took its turn, Woody soaked the arrows in a mixture of what would bring death a lot quicker. His Indian friends had shown him how to gather poisons, in times when one needed quick silent deaths. In Woody's mind every man at the ranch had a reason to die, just because they were a friend of Danny Moore.

From the branch of a magnificent Oak tree, Woody made a bow and he used a thin leather strap for the string. Waiting until the night's darkest hours, Woody began his hunt to kill as many as he could. With arrows or his Bowie knife, the silent deaths left bodies of men lying on the ground everywhere.

Now closer to the ranch, Woody would have to slip in and kill the point man once inside. Making his way to the back door of the ranch, the moon cast a dim glow as he listened. Right behind him stood someone leaving him to do what any right thinking man would do. He raised his hands up high. The trick worked because he was still alive as the voice broke the silent night." "You been killing a lot of men tonight." Woody stood motionless waiting for the right moment he could also kill whoever stood behind him. "You could have killed me, stupid." Woody's mind raced on as he wanted to try his lightning speed draw but turning around might be his death.

The sounds of spurs told Woody just how close the man was from his back and walking up behind him he knew the gunman had to be pointing a gun at him. The voice spoke once again. Woody was puzzled at how low the gunman was speaking, "Why did you take so damn long to get here?" Now Woody was quite surprised because the gunman thought he was on his side.

With his hands still in the air, Woody began turning to face the gunman, "I tried to get here sooner than this." He was for real in what he told the gunman.

The gunman never realized Woody was not on his side and spoke in a very low voice, "When we get the money, we will have to split up because you could get me killed with your stupid ways." Still holding his hands in the air, the gunman told Woody, "Put your stupid hands down and this will be the last time, I work with you no matter what Daniels says." The gunman had been sent to rob the ranch and had thought Woody was the one sent to help.

Once Woody put his hands down he knew he'd have a chance to kill the gunman in front of him. Puzzled, he asked in a low voice, "What do we do now?"

"You mean to tell me Daniels sent you here, without a clue who I am or what to do?" the gunman asked.

Woody would now play along and said, "All I know is that you're the boss."

The gunman smiled and as the moon's dim light hit his mouth, his gold teeth shined. His head rose showing Woody he would take the compliment as told. "We go inside and wake up this man by the name of Danny Moore, make him open up the safe and take the money."

Now Woody knew this man in front of him would die, but would use him as long as he could. He held out his hand to shake the gunman's hand.

"We don't have time for stupid things like that. Let's get to work." The gunman said.

Woody felt like killing him at that point, but asked, "How do we get inside?"

"I been here three weeks stupid and know everything," the gunman said smiling again. He paused for a moment then looked around and back at Woody saying, "They think I'm a dumb work hand, but I'm smarter than all of them." Pushing Woody to one side, the gunman said, "I left a window unlocked to get in stupid, Now come on. "

Being called stupid was getting old and he really felt like beating the crap out of the gunman instead of killing him, Woody let him lead the way. Once inside, the gunman walked down the hall and up the stairs to where Danny Moore would be asleep. The slap across his face awoke him up, kicking trying to grab anything in front of him. The gunman spoke and stuck the barrel of his gun into his mouth. "If you want to die stupid, just make a sound."

Danny Moore was as still as a rock on the bed.

"Get up slow and open the safe or die."

Danny Moore got out of bed making his way to the safe, pulling out handfuls of money and gold. The gunmen grabbed the pillowcase from the bed and began to fill it up. Woody stood in shock at what he had just seen and could not believe his eyes. He started to put together what would only make sense.

"I'd been better without you," the gunman said looking at Woody."

"We'll take Danny Moore in case his men ride up on us," Woody spoke in a low cold voice.

CHAPTER NINETEEN

In the pitch black darkness of the night, in Woody's mind it almost all came to an end. Killing Danny Moore Jr. would be a pleasure and to also see the pain that punishment would bring death as slow as possible. He could only hope to erase the awful memories of his own family's death. But no matter how many times someone died in his path, he would forever miss Frank and Maggie.

The gunman up in front led the way out from the ranch. Moore's hands were tied to the saddle horn. A few yards away Woody tried to study Moore's ways. As he followed behind them, he never let go of his .44 pistol. The only reason he hadn't already killed Moore was because, Woody needed to somehow see the reaction in the point man's eyes.

Any minute the gunman in front who'd keep calling Woody stupid would do it again. Passing the graveyard the white picket fence glowed in the dim moonlight. It was then the gunman yelled, "Hurry up, stupid." Woody dug the spurs he'd gotten from Galindo many years ago into the paint's sides. As his horse raced forward, Woody pulled out his Bowie knife. In one quick slash, the gunman's throat was bleeding. Although he held his hand over the gash, blood poured out between his fingers as he looked at Woody for the last time.

Moore's eyes held a fear he would also die right then, but Woody told him, "If you call me stupid, I'll kill you as well."

Moore kicked his horse's sides to speed up a little to ride beside

Woody and said, "Mister, I have no idea who you are or why you robbed me, but keep the money for yourself. Just please don't kill me."

Woody slapped Moore's face and took the horse's reins in his hands to pull the other horse along.

Riding a few hours, no one had said a word, then Moore spoke up, "Mister, where in the hell are you taking me?"

Woody stopped the paint and got off untying Moore's hands saying, "Had to find a tree strong enough to hold your body and from the looks of it, this one here will do."

Moore's eyes widened and even though it was dark, Woody could tell. Instilling fear in Moore was Woody's plan, then the painful punishment would follow. It was then Moore began begging for his life. "Mister, you're making an awful mistake. Just take the money and please let me go."

"You always killed after you got the money, so now it's your turn to die," Woody said as he threw the rope over the tree limb.

"Mister, so help me God, I've never killed anyone," Moore cried.

"I never seen you kill anyone, but you sure as hell pointed the way," Woody replied as he began beating Moore's face with his fist.

"Please mister, just tell me what you're talking about pointing the way," Moore begged. His cries for his life were now stronger than ever as Woody placed the rope around his neck.

"You're the point man for wagon trains and many people died

including my parents because of you," He answered as he pulled the rope tight around Moore's neck.

"Oh my God! You're making an awful mistake," Moore screamed while Woody tied the loose end of the rope to the saddle horn.

"It wasn't me. It was my twin brother. He's the point man for the wagon trains, I never knew anyone being killed."

Woody looked at Moore and in the moon's glow, he could see his tears rolling down his face. He began untying the rope from Moore's neck and asked, "How can you prove it?"

"Only my father and mother know we are twins, but they're both dead mister," Moore said still crying.

Woody could not kill Moore until he knew for sure he had the right man. From what the old man and woman who lived in the small cabin in the meadows had told him, none of them said a thing about twins. He started a fire as he said, "I been looking for twelve years to kill a man named Danny Moore. In my path to you, I met a couple in the meadows on the other side of these mountains." As he began a meal he told Moore, "The old man said that he'd killed a Danny Moore, Sr. Then went on saying that his wife the old lady there, had been raped and had a child. He never said nothing about twins." Moore stood up and Woody quickly pulled his pistol out saying, "If you ever spook me like that again, I'll shoot you on the spot."

Moore now needed answers just like Woody did, but his was to know about the old lady in the meadows. "Mister, please let's go speak with them."

Now Woody was puzzled and if he didn't find out, it would haunt him forever. He had promised Carlos not to tell anyone of the passage through the waterfall. So, the trip around the mountains would now take a little over a week. If, in fact, Moore had a twin brother, Woody may have his hands full, but he would have let this one go.

Camps at night were just the same as all the rest, coffee, beans and chili, sometimes Rattlesnakes or rabbit. Around the bend, maybe a day's ride, the meadows would come into view. But to Woody's luck, the next day's smoky clouds up ahead told the cabin was on fire and maybe the old couple had been killed.

Looking on many riders, most likely outlaws fled away. Woody quickly pulled out his buffalo rifle still sitting on the paint and loaded it. Steadily aiming at the group of fleeing men, he told Moore, "Stay on your horse and don't piss me off." The booming sound of the buffalo rifle echoed in the mountains. One outlaw toppled over his horse dead. Woody reloaded his buffalo rifle, the thundering boom left another soul on the ground dead. The third one landed on his face dead, but the others seemed to be too far away. So, he quickly moved on in the direction of the burning cabin. No one inside would survive the flames. Woody and Moore looked at each other. Speaking first, Woody told Moore, "Now there's no one who can make your bond."

"At least let me dig my own grave mister," Moore said as his head dropped to the ground.

The sound of voices told the old couple it was Woody and someone else. They opened a cellar door about twenty yards away from the burning cabin. Woody rushed to help the old man out of the cellar and was about to help the old lady. Moore jumped off his horse, and with his hands still tied, he tried to help the old lady. Reaching for his hands, she froze staring at Moore saying to herself, "Oh my God. It can't be you." Her husband, Woody and Moore all looked at each other because they couldn't understand what she meant. As she stepped out of the cellar, she fell to her knees crying.

"How did you know so fast who I am?" Moore asked, quickly kneeling next to her.

She pointed to his ear saying, "Your father wanted to tell you both apart and marked you both by cutting the tip of one ear off each one."

Moore hugged the old lady as Woody walked up to them while he asked, "Is the other twin cut on the same ear?"

She reached for her husband saying, "I'm sorry I didn't tell you I'd had twins." Wiping away tears from her eyes, she continued, "It was hard saying I'd lost one son, but to have to say two would have killed me."

"Mister, you got the wrong man," Moore said as tears rolled down his face while he looked at Woody. "And I ask of you to let us be."

"Is the other twin cut on the same ear?" Woody asked again kneeling down next to the old lady.

"The other's ear is cut on the right side, just like this one's here on the left," she answered shaking her head no.

Now Woody could set a better trail to seek out the man he most wanted to kill. But where to find that man would be hell to know. Rounding up the old couple's horses and hitching them to a wagon had taken almost the whole day. The outlaws would no longer come back to mess with the old couple, due to the booming buffalo rifle that had left three dead and would kill again.

Camping out next to the cellar while the old couple and Moore slept inside, Woody could watch out for any trouble that might come their way. The squeak of the cellar door told him someone was coming out. He stood next to his camp fire, the old man only stuck half his body out holding a bottle of whiskey. He waved it towards Woody asking, "How about a drink?"

"You just made my day old man," he said. It was like a dream come true seeing that whiskey bottle. He leaned over the get the bottle asking, "How's your wife taking the news of her son?"

"She's the happiest I've seen her in a very long time," He answered smiling and reaching to shake Woody's hand. "Thank you Woody," Not many people had ever told Woody "thank you" and it made him feel good inside knowing he'd done something good. After a few hours sipping on the whiskey, Woody began to feel warm inside and somehow needed to move on.

As the dawn's early light began to brighten the meadows, Woody had been long gone. But he could still see the place where the old couple and Moore were. Moore had gathered his holster where Woody had left it and mounted his horses. As he started rounding the cattle, Woody could tell everything was going to be okay. Moore was taking his mother home with him and the old man as well.

The reason Woody had thought to leave was because in his mind, he knew he'd be asked to stay at Moore's ranch. He had another plan which would be, to keep searching for the real killer Moore. Identifying the other twin would now be much easier, because of the cut on his right ear. Leaving Mexico, he had one more stop to make, but first, he wanted to get cleaned up a bit.

Woody rode until he found the trail where he'd spent the night and met the young school teacher. He thought to get a good rest, but the buzzards in the sky told another story.

Setting a good fast pace, Woody looked on for any signs of an ambush. The roaming pack of wolves was what assured him it would be okay to move in faster. If the pack of wolves kept going against the wind, they would sense any danger up ahead.

Tracks on the ground of dry horseshoes told Woody riders had ridden by a few days ago, while it had been raining. The little village came into view. He rode his paint down the path to the first stone house. He dismounted his horse and could see bodies lying down dead everywhere. Even the horses and cattle had been shot. Motionless the wind seemed to bring a gentle whisper in his ears. He could clearly hear Maggie's voice.

It was then Woody knew what he had to do from then on and it was to hunt down ruthless killers. But to wear a badge would only put him in the eyes of everyone. Reading tracks and signs of how the people had been killed, he could tell by the wagon tracks someone had gotten away.

Following the tracks for two days, Woody dismounted his paint. On the trail laid a little rag doll covered in blood. This told him a child or children were in the wagon up ahead, pouring water from his canteen on the doll and wrapping it up in dry weeds would soak up the moisture along with the color of blood.

Riding on until nighttime, a campfire stood alone. Woody walked next to the paint. The voice of a man Woody could now hear was the beautiful Mexican teacher's father. She stood next to him staring into the fire. On the ground, a dozen little boys and girls sat asking for food and crying. Woody understood their pain and could easily relate to their needs.

Moving closer, Woody yelled out, "Hello camp fire." Then he put his hands in the air walking into view.

"Gringo, what are you doing way out here?" said the voice of the man Woody had spoken to before.

Woody reached out to shake the man's hand tossing the saddlebags to Ruthy Cantu saying, "There's beef jerky and carrots in there."

She looked at Woody puzzled and she knew he wanted to feed the children. All she could say was, "Thank you."

Unsaddling his paint, Woody wondered what kind of men would do such a thing to anyone. He wiped away the tears no one but he knew of as they ran down his face.

"Woody, you are heaven sent, you know that?" asked the gentle voice of Ruthy Cantu that made Woody turn around.

"If there's an angel among us tonight it must be you because, you're the most beautiful woman I've ever set eyes on," He said looking up at the stars. Ruthy's smile could be seen by the glow of the moon as he stood motionless. She tiptoed and gave him a kiss on his left cheek. He so badly needed to take her in his arms, but all the little children were still awake.

Walking up to the campfire, Woody told the man, "I really never caught your name sir."

"That's because I never threw it at you," the Mexican man said looking at Woody smiling. "My name is Joe Cantu and I'm glad you're with us tonight."

Woody walked around the campfire kneeling down beside a little girl, she covered her face with both hands as she cried silently. Placing one hand on her shoulder Woody told her, "It's okay. Why do you cry?"

Ruthy sat next to the little girl looking at Woody saying, "She cannot hear you nor speak to you."

He picked up the little girl in both arms; she hugged his neck placing her head against the side of his. He turned to Ruthy asking, "Why does she cry like this?"

"She's been crying for two days now ever since she lost her rag doll," Ruthy said softly standing beside Woody.

He smiled at Ruthy walking over to his paint. With one arm still holding the little girl, he reached with his other hand to undo the string. It held the rag doll he'd found on the trail. There was no doubt in his mind who the rag doll belonged to.

"Found it on the trail covered in blood," he said handing it to Ruthy. "It should be okay now." She untied the vines around it and handed it back to Woody.

Softly tapping the rag doll against his leg to loosen and puff it up again, Woody walked toward the fire laying it on a rock. Removing his hat, he placed it over the rag doll. Once the little girl had been put down beside the fire, she looked at Woody but kept crying. He pointed to his hat so she could see it on the rock. He began to dance around it. Kneeling beside his hat, he slowly lifted it up. With the fire's glow, the little girl stopped crying and stood to get her rag doll.

Ruthy studied Woody carefully as she could sense he was really heaven sent saying, "Only an angel could do such a thing."

Sitting beside the little girl, Woody winked at Ruthy. He looked down at the little girl hugging her rag doll. She ate beef jerky and no longer seemed to be crying.

Joe Cantu stood beside Woody and said in a low voice, "I've heard of angels before, but never thought they packed a gun."

He looked at him and continued, "Those men who shot up our village are out there somewhere and they're meaner than a pack of wolves." Joe Cantu stood still for a minute and told Woody,"It's a full moon tonight , plenty of glow to see if anyone rides up." Not giving Woody time to speak, he could tell he was tired. "Get some rest. I'll hold first watch."

The chances of Woody and Ruthy to get to know each other that night had been set aside. Joe Cantu walked around the campground all night. Yards away Ruthy lay surrounded by the children. The little girl slept peacefully hugging her rag doll.

CHAPTER TWENTY

Almost a week had passed since Woody had given the little girl her rag doll. As the children played among each other, Ruthy cooked whatever the day's hunt had brought. Woody and Joe sat apart making plans for the children's safety as Ruthy's voice went out towards the children, "Run for cover!"

Up ahead a band of outlaws stampeded towards the camp. The dust cloud of horses had been behind Woody and Joe. "Watch out behind you, Woody!" Ruthy shouted as the lead outlaw's horse stomped beside Woody. Before he dove to the ground, he'd pulled out his .44 revolver shooting twice into the outlaw's side. Falling over, the outlaw's body landed only yards away from Joe's path as he raced to the children. Woody's gun went off again as he knelt on one knee shooting towards the outlaws. Three more men toppled over their horses dead before they hit the ground. Reaching behind his holster belt he pulled out his extra .44 pistol he'd always kept just in case. Ruthy's eyes couldn't believe how he'd been so quick.

Joe's attempt to bring the children back together caused him to catch a slug to his lower back from one of the outlaws as he lay motionless on the ground. Six shots into the air attempting to kill the last outlaw, he weaved into the cloud of dust causing Woody to miss. But as the dust flew sideways, the outlaw's body came into sight once more.

Standing up, Woody no longer had bullets in his second gun. He reached for his Bowie knife and swung towards the last outlaw who had been the one who shot Joe in the back. The knife hit the middle of the outlaw's chest as he stormed past Woody. With one leaping move, Woody was in the air landing behind the outlaw's saddle. Reaching in front of him, Woody pulled out his Bowie knife from the outlaw's chest and then slid it across his throat. He then pushed him off his horse. Rearing up on its hind legs, Woody pulled at the reins to make the horse spin towards the camp. Jumping off beside Joe, he spoke as he motioned for Ruthy. "He'll be okay. It's to one side." Cutting away Joe's shirt, he carried Joe's body to the wagon's tailgate.

While Ruthy laid a bed roll out for her father to be put on, she said, "There's no doctors anywhere. What are we going to do?"

Woody looked at Ruthy's crying eyes, and said, "Trust me; he'll be okay." Letting go of her hand, she stumbled on her way gathering the children.

Joe's voice called for Woody, "Son, can you remove the slug?"

"Yes, but it will be painful as hell," Woody said in a low tone of voice.

Joe was tougher than Woody had thought and surprised Woody by asking, "Painful for you or me?" Woody could tell Joe would be okay, but would be in pain he had come to know many times over.

The night took its toll as the moon's glow over the camp gave enough light to see. Woody and Ruthy sat speechless looking at each other as the children slept. Joe's body lay still as if half dead, but he would survive because of Woody. "I am very grateful for your help Woody," Ruthy whispered breaking the silence. She moved closer and whispered again, "You were very quick with your guns and the Bowie knife." Taking his hand in hers, she told him, "I have never met a man so young, yet so clever and brave as you. "

It was then Woody knew he could take advantage of Ruthy, but being the gentleman he was, he whispered, "You're the first woman I will not take advantage of in a moment as this."

Puzzled, Ruthy asked, "What do you mean 'take advantage of in a moment like this'?"

"Just because I saved everyone today doesn't mean I'll try to kiss you right now," he said softly looking up at the moon.

"Carlyle Winston Causey, then it will be me to take advantage of you," she leaned over speaking in his ear. As her lips touched Woody's, he could only taste the sweetness of her tender long kiss. Standing up she pulled at Woody's hand taking a blanket from his bedroll saying, "Come with me cowboy."A short distance from the camp, Ruthy laid the blanket down on the ground. She stood with Woody in the moon's glow kissing him once again. "We don't have much time until daylight," she said gently in Woody's ear.

Woody no longer cared about taking advantage and began to pull off Ruthy's clothes as well as his. Lost in making love, each one moaned for more. The dawn's light soon would peep over the camp.

Hours later the sun's heat beamed down on the wagon canopy as Joe laid within. The children all sat around him as Ruthy begin singing to them. Listening Woody studied the mountains for clues of water, something in times such as this was a must.

The paint tied to the back of the wagon tailgate plodded along. Stopping the wagon turning it into some boulders, Woody told Ruthy, "We got more company." Mounting the paint, he asked her, "Do you know how to use that rifle?" She nodded yes reaching for it.

"No matter what, don't let anyone come close to this wagon, shoot to kill," he said.

Digging the spurs into the paint's side, Woody was gone in no time at all. Straight towards another band of most likely outlaws, he would show no signs of weakness. Only one rider stood off alone as he rode towards Woody. In moments, the two rode side by side back to the wagon. The others rode close by. Woody's waves to Ruthy meant everything was okay. The band of men were self-made bounty hunters, hunting outlaws for justice.

All eight men stood tall packing extra horses with food and water for their journey. Rugged looking men who had the looks of never smiling or laughing in moments seemed to find a playful time with the children. Also fed them and gave them water. Ruthy studied Woody as he spoke to the leader of the bounty hunters because he pointed back to the children every once in a while.

After supper, Ruthy asked to speak to Woody alone. In the moon-lit night, Ruthy and Woody walked together as she asked, "Why did you keep pointing to the children, when you were speaking to the bounty hunter?"

He smiled joking towards her answering. "I told them what happened and how we all got here." He looked at the moon for a while before he spoke again, "Each man back there lost a child or two. That's why they formed a band of bounty hunters to track down the killers." As he took her hand in his, he started pulling her close to him. "They would like to speak with you and your dad to see if they can give the children homes," he said.

Ruthy stood speechless for a moment, then said, "You are heaven sent Woody."

"Those men are heaven sent and each one has a wife who sits alone at home waiting for them," He said looking into the moon's light again.

Woody told Ruthy their story. The band of men had formed into self-made bounty hunters, who promised each other to hunt down the killer of their children. From what he was told by the leader.

The children had all been outside playing when out of nowhere, a bunch of renegade outlaws stormed the street. Shooting everything and anyone as they rode past the small town up ahead. The five men Woody had killed were the last ones, the bounty hunters were looking for. Each man now had a lot of respect for what he was doing. Helping Ruthy's father and the children. They would do anything for him because, he'd killed the five they thought had gotten away.

Walking back to camp, Ruthy still held Woody's hand and told him, "My father will be grateful to know homes for the children might be found. But only one child will never be taken away from me. She's the one who cannot speak nor hear." She looked at Woody for a while lowering her head as tears ran down her cheeks. "Her name is Sonia and until her mother was shot to death right before her eyes, she could speak. I honestly believe she can hear, but somehow avoids sounds."

"Then someday when her fears subside, she will speak again," He said while he hugged Ruthy. "We will both keep her as ours if you care to be with me," He whispered in her ear.

Ruthy's eyes blinked away tears because now she really knew in her heart, Woody had been heaven sent into her life. "I will honor you forever Carlyle Winston Causey," she said softly while in his arms. She gave him a long sweet kiss as the moon danced away that night. Love had found its way into Woody's life once more. Ruthy, as well as little Sonia, were gifts sent from heaven.

The sounds of men getting breakfast ready for the children awoke everyone and the dawn's light clearly laid upon the camp. A few men helped Joe lay on soft bedrolls from blankets each man had piled up for him.

Woody watched Sonia's every move because he knew in his heart she would be his little girl. If her fears would someday go away, she might speak to him or Ruthy.

Joe clapping his hands was a way to gather the children and they would all run next to him. But Sonia's expressions stayed the same as Joe looked her way. It seemed to Woody that Joe also knew that she would someday hear and speak. The two men looked at each other as if they had spoken without words. They understood and knew what each child was going through. Sonia being the smallest to see her mother shot to death had a fear deep inside her heart and soul.

On the trail to the little town only miles away, the children rode on the horses with the men. By mid-afternoon, the town would come into view and everyone could get cleaned up a bit.

Joe sat inside the wagon speaking to Woody as he guided the wagon towards the town, "I came through here once when I was young," He rubbed his chin remembering something. "Settlers were barely moving in and had to live in the back of wagons until a place was built for their families," Joe said.

Woody stopped the wagon helping Joe to the front seat saying, "I think you should see something Joe."

Woody pointed to the buildings up ahead, Joe let out a sigh saying softly to himself, "Wow, that's amazing." The wooden buildings were in two straight lines forming a small town which was named Italldo. As the wagon made its way through the rutted road; the people of the town stood on wooden porches watching.

The self-made bounty hunters each stopped at their own places. The children began waving to the women who were in shock to see so many children. Bundles of joy had seemed to arrive that day. The women hurried to help the children off the horses. Little Sonia stood on the seat holding her rag doll. Woody cut his eyes her way, but kept his head straight saying, "We'll build a nice place for us."

"You saved us all Woody and I'm in debt to you," Joe said.

Woody could only turn to Ruthy reaching for her hand saying, "I have been blessed ten times over."

The leader of the bounty hunters had lost himself in the midst, walked up saying to all of them, "Everybody can stay at my place."

He waved at Woody to come with him.

To one side of the buildings stood a huge house which was his home. Knocking at the door, his wife, a half breed white and Indian looked towards the children. Then she looked over at the wagon at Ruthy. Speaking to her husband, she openly welcomed everyone to come in. Beautiful paintings outlined the walls and the rugs on the wooden floor seemed to speak to Woody's mind.

Stairs led up to other parts of the huge house. Outside the other men helped Joe carrying him inside. The bounty hunter's name was Maxwell. According to what the men were telling Joe, he seemed to own the town as well.

As Joe was being helped inside, Maxwell told them, "He'll stay in the bottom rooms to the left there boys," He pointed the way.

Inside the room, Joe was laid on the bed to rest. Woody walked in saying, "Looks like you got the best room in the house." On the walls, hunting trophies seemed as if they were still alive.

"Yeah, it sure does," He answered Woody as he pointed to a gun rack that held a buffalo Rifle like Woody's.

Walking up to it, he noticed it was identical to his. "I've got a buffalo rifle just like that one," he said.

Maxwell smiled at Woody saying, "There were once two of these owned by a well known man many years ago. Can't really recall his name, I bought this one from him as well as all these hunting trophies on these walls." He looked up at the ceiling for a while as he held his chin, "Hell, now I remember his name. It was Frank Casey or Causey." He then walked up to Woody asking to see his buffalo rifle.

Woody nodded his head as he heard Maxwell speak of a Casey or Causey. Then the story his father once told him made its way to the surface of his mind. Lost in his thoughts, Ruthy walked beside him placing her hand on his shoulder."Are you okay Woody?" she asked bringing him out of his trance.

He turned his head towards the buffalo rifle and again wondered if it could have once belonged to his father. "Let's all get cleaned up a bit, then we'll talk about guns;" Maxwell told Woody.

Unloading the wagon Ruthy's eyes kept cutting Woody's way.

He hung the leather scabbard on his shoulders that carried the buffalo rifle inside. The women of the town waited for Ruthy on the porch to speak with her. Puzzled she stopped as she looked back at Woody then towards the women. "Is there something wrong?" she asked.

Each woman reached to help Ruthy with her belongings. One of them said, "These children need a good meal and a nice place to rest." The women turned towards the children as each one seemed to know which one they would care for. "Please let us help you. You must be tired after the long ride," another called out.

Ruthy was exhausted but would never think to admit it to anyone. She loved all the children as if each one was her own.

Woody walked past Ruthy answering the women for her, "She would be delighted for your hospitality if the children do not mind. "

With big smiles, the children had already been picking out who they might go with and all it would take was Ruthy's okay. Looking back at the children, she broke a smile while all of them looked on. "I suppose it's okay."

The children's cheers and applause spoke for itself that day. Each child might as well have been given a home. Hugging the children, each woman walked away promising candy and toys to each child. Only one child remained on the wooden porch, but just for a moment as Woody reached down to pick up Sonia's tiny body.

Walking into the house, Woody spoke to Ruthy, but meant for Sonia to know she would stay with both of them. "We will all three stay together." Sonia's little head now rested on Woody's shoulder telling him she was tired and needed rest.

Walking behind Maxwell, Ruthy spoke to him as they made their way up the stairs. "You have a very nice home."

Once at the top of the stairs, Maxwell pointed towards a door saying, "Took me around four years to get it the way I wanted." He then opened the door for Ruthy and Woody to step inside. No words were needed as each man shook hands.

Maxwell's wife's voice came from down below, "Supper's at five." A good nap and meal would do everyone just fine.

Downstairs, Maxwell and Joe talked about the children and how they would all have a home. A knock at the door surprised Joe as a woman spoke, "Someone called for a doctor?"

Maxwell answered, "Yes ma'am. He did," pointing at Joe smiling he left the room.

Closing the door behind her, she asked, "You surprised to see a woman doctor?" Before he could answer, she held the palm of her hand on his forehead. Her thumb lifted his left eyelid. She was now only inches away from his face. She said, "Well, now days I hear we don't need rain dances to get rain." Lifting his other eyelid, she continued, "Clear eyes, just a little watery from the pain." She stood straight up digging into her doctor's bag saying, "Around here and of course as they say now days, this is good for pain." Pulling out a bottle of whiskey, Joe's eyes glowed as he reached for it. Popping the top of the bottle, she took a big swig saying, "Sure hurts to see you lying there."

His mouth dropped open in shock, but soon began smiling as she handed him the bottle. "One joke deserves another cowboy."

"A woman doctor," Joe said smiling after taking a big swig of whiskey. "How did that come about?"

The room was quiet for a moment as she dug into her bag then turned to face Joe, "Can you move your legs?"

He took another swallow of whiskey and handed the bottle back to the doctor saying, "This time tomorrow, I'll be ready to dance."

Putting the top back on the bottle, she cut her eyes back at Joe saying, "Just like all the men here, just a dance will do. "

He pulled himself up with both arms leaning on the headboard and said, "Laughter can be good medicine for pain and the heart as well."

She looked up at him saying, "I haven't had much of either in a while now." The room was quiet again and no more words were spoken for a while. After cleaning his wounds, she told him, I'll be back tomorrow to check on you."

As she opened the door to leave, Joe told her, "Thank you doctor."

"Take care cowboy," she said stopping and looking back at Joe.

"Do you have a name?" He quickly asked.

She looked at him for a moment, then said, "Tracey, Dr. Tracey." She leaned on the door asking, "And yours is?"

He studied her for a while, then said, "Joe the rain dancer."

Tracey shook her head and cracked a smile as she closed the door behind her. Outside she stood for a while. How she became a doctor began to float in her mind. Inside the room, Joe wondered if Tracey was a married woman.

CHAPTER TWENTY-ONE

A few months had passed and Joe was now up and about sometimes helping Woody build a small cabin right outside of town.

Ruthy spent time with the women. Each day that went by it seemed that, Woody drank more and more which made it bad for his poor liver. At times when he spit on the ground, blood found its way out of him. But not caring, he would never tell anyone keeping it to himself.

One brisk morning before dawn's light hit Italldo, The sound of clicking spurs could barely be heard. Woody walked towards the saloon. To one side of the town a few tumbleweeds raced across the flat land. Tomorrow they might be blowing in another direction. The town sat in an alley of mountains on each side. The sound of a rooster's early morning crowing began to awake everyone. Maxwell had been up for hours. Looking out his window, he could barely make out the figure of Woody. Cutting his eyes down to his night stand he looked at the picture of his only son. A bottle of whiskey stood next to it. He vowed never to open it out of respect to his son. Woody was heading to the saloon where Maxwell's son had lost his life in a gunfight. Quietly walking out of his bedroom as to not wake his wife. He grabbed his guns and headed towards the saloon.

Woody had just stepped inside, "The Broken Glass Saloon." The swinging double doors opened up as he pushed them apart. The bartender, Buck, wiped shot glasses clean as he watched Woody come in. He cut his eyes to two gunslingers who had stayed all night. One was eating his breakfast. The other one sat with both his boots on top of the table, sipping on a bottle of whiskey.

Buck knew Woody would always point to a bottle of whiskey.

He quickly set it down in front of him saying, "Get it and leave as fast as you can, please."

Woody looked at Buck smiling and asked, "Why are you whispering? You never done that before. Is everything okay?" Popping the top off the bottle, he took a big swig and turned to see who Buck was looking at.

The gunslinger who'd been eating stared at Woody and stood up asking, "Mister, you got a problem with me eating or do you need a bite?"

Woody looked back at Buck whispering, "Is this what's got you worried?"

The other gunslinger now stood up and faced Woody saying,

"Hey farmboy. You hear my brother talking to you?"

Woody took another swallow then placed the bottle back on the bar. "Half the town's probably asleep and if any shots are fired, they're going to blame me for the noise," He told them in a low voice.

Both gunslingers now stood glaring at Woody. "Awa!" one of them said, "You sure are a joking boy."

The other one placed his hand on his brother's chest and said, "If any shots are fired, no one can blame you cause you'll be dead mister."

Their laughter got quiet as Maxwell walked inside standing next to Woody. Both gunslingers looked at each other for only a moment. "You need your daddy's back up?" one of them asked. They started laughing again as Woody walked out the doors. Maxwell followed as the other gunslinger said, "Now that's what I call respect."

Woody stopped in the street looking Maxwell in the eye asking him, "What are doing here?"

Maxwell looked at Woody for a while then said, "I haven't known you very long, but I kinda took a liking to you son."

Woody studied Maxwell for a minute then replied, "I kinda like you as well. That's why I walked away back there. But, I feel that any minute them two gunslingers are going to step out them doors. I need you to step on out of the way please."

Maxwell's eyes started to sparkle as he remembered his son saying, "I'll fight my own fights." He looked at Woody blinking tears saying, "I lost my only son in that bar and you remind me so much of him."

The double doors swung open as the two gunslingers walked out calling to Woody and Maxwell, "You two shouldn't carry guns if you intend on walking away from gunfights."

"If you both want a fight, it's with me. Not the old man," Woody said now facing both of them.

One gunslinger walked out into the street. The other followed but stayed away from his brother.

In Woody's mind, there was no doubt a gunfight was about to happen. He walked away from Maxwell as he whispered to him, "Do not follow me anymore." Maxwell's draw against the two gunslingers would be no match and somehow all three men knew it. Woody spit blood onto the ground saying, "I will not wait on you two all day." Both gunslingers went for their guns as Maxwell froze in his boots. In one quick motion, Woody drew his .44 revolver out. Two shots rang out before either of the two cleared leather. The bodies of the two gunslingers dropped to the ground.

Buck stepped outside shaking his head saying, "I've never seen a man draw one gun so fast and kill two men at once."

Woody spun his gun on one finger letting it drop into the holster. Walking over to the two dead gunmen he said, "Bury them in the same hole." Stepping over them he looked back at Maxwell. He smiled and asked, "You coming dad?"

Maxwell's body unfroze as he took a step towards Woody with a smile from ear to ear. "You're pretty damn fast with that gun son."

"The gun seems to be a way of life out here, a friend of mine told me one day," Woody told Maxwell as they walked away.

"Your friend, was he a gunslinger?" Maxwell asked Woody walking beside him.

Woody stopped and looked at Maxwell for a while then said, "My friend, well you could say he was. In fact he's U. S. Marshall Matt Bryan. Both he and his father Carlos Bryan passed on the talent of knowing how and when to use a gun."

"Well, I'll be damned. I know both of them. Half Spanish right?" Maxwell quickly replied.

"That's them and they taught me to speak Spanish," Woody said with a big smile on his face.

Together they both headed to Maxwell's house. Everyone began coming out into the streets. Buck spoke of Woody's lightning speed draw and how he'd killed the two gunslingers at one time before they cleared leather. Italldo would soon be known to have its own gunslinger. Others wanting to make a name for themselves would come calling.

Standing at the door, Ruthy looked at Woody and asked, "Are you okay?"

He smiled at her reaching for her hand saying, "Everything is okay, but I forgot my bottle of whiskey back there."

Maxwell motioned for both of them to step inside and said, "I'll send for a new bottle in a few minutes."

At the top of the stairs little Sonia looked on, holding her rag doll tightly because she seemed to be afraid. Woody and Maxwell looked at her, then at each other. Both had thought the same thing about her. If she could not hear, why was she so afraid? Woody took another look at her and walked up the stairs speaking out loud, "It's okay honey,

I'm fine." Somehow, he knew little Sonia soon would let go of her fears within her heart and speak to him.

Joe had seen the entire gunfight from the windows of his room, because he'd heard Maxwell when he left. Walking back down the steps with little Sonia in his arms, Woody could now see into Joe's room. The curtains slightly blew with the wind coming in and a rifle was leaning against the window. Joe had been ready to shoot the gunmen if necessary. Woody looked at Joe nodding to let him know he was glad he had his back. Joe nodded with a puzzled look thinking to himself how Woody could have known. "What makes you so clever has stunned me since the first day we met you and now you seem to amaze me even more."

"Nature speaks to us at times as do the human acts we tend to do each day," He said smiling passing beside Joe.

"Now you got me very surprised as well as confused," Joe told Woody more puzzled than ever as they walked into the kitchen for breakfast.

"I noticed as I was walking down the steps looking into your room, the curtains blew with the wind and a rifle leaned against the window," Woody told Joe pulling out a chair from the table, setting little Sonia down. "You were ready to back me up, if you'd closed the window or even the door, I'd never have known," he said to Joe smiling.

Joe smiled back at Woody, but spoke to Maxwell, "See, I told you this kid's sharp as an arrow."

"Not only is he sharp, but quicker than I could have ever imagined," he answered. "In fact, I've never seen anyone so fast." Maxwell said.

Ruthy looked at Woody and now knew someone else had died from his gun and asked, "How many were there, Woody?"

"Only two, but they chose to die," he told her as he turned towards her.

Through breakfast, no one spoke, only Woody as he kept speaking to little Sonia, like he'd done so many times each day. "Our cabin is almost finished and there's a big tree next to it. I'll hang a swing for you." Maxwell's wife Sue stood over the iron stove and winked at Sonia. Woody acted as if he'd not seen the wink and cut his eyes to Sonia who was now smiling at her.

For some strange reason, Sue was the only one to make little Sonia react in any kind of way. Being half Indian and living almost half her life around the white people, had made her care more for the young ones than the old. The older ones spoke to her with their eyes instead of with their mouths. When they did speak to her, it was always and only for the respect of Maxwell.

Maxwell's voice made everyone look at him as he told Joe, "You're very welcome to stay here with me Joe. I could use a good foreman."

Joe looked at Woody then at Ruthy and said, "Guess you two will be okay." Then he looked at little Sonia and told her, "I'll come by to see you all each day. Besides the cabin is only a few miles from town."

"Good, I'll take that as a yes," Maxwell said standing up reaching for his hat. "See you out behind the house shortly."

Joe stood up himself pushing the chair to the table, holding onto it while he looked at Woody, "Carlyle Winston Causey, you're a hell of a man." Somehow, he knew Woody had something to do with

Maxwell's offer to make him foreman. He reached over the table to shake his hand saying, "First I've got to go see someone, then I'll speak to Maxwell."

As Joe began walking away from the table, Woody told him, "Give my regards to the Doc."

"I just can't put a finger on it yet, how you know so much," Joe said after he stopped walking and turned to look at Woody. "But you are one clever young man."

"So I guess you'd like to know how I knew, right?" Woody asked smiling at Joe.

"Enlighten me a bit if you can," Joe replied as he put on his hat and tucked his shirt inside his pants.

Woody's mind danced a while as he could remember his father^ Frank wearing his best clothes when taking Maggie to a picnic.

But only he would keep the memory in his mind as he looked at Joe explaining, "You didn't eat much and you're wearing your best clothes."

Joe shook his head as he looked at Ruthy saying, "He's good, very good." He then walked out the door with a big grin on his face.

"Thank you Woody," Ruthy told him reaching over to his hand. "My father really likes you."

"Let's go for a buggy ride today," he said standing up. Little Sonia looked up at Sue and smiled again. Woody caught her smile from the corner of his eye and said, "I'll go get the buggy ready," talking up to Sue, he whispered. "Thanks"

Sue looked at Woody with curious eyes as she stared at him. "They're very lucky to have you," she told him. "May the spirits keep an eye on you."

As little Sonia and Ruthy sat on a blanket, Woody started a fire with his two arrowhead flint rocks. After a few hours, Sonia slept peacefully in the shade of a tree. Ruthy pointed for Woody to see three riders making their way to town. He could tell they weren't ranch hands by the way they rode right next to each other. They each wore long black dusters, the bulges under their coats let him know they packed guns on each side as they rode by and on to town.

Ruthy studied Woody and could tell it excited him. Somehow, he wasn't hiding it anymore each time trouble loomed. They sat looking at each other for a while, then Ruthy spoke softly not to wake up Sonia, "How many men have you killed Woody?"

"It's not the count of dead men that matters, it's how many times I've stayed alive," he said standing up. "Besides what makes you worry like that?"

Ruthy stood up and replied, "My father told me that if a man has killed many, he will soon come to crave death."

"Did he say which death?" he asked hugging Ruthy. "Others or of his own?"

She smiled as she kissed him saying, "You're something else Woody."

Rolling back into town Maxwell and Joe had spoken to the three men. As he rode by, Woody could tell and feel all three men had their eyes on him. Moments later, Maxwell spoke while Woody and Joe stood listening, "Woody, these men are family to the two brothers you killed a few hours ago?"

"Do they know it was their choice to die?" Woody asked Maxwell smiling.

He pulled Woody closer to him and Joe saying, "We'll hide you a while until they leave town."

He looked at Maxwell then at Joe saying, "A real man never hides from death and should never let anyone know if he is in fear."

Walking out into the street, Woody called out to the three men, "Hello there." He kept walking towards them.

All three men got off their horses to face Woody. "You men looking for the killer of the two brothers who died earlier today?" Maxwell and Joe stood yards behind him ready to die for their friend.

One of the three men took a step forward saying, "I've see you before, If I'm right, you're that kid who lived through the slaughter of the wagon master and his men coming out of Lubbock."

"Knowing and doing are two different things mister," Woody said taking a step closer. "What's your pick?"

"We belong to the Carlos Bryan outfit in Lubbock and we're here to find out what happened to the two young men," another one said taking a step closer to the first. "They left earlier today and they never made it back to camp."

"Well I'll be damned. You're that kid and you're a good friend of Matt Bryan and his father Carlos," the third man said. "We got no beef with you. We only need to know what to tell Carlos about the two young men."

"They found what they came looking for and it was two of them against me," Woody told them taking another step closer.

He pointed all around him as people walked in the streets, "Everyone will tell you the same."

Death had passed by Italldo that day. The three men walked into The Broken Glass Saloon for a meal and a drink. Knowing Matt Bryan and his father might have saved Woody or maybe the three men.

Felix Flores, Jr.

CHAPTER TWENTY-TWO

The booming sound of a buffalo rifle echoed inside Woody's mind. Then the distant sound of Maggie's voice followed as flames of gunfire danced their way into his dream. For 13 years, the dreams would turn into nightmares. To awake from one, had become part of his life. Staring into the darkness within the cabin he sat up.

Again wanting to saddle up and finish the hunt that would someday, bring Danny Moore to his death. Ruthy slept peacefully beside him, but as the moon's flow shot into the window, His eyes focused on where little Sonia was supposed to be asleep. The empty spot made him stand up and walk into the front room. The cool breeze touching his face from the open door. Made him pull the hammer back on his Colt .44 that he'd slept with so many nights.

Moving towards the open door Sonia's voice softly spoke. He stayed out sight waiting to see who she was speaking with. He heard someone or something run away. Stepping closer to her, he didn't make a sound. He stood in silence listening to footsteps.

No one or nothing seemed to be out there. Little Sonia slowly turned around and walked back to her bed carrying her rag doll.

Woody now knew that she had been sleep walking. But the running footsteps could not have been part of her dream. They'd been, loud enough for Woody to hear. Still awake he laid in bed as Ruthy and Sonia slept. Acting as if he was asleep he laid listening. Even though she had been sleep walking, Sonia had spoken that night. But when awake, she would not speak from the fear still holding her.

Ruthy began her daily chores after making breakfast.

Woody was outside following footsteps. Someone wearing moccasins had left a trail, until they mounted a horse and rode toward town. Puzzled Woody couldn't understand how he had heard footsteps, if the person had been wearing moccasins. As the shadow of an eagle passed by, Woody looked towards the sky. His Indian spirits were always with him. Drumbeats echoed gently in his mind. Needing to know who or why someone had come to the cabin at night, was a must because Sonia had spoken to them.

Saddling up his horse, he rode into town alone. Once at Maxwell's house, he dismounted his horse. Maxwell ran out the door saying, "It's Sue, she seems to be having a stroke." Woody ran across the street to the doctor's office for help.

As the door opened, Joe stood watching Woody calling for the doctor. Stepping outside the door Joe asked, "What's wrong?"

Woody could only say, "Sue is having a stroke of some kind."

After hours of waiting in Maxwell's study, the doctor walked in with the news, "She will be okay now. Just seems to be in some sort of shock.

Maxwell, Joe and Woody walked into the bedroom where Sue was sleeping. Woody couldn't believe what he was looking at, but kept it to himself. Next to the bed on the floor a pair of moccasins laid on top of another rag doll like little Sonia's. As he placed a face on who'd been at the cabin the night before, he sat next to Sue. In a low tone, Woody sang in a native tongue, while holding on to her hand. The sprits danced among Sue, Outside on the streets everyone gathered to see what had happened. Waking up, Sue told Woody, "You must get them out of that cabin for their safety as well as yours."

"Why did you run?" Woody asked puzzled.

"I could not stay because if she had awakened, she would never have been able to speak with you."

"Will she speak to me when I get back?" he asked standing up more perplexed than ever.

Sue blinked away tears and told Woody in a whisper, "If it's not too late."

Woody could tell something had made her speak within her to him and only the spirits could do such a thing. Quickly walking out the door, he mounted his paint riding as fast as he could back to the cabin. On the way, four riders passed to his left into town. Not caring who or why they came, he kept riding in a lightning pace. In the distance, the smoke in the sky told Woody that the cabin was on fire.

Dismounting the paint while it still ran, Woody ran towards the front door. The flames shooting out kept him from going inside. He stood looking towards the buggy he'd used many times for their picnic rides.

Hanging from the buggy wheel, Ruthy's dress blew with the wind. Running next to the buggy, he froze for a moment. His eyes looked upon Ruthy's naked body with bullet holes marking her death. Covering her body with her dress, he wiped away rolling tears, searching for little Sonia. Behind the cabin, inside the pile of chopped wood, little Sonia's crying got louder and louder as Woody approached. Holding onto her little rag doll, her big brown eyes gazed up at Woody whom she had fallen in love with the moment she'd met him. As he picked her up, the warmth of her blood against his hand told him she was badly hurt.

Carrying her to the buggy, he laid her on the seat. As he pulled out a handkerchief from his back pocket, to wipe away the blood, He could tell she was losing blood fast. There would be no way he could make it back in time to the doctor's house. Sue had told Woody she would speak to him. The spirits had told her, but he never imagined it would ever be her last words to him or anyone else, "He came again," she said.

Woody listened as she spoke moving closer asking, "Who was he?"

Her tiny body wasn't moving anymore, but she moved her tiny lips whispering, "The man with the burnt face."Her eyes slowly closed as her head rolled to one side.

Soaked in blood, Woody cried out yelling up towards the sky, "Nooo."

Hours later as Woody rode the buggy into town, everyone stood looking as he slowly made his way towards Maxwell's house.

In minutes, they all waited around the buggy with tears in their eyes.

Maxwell walked outside besides Woody saying, "My wife told me everything about the spirits letting her know this was to be."

"Little Sonia spoke to me just like Sue said she would,"

Woody told Maxwell untying the paint from the buggy. "A man with a burnt face did it," he said wiping away tears.

"We must bury your loved ones first, then look for him," Maxwell replied placing his hand on Woody's shoulder.

Woody nodded looking at Maxwell saying, "After I kill him, I'll be leaving."

Maxwell already knew who the burnt face man was and knew he was fast with his guns as well. Still holding on to Woody's shoulders he said, "Sue told me the spirits gave her a vision of the burnt face man shooting you."

Woody stood still looking up at the sky grinding his teeth saying, "So be it."

Maxwell pointed to the bodies asking for help to get them ready to bury. "Come with me Carlyle Winston Causey," he told Woody walking into his house. "We have to make plans to face the burnt face man because he is very quick with both of his guns."

"Do you know where he is at?" Woody called out to Maxwell stopping at the bottom step.

Maxwell turned to face Woody saying, "The day my son lost his life, I told him I needed to speak with him before he chose to fight." As he wiped away tears from his eyes he said, "Please don't be a fool. Just wait until your loved ones are buried, then you can go as you wish to face their killers."

Woody's craving to kill didn't want to wait, but somehow Maxwell was making sense. "At least tell me where to find him or them."

He stuck out his hand to shake Woody's saying, "That's fair enough because it's your right to know." With his other hand he pointed to the mountains saying, "You'll find the burnt face man with a dozen no good for life outlaws like him at the Double X Ranch." Squeezing his hand to get his attention he said, "The fight cannot take place there or you will never make it out alive."

Once inside Maxwell asked Woody to have a seat. Walking over to the window watching the townspeople carry away Ruthy and Little Sonia's bodies while he spoke. "No man has come back after going to look at the Double X Ranch alone." Sipping on a bottle of whiskey after many years of not drinking in respect to his son's death. He now drank as he told Woody, "You told me that Marshal Matt Bryan and his father Carlos Bryan shared the use of their talents with you." Taking another big swig Maxwell continued, "The same two men who taught you, also taught that rotten dog with the burnt face."

Woody's mind could only imagine how fast the burnt face man might be. He could hear Matt and Carlos Bryan say, "To kill you must know how and when."

Maxwell's voice awoke Woody from his thoughts as he said, "The burnt face man's name is Terry Coleman and he's quicker than a rattlesnake with both his hands."

Maxwell handed Woody the whiskey bottle, he stood up, took another drink and asked, "Why is he so rotten now?"

Maxwell looked at Woody for a while then told him, "Many years ago a fire started in a building next to the general store and Coleman's wife was asleep inside." Taking another big swig, he said, "Coleman made his way inside the burning building and in moments he stepped outside with his wife dead in his arms." Woody listened as Maxwell said, "From that day forward everyone called him the burnt face man. It dug a hole in his soul making him bitter and meaner than hell."

Pulling out his pistol making sure it was loaded and dropping it back in his holster, Woody asked, "How did the fire start?"

Turning his back from Woody, Maxwell walked over to the window looking outside and told him, "That's the son of a bitch who killed my son in a gun fight. I lit his building on fire hoping to kill him but instead his wife died."

Taking another drink from the bottle then placed it down on the table, Woody told Maxwell, "Well, I'm going to make sure he dies right before my eyes, for what he did to Ruthy and little Sonia."

Maxwell turned back around facing Woody saying, "Those three men who work for Carlos Bryan are still in town and from what the word is on the streets, you're a friend of theirs."

Woody made sure his hat was snug on his head as he walked to the door while he said, "I've got to clean up a bit and get my head straight so I can face Terry Coleman and his bunch."

"What part of you not being able to do that, did you not understand?"

Maxwell yelled loudly.

With a cold glint in his eyes, Woody looked back at Maxwell saying, "Far as anyone ever knowing, only another Carlos Bryan trained gunman will die, if it's me or him."

Maxwell walked over beside Woody telling him, "You're much different than Terry Coleman. You kill for a reason, but he kills for pleasure."

"You're a good man Maxwell and I appreciate your concern,' Woody said glancing at Maxwell from top to bottom. "But a man has to do what a man has to do and at times no matter what the outcome. "

Maxwell's eyes blinked back tears and said, "You're one hell of a good kid in my book, but you're gun-ho even though you don't know what it means."

"I'm sure you're going to try and tell me, right?" Woody asked taking one more swig of whiskey.

"Talking to you right now is no good, so I've got to show you something," Maxwell answered reaching for the bottle. HE closed the door and walked over to a wooden chest on the floor. As Woody looked on, Maxwell pulled out a wooden case with the letters "FC" carved on top. "When I bought the buffalo rifle, this came with it." As he opened the case, a reddish cloth held something rolled up in it. Gently placing the cloth on the table, Maxwell unrolled the cloth revealing a long metal telescope with glass lenses on each end. Woody had never seen anything like it and asked Maxwell what it was for. Handing it to Woody, he answred, "Look through it into those mountains."

Through the window, Woody looked at the mountains and was amazed at how close they seemed to be. "What is this thing for?"

Maxwell walked over to the rack and took down the buffalo rifle he'd bought from Woody's father many years ago saying,

"What you're holding is called a telescope and it mounts on top of the buffalo rifle." Woody listened as Maxwell attached the two together. "Only when you're about to shoot will you have to put the two together just like I did." He took the two apart and rolled the telescope back in the reddish cloth. While closing the wooden case he said, "Take it and use it to take down Terry Coleman and his men."

"How much do you want for it?" Woody asked shaking Maxwell's hand.

He looked into Woody's eyes saying, "I believe this rightly belongs to you because FC was Frank Causey, your father."

Still looking at Maxwell, Woody nodded because he knew he needed Terry Coleman dead just as bad as he did.

Felix Flores, Jr.

CHAPTER TWENTY-THREE

The gentle cool breeze of the starlit night sent, Woody's campfire flames leaping upwards, behind boulders where he'd camped out nearly a week. Each night through the telescope alone, Woody studied the Double X Ranch. Terry Coleman and his men like clockwork partied nightly until they no longer could stand.

As lanterns lit up the wooden porch, Terry Coleman came into view; others stepped out onto the ground to watch a fight that had broken out. Attaching the telescope to the buffalo rifle, Woody stuck a slug in it. Looking through the telescope, he found the midsection of Terry Coleman's chest. He told himself, "This is for all your bad deeds," then pulled the trigger as the echoes rang out in the night. Quickly reloading, he pointed the buffalo rifle again. Finding the burnt man's right hand man was quite easy.

Through the telescope Woody could tell by him giving orders to the others, that he would be the next one to die. Another echo rang out leaving yet some other few men dead adding to Woody's deadly count.

The booming noise of the buffalo rifle, caused Woody's paint to rear up while Woody spoke to it, "Easy, boy. Easy," Reaching to calm it down, he tripped on a rock causing him to fall. The hard blow to his head knocked him out cold.

Splashes of water from someone's canteen awoke Woody, he reached for his gun. The empty holster made him reach for his Bowie knife, but it was gone as well. Without protection, Woody tried to stand up as quick as he could. A boot to his chest held him down as he heard a voice say, "We already know you carry a gun behind your holsters belt, so take it easy son. We're on your side."

Woody glanced up and with the flames of the campfire, he could see the three men clearly. "Carlos Bryan's men, right?"

The boot was removed from his chest as the cowboy said, "Yeah, that's right and we're here to help bring down those cowards at the Double X Ranch, if you don't mind?"

"How long have I been out?" Woody asked sitting up rubbing the side of his head where he'd hit the rock.

"Not long," the voice answered. "Them two shots rang out pretty loud and soon they'll come calling, we got to move around," the cowboy said after pausing a moment.

After putting the fire out, all four men rode off into the dark night. Beside each other, Woody said, "Thought it best to kill Terry Coleman and as many with my buffalo rifle, but as you all know I fell and knocked myself out." All three men laughed, but Woody could tell they meant no harm and asked them, "What's your names, boys?"

They all laughed again because Woody was the youngest and they were way older than any boy. One spoke up, "I'm Taylor, this is Bo and Jack."

Woody nodded in the glow of the moon to the other men saying, "I suppose that all you three are good with guns?" All three men kept quiet telling him the answer was yes. Breaking the silence, Woody said, "Glad to have you on my side."

"Any friend of Carlos Bryan is a friend of ours until the end," Taylor said with a deep voice that told of a man with much experience.

Letting the words soak in a while Woody said, "Terry Coleman was once a friend of Carlos Bryan and his son Matt Bryan, hear they taught him how to use a gun," Bo answered as they kept riding, "You could say so, but Terry Coleman always had in mind not to do the right things in life."

All four men rode in the dark night until the morning dawn sent its light over the mountains. Dismounting their horses Taylor said, "This is a good place to make our stand." Bo took all four horses by the reins guiding them behind some boulders. Like clockwork each man did something without speaking a word, as the cool breeze kept them awake.

"Why do we need a camp fire? Won't it give us away?" Woody asked.

Jack's smile made Woody wonder even more and answered, "We're outnumbered and we got to outwit our company or we all die."

"The camp fire's smoke will give us up, won't it?" Woody asked still puzzled.

Taylor's deep voice replied, "We all three been in and out of fights at night and even daytime." Standing beside Woody, he pointed to other boulders higher from the camp fire saying, "While the smoke invites them here, we'll be up there plucking them off like ducks in a pond."

Woody asked all three men the same thing as he moved to his paint to undo one buffalo rifle, "Anyone ever use one of these before?"

They each shook their heads moving towards Woody who handed it to Bo. After they each held it for a while, he told them, "It's the same as a .44-40 Winchster, but the kick is much stronger."As each one smiled, Woody could tell they wanted to try it so he told them, "Take turns using this one and I'll use the other one with the telescope."

Hours passed as the fire sent smoke upwards and Terry Coleman's men could easily tell where Woody's camp was. Woody's mind wondered off for a moment. He could still see the beautiful flowers he'd left on Ruthy and little Sonia's graves. Then the booming sound of the buffalo rifle Bo had fired brought him out of his peaceful moment. More shots rang out down below as Jack and Taylor kept the Double X Ranch men at bay.

Through the telescope, Woody found his target of a man to his left trying to sneak up on them he said, "Nice try, but not good enough." Pulling the trigger, the booming sound froze everyone and in seconds the falling body of the dead man told the others to back off.

"Let's get out of here!" one of them shouted. More than a dozen men quickly tried to move out, Jack and Tayor's .44-40 Winchesters rang out until every man lay dead down below.

Woody had made friends for life as each man had put their lives in harm's way for him. Jack called out standing down below, "They're all dead except for the ones at the Double X Ranch."

Taylor's voice sounded hungry and said, "What the hell are we all waiting for? Let's go get them before sunset or we'll lose a few."

Not knowing how many lay in wait. Woody, Taylor, Jack and Bo rode towards the Double X Ranch with only one thing on their mind.

It was to kill anyone on sight. The overhead entrance read "Double X Ranch" but seemed to be like a ghost town. As all four riders dismounted their horses, they walked towards the ranch.

"The curtains to the left of the ranch moved," Taylor told the rest of them. "Be careful, they might come out shooting at us."

Woody placed his hand over the butt of his gun saying, "The door is opening up very slow.

A woman's voice called out to them, "Please don't shoot! We're all women in here."

Walking closer, Taylor answered, "It's okay. You can all come out of there."

Like the first they all walked out in fear, Woody made his way to one side of the Double X Ranch. Beside the ranch, a rutted road led into the mountains. Woody wondered where it might end up. Through an opened window, another voice caused him to spin around with his gun ready to shoot. As he locked eyes with her he asked, "Why didn't you come out with the rest and who are you speaking with in there?"

She reached to one side of her saying, "My son." Then she pulled a little boy into view.

Woody put his pistol into the holster asking, "Is there anyone else inside?"

She picked up the boy placing him outside the window onto the ground, crawling out saying, "I just don't need him hurt mister. You can have me anyway you want, but please don't hurt my son."

Woody knelt beside him and said, "My name is Woody. What's yours?"

He looked up at his mother then at Woody saying, "Tommy."

Woody put out his hand to shake his hand saying, "Nice to meet you, Tommy."

The little boy smiled at Woody then looked up to his mother saying, "It's okay, Mom. This cowboy looks and sounds different than the rest."

Woody stood straight up while keeping his eyes on the woman saying, "There's no need for the gun behind your belt ma'am." Holding his hand out so she could hand over the gun he said, "It's okay. Like Tommy said, I'm different and mean no harm."

Her wondering eyes looked at Woody saying, "My name is Roxie mister. Or should I say Woody?"

Woody smiled and kept his hand out for her to hand over her gun saying, "Your eyes spoke to me and in a way they seem to tell me how I knew you had a gun."

Roxie nodded and answered, "You are different in a way and then again you are a very clever young man."

Woody grabbed the gun in his left hand and reached with his right one shaking hands with Roxie saying, "Seen the gun when you bent over to pick up the boy and placed him out the window."

He took a good look inside the window asking, "Is there anyone else in there?"

"All the men left and never came back until you all showed up," she said, kneeling to hug Tommy.

Taking off his hat, Woody told Roxie, "I hope those men were not relatives of yours?"

"Oh, for heaven's sake, no!" she quickly answered. "Them bastards took half of us from our little town which leads through those mountains." As Woody looked at the mountains, she continued, "It's been about three and a half years going on four." Crying she picked up Tommy saying, "I had him here but I don't know which one of them bastards is the father, because I belonged to them all at one point."

Woody took a step closer and told Roxie, "They're all dead now and if you'd like I'll see to it that you make it back to your little town?"

Roxie's eyes couldn't hold back her tears as she said, "Oh mister, please tell me I heard you right and I ain't dreaming."

Woody took off his hat and placed it on Tommy's head saying, "We'll leave in the morning and the others are welcome to come along." Studying the rutted road told Woody not long ago on a rainy day, a wagon or two had been carrying a heavy load. Looking back at Roxie he said, "Them women out front, some just got here a week or two ago?"

She looked at him for a moment studying him a while. In her mind, she thought not only was he heaven sent, but also a very clever young man. She answered, "Yes, you're exactly right. How did you figure that out so quick?"

He winked at Tommy and smiled saying, "Took a wild guess."

He walked back to the front of the ranch as Roxie and little Tommy followed.

Taylor stood on the porch speaking to the women while Bo and Jack each drug the bodies of the two men Woody had shot with the buffalo rifle the day before.

Later that night, everyone sat inside the Double X Ranch. Each woman took turns telling the men how they were taken and brought to the Double X Ranch to only please all the outlaws.

Jack sat outside alone keeping an eye out for trouble. In moments the door opened. Roxie came outside with food and a bottle of whiskey for him saying, "Just thought you'd need a bite to eat and something to keep you warm."

He stood up removing his hat telling her, "Thank you ma'am. My name is Jack Stone. What's yours?"

She looked at Jack smiling and answered, "Roxie." She handed him the food and whiskey saying, "I'll get a few women to watch out for the rest of the night. If we're leaving in the morning, you'll need all the rest you can get." Jack's eyes studied her with the glow of the night with curiosity as she could read his thoughts. "Guess no one told you yet that Woody's taking everyone of us women back to our little town. Maybe I should not have said a word about it."

Jack took a few bites of food standing next to Roxie. After chasing it down with a big swig of whiskey he said, "Taylor, Bo and I work for a very wealthy man named Carlos Bryan who has a son who's a U. S. Marshal." Taking another swallow, he smiled at her saying, "We got orders to see to it that young man Woody never needs to ask for anything." Handing the whiskey bottle to Roxie, he told her, "Our boss put out the word all over this territory to all his men to go out of their way for him. So that means we'll all leave in the morning if Woody wishes."

Roxie took a small sip then looked at Jack and took a big swig before handing the bottle to him asking. "Your boss, Carlos Bryan, is he a lawman like his son?"

"Mr. Bryan raises horses and hates bad men, so you're in good company ma'am," Jack said as he sat down motioning for Roxie to sit down beside him. "He also has men all through this territory and then some."

Roxie took a deep breath studying Jack a while saying, "You better get some rest. I'll watch out tonight along with a few women, okay?"

Jack stood up shaking her hand saying, "Thanks a lot." I'll let the men know."

Roxie and a few women walked around the ranch that night as Woody,

Taylor, Bo and Jack slept peacefully for the journey through the mountains come morning.

CHAPTER TWENTY-FOUR

Three days of riding only brought another night where camp would be as usual. But for Tommy it all felt good because at times, Woody would let him ride horseback. Suddenly Taylor's voice filled the camp, "We got company." Riding past the second wagon, he told them the same thing.

Dismounting their horses Taylor and Bo jumped off beside the first wagon and Taylor asked, "You ladies know how to shoot a rifle?"

Jack brought the wagon to a halt behind the one Roxie had been driving and said, "Everyone try and get under the wagons as fast as you can."

Woody kept his eyes glued to the hundred or so galloping horses heading their way. Quickly dismounting his horse, he reached for his buffalo rifle and shot a round into the sky. The thundering boom echoed throughout the land. Tommy's eyes seemed to pop out of his head in shock to hear such a sound. Woody looked back at everyone saying, "It's okay. Just don't panic. Stay under the wagons please." The telescope had not been on his buffalo rifle, so he had to pull it out of his saddlebags. As he looked through it, a smile no one could see broke out on his face.

"Can you get a good look at them?" Taylor asked as the smile disappeared from Woody's face.

"If I don't make it back, die with a good fight against them," Woody answered handing the telescope to Taylor.

He stood still while Woody jumped on his paint and rode off. Through his teeth, Taylor told himself, "Crazy kid."

Tommy knelt under the wagon beside Roxie with his mouth wide open, still in shock from the sound of the buffalo rifle. Bo and Jack stood alongside Taylor watching Woody ride out alone. Bo's voice broke the silence, "I've heard a lot about his kid and today I'll see if the rumors are true."

Pulling his gun out of his holster to see if it was loaded, Jack said, "At least he didn't show any signs of fear."

Taylor's eyes looked ahead as he handed the telescope to Bo saying, "Must be about a good hundred or so red men." He jumped on his horse sitting atop it like a commanding officer in an army ready to charge.

Bo handed the telescope to Jack and said, "I'll be damn."

Up ahead Woody waved his hat at the red men as he came to a stop. After a long time, Woody stood out alone as the red men, better known as Indians, Started dividing into two sides forming two long lines for the wagons to pass through. Bo was the first to speak, "Everyone back on the wagons and keep very still."

Taylor rode next to the first as Roxie rode on. Then Jack rode as close to the second wagon saying to everyone, "He's magic or crazy as hell, but he did it!"

Woody sat on the paint as he waved the wagons through. Tommy didn't care about the red men, because Woody was now his hero and kept looking at him. Once he was close to seeing Woody's smiling face; he winked at him and melted Tommy into his mother's lap with a big grin. Roxie wanted so bad to tell Woody thanks, but kept looking ahead as the chills on the back of her neck went away.

After the second wagon passed the two lines of Indians, all the warriors sent out shouts into the sky as they raced off into the open land.

The darkness of the night crept in as Woody called out to Taylor and the rest, "We'll make camp here for the night."

A few hours passed and the women sat around the campfire listening to Bo talk about Woody. He listened as Bo went on about how at age fifteen he had been the only one to survive a wagon massacre. In Woody's mind, Bo's voice echoed far away while his thoughts danced back to the night his mother yelled, "Run!" Roxie and the rest of the women watched him as Woody was lost in thought.

Taylor's voice brought Woody out of his daydream and he noticed everyone looking at him. Standing straight up, Woody pointed his finger at Bo, and said, "There were two survivors that day.

Me and a little black dog I named More."

Jack stood up poking a long dry limb into the fire saying, "Heard the dog grew up real big and died helping you in a gun battle."

Woody stood still for a moment looking at Jack and said, "I lost a lot of people I loved in my day and that dog was one of them kind of animals that grew in your heart like a human being."

Roxie called out to Tommy, "It's bedtime little cowboy." Tommy never took his eyes off Woody and froze a while. Even though Tommy was much younger than Woody was at the time of his first wagon train, He could see himself in Tommy's eyes and needed to let him know he was really and truly a good man. However, for now only a smile gave Tommy a good feeling about Woody.

Taylor whispered to Woody so no one could hear, "That boy sure looks up to you Woody."

He turned around looking at Taylor in the dim glow of the night, placed a hand on his shoulder telling him "That young boy looks up to all of us men here tonight. Because in his eyes, we are real cowboys and it's our job to see to it that we fulfill our duties as such." He nodded to Taylor as he walked away. He was at least twice as old as Woody, but in his eyes, Woody displayed a much bigger role.

Around the campfire, everyone found a spot for their bed rolls. Roxie and Tommy under the wagon as Woody looked on.

After unsaddling his paint, he took the saddle to Tommy saying, "Out here in the open country, real cowboys use saddles as pillows and this one's yours tonight."

Tommy's eyes glowed with happiness as Roxie helped him pull the saddle under the wagon. He began to stand up and leave, but Roxie's voice held him a moment longer, "You're heaven sent, Woody and a very good man."

Woody touched his hat with two fingers nodding at Roxie. Then he looked at Tommy winking at him. He seemed to melt with joy then laid his head on the saddle.

Walking away Woody remembered how he'd once thought of the wagon master and his men being all good men before they turned on everyone. Then he could clearly hear his mother say, "Woody, you need to pay attention where and how far we travel because someday, my son, you may become a great leader yourself."

Kneeling next to some rocks, Woody silently prayed as Tommy told Roxie, "Look Mommy, Woody's crying."

She hugged her son and told him, "He's not crying. He's thanking God for today and asking for guidance in tomorrow's journey."

Felix Flores, Jr.

CHAPTER TWENTY-FIVE

Riding his paint Woody lowered his head while closing his eyes. In the distance, the howls of wolves could be heard as they hunted in the darkness of the night. The peaceful wind blew against his chest as the aroma of burnt mesquite told him that, someone camped out in the open country. Not being able to see the campfire let him know that a cliff would be ahead of him. Moving on Woody let the paint set the pace while he kept his eyes wide open. Searching for a sign of a fire or sounds of anything to let him know someone was around; Woody dismounted the paint and walked next to it. After a moment standing at the edge of a cliff, he looked down. With the glow of the moon, he could easily count up to ten men huddling around a campfire.

Heading back to the wagons no longer existed because the click of a gun's hammer took it all away. The voice he heard was a whispering demand not to be foolish, "Put your hands up very slow and turn around."

As Woody obeyed, he could only hope for a chance to defend himself before taken down to the others. Who might kill him on the spot and go back to sleep.

Out of the corner o£ his left eye, Woody caught another man's silhouette as it moved towards him saying. "Tie him up and let's take the others alive if we can."

"I ain't part of them down there." Woody said not moving.

"Of course you are, that's why you're the lookout man for tonight." the first one replied, not believing him.

Not wanting to upset them, Woody could tell these two men were not with the ones down below. He tried his luck by saying, "Mister, if you think I'm with them, who are y'all with? Because I thought for sure y'all were with them."

The one to Woody's left said, "Then what the hell are you doing way out here in the middle of nowhere alone?"

Woody didn't want to show his hand, so he played it by ear and answered, "I'm searching for wanted men."

Both men now stood in front of Woody and as the moon's glow hit their chests, the shining tin stars spoke for both of them.

Now Woody could see it would be okay to speak of the wagons full of women and Tommy. But before Woody could say anything, three clicks of gun hammers behind the two lawmen made them freeze on the spot. "We ain't with them down there either, but with this one here. Killings will start if he's hurt."

Both lawmen raised their hands in the darkness as Woody made out the voice saying, "Taylor, looks like both of these men are lawmen and thought I'd be part of them down below."

"You okay boy?" Taylor asked with a low cold voice.

Woody stepped between the lawmen saying, "I'm all right, Thanks for coming along."

One of the lawmen knelt down pointing to his right, "We need to try and take these men alive if we can because one of them can tell us where Danny Moore is hiding." Still pointing he continued, "There's a trail, but it's very dangerous."

Kneeling next to the lawman after a second, Woody asked, "Did you say Danny Moore?"

"Been trying to catch him for a while now but no luck," the lawman said standing back up.

Woody was silent for a moment then spoke quietly, "I've been looking for him almost 14 years.

"I'm U.S. Marshal Trent Stone and this is U.S. Deputy Mike Dune," the lawman told Woody and the rest.

After everyone shook hands and said their names, both lawmen stood in front of him. The name of Carlyle Winston Causey, better known as Woody, had caused a great deal of respect.

Each one of them kept standing as if they were waiting to hear him give them orders. Taylor whispered to Woody because he'd understood the reactions of Stone and Dune hearing his full name, "Woody, how you want to do this?"

His voice was calm as Woody took control saying, "Come daylight a click of a gun to each one's head will awaken them. The first one to resist dies on the spot."

All six men had chosen the spot next to the sleeping camp.

As the dawn's light hit the edge of camp the clicks of guns and rifles began to wake each man up from his bad dreams, shocked to be looking down the barrel of a gun.

Woody's gun pressed down on the forehead of a big fat cowboy; the click of his gun awoke him. He looked up at Woody with bug-eyed fear. But once Woody pulled back the gun from his head, the big fat cowboy took another look at him saying, "When you send a boy to do a man's job, the boy could wind up dead." He cried pulling his gun out of his bedroll. But Woody wasn't in any mood to play games. He'd given the order to kill if anyone tried to resist. The bullet hit the big fat cowboy square between the eyes and as he fell over dead. Everyone's eyes watched Woody then each other.

"Anyone else want to die?" Woody asked. He had instilled fear into the rest and knew he could get answers if he asked. Kicking the big fat cowboy's bed roll over his dead body, Woody said in a low tone, "No one gets buried if they die because the buzzards need to eat like us." He took a few steps looking at another outlaw in his eyes and asked, "You feel lucky?"

He closed his eyes and whimpered, "No sir!"

Woody could tell the outlaw would talk if asked questions. "Everyone stand up, Get dressed but leave your boots where they are." With ropes tied from their wrists the long line of men moved as ordered.

Once the women came into view, Woody spoke to Taylor. He repeated what Woody told him, "Any lady need a horse feel free to have one."

Marshal Stone rode next to Woody and told him, "Heard many stories about you son. Just need you to know many people back home will honor you for what you stand for."

Woody looked at him and told him, "Come a few hours, I'll take one of our prisoners off our trail for questioning. If I don't come back with him, it will mean he didn't talk."

Deputy Dune had been riding close enough to them. "Maybe you need to take two at a time, save a trip or two."

As Woody looked at Dune and back at Stone, a smile overtook all three men as he said, "Sounds good to me."

Tommy's eyes gazed towards Woody as he rode off with two outlaws and asked Roxie, "Is he coming back Mom?"

"He'll be back, but the other two may not," She said knowing what Woody was going to do with the two men. Hugging Tommy she told him, "When we make it back to my real home, it's going to be all yours too okay?"

Tommy's eyes closed and he laid his head on Roxie's lap for a nap.

Felix Flores, Jr.

CHAPTER TWENTY-SIX

Sunset divided Woody from the wagons as he dismounted his paint. The two outlaws fell to the ground as the rope gave slack from being dragged. As he pulled out his Bowie knife, one of the outlaws said, "Mister, whatever you intend on doing to us, I beg you, please don't kill me."

Woody untied the rope from the other one first and asked, "Where can I find Danny Moore?"

Shaking from head to toe, the outlaw answered quickly, "I heard your name back there and I heard a lot of stories about you as well." Pointing to Woody's canteen he asked, "May I have a drink of water, please?"

Holding the Bowie knife in front of the outlaw's face, Woody said, "The only water you'll ever get is if it rains in the next minute or so, cause you're going to die if you don't answer my question."

The outlaw's eyes grew in fear of Woody cutting his face and answered in a crying voice, "I have no idea where he is now, all I know is that we were to meet him in a cave somewhere."

The other outlaw shouted, "Shut up, coward!"

Woody smiled and said, "I won't kill him because he talked, but I got a feeling you'll have to die." Stepping closer he grabbed the one he said he wouldn't kill. Holding on to the back of his hair, he plucked his eyes out in front of the other. Pushing him sideways, Woody told the other, "Well now looks like it's your turn to talk or die."

As the first outlaw screamed in agony, the second one fell to his knees begging for his life. Woody stood in front of him leaning over him placing the blade of his Bowie knife flat on his shoulder. "I hate getting this Bowie knife bloody twice in one day." Cleaning his knife with the outlaws's shirt, Woody smiled at him asking, "Where' s the cave at?"

Closing his eyes, the outlaw answered, "The cave next to the ranch on the left of those mountains." He pointed in the direction where Woody had rescued the women. He kicked the outlaw's face sending him falling backwards. Lightning fast he stuck his Bowie knife back in its leather sheath, pulling his Colt .44 pistol out shooting the outlaw's face until the gun was empty.

Still pulling the trigger he went into a trance needing to kill Danny Moore so bad.

Moments later the shrieks of pain from the other outlaw rang in Woody's ears, He awoke looking down into the dead outlaw's face. After reloading his gun, Woody walked over to the paint and walking along with it until he could no longer hear the outlaw's wailing.

Craving to kill Danny Moore subsided in Woody's mind and in his heart he knew it would be a must to do so. Even though it was dark. Woody knew it was blood he was spitting out because he could taste it and it was getting worse as time went on. But, the only painkiller would be the drink after he spit again.

As the night wore on, Woody could see the wagons' camp fire. He knew the women and Tommy would be safe if he had to leave them. Come morning he would speak with Marshal Stone and Deputy Dune of his plan. To go wait near the cave by the ranch where he'd saved the women and Tommy. Rolling out his bedroll Woody laid out alone in the open land. The stars flickering above him helped him sleep.

The paint had become more than just a ride from place to place. He now awakened Woody by pushing his nose on his shoulder. Woody looked up with a smile as his paint stood over him, ready for whatever that day had in store for them. Washing his face, he poured water into his hat for his paint to drink. Rinsing his hat out he placed it on his head, riding towards the awakening wagon camp.

Marshal Stone and Deputy Dune stood alongside Bo, Jack and Taylor as the women cooked a quick meal for everyone. As Woody dismounted his paint, Tommy sat under the shade of the wagon. Watching and smiling because he liked Woody more than anyone could ever tell.

After breakfast the wagons were on their way again. Tommy looked back asking Roxie, "Why is Woody and the two lawmen not coming?"

Roxie stopped the wagon motioning for Taylor to come over. Moments later Tommy shed tears from his eyes as the wagons pulled farther from Woody. Only a few miles away from the wagons, Woody stopped the paint and froze in shock to hear, "Woody, you need to pay attention where and how far we travel because someday, my son, you may become a great leader yourself." Dismounting his horse, it was then he understood his mother's words more clearly and smiled to himself.

Marshal Stone and Deputy Dune also dismounted their horses. As he looked at them, Woody could tell although he was so young compared to both of them. He was in full control. To Woody, Danny Moore was and would always be a must to find and kill someday, but there was something else that needed more attention. "I don't know how much you two lawmen crave to find and kill Danny Moore,

I feel like we just let down three good men. Jack, Bo and Taylor need our help to see those women to safety first." Mounting their horses they all nodded to each other, agreeing as a trail of dust was left behind galloping towards the wagons.

Roxie wiped away a tear from her eye as she looked back at her son because he'd never given up on Woody coming back. She called out to him, "Son."

"Look Mom, Woody and the lawmen are coming back!" he yelled.

Once beside the wagons, Woody shook Bo, Jack and Taylor's hands and rode around tilting his hat at the women saying, "We'll ride with you until the next town because your safety is much more important . Riding closer to the wagon Tommy rode in, Woody asked, "How'd you like to ride horseback?"

His eyes grew wide with excitement and couldn't wait as he leaped into Woody's arms from the wagon. Everyone laughed as he caught Tommy midair. Dismounting his paint he said, "This is a good horse, all you got to do is sit on him and he'll take you on a ride."

Tommy grinned from ear to ear as Taylor glanced at Woody and rode beside the paint letting him know he had Tommy's back. Woody nodded at Taylor and winked at Tommy. He felt so big in the saddle and yelled at Roxie, "Mom throw me my hat."

Woody jumped onto the wagon as Roxie handed Tommy's hat to him. Woody tossed it to Tommy as Taylor said, "We need a lead man. "How about leading this wagon train Tommy?"

He looked over to Roxie asking her, "Can I Mom?"

She smiled looking at Woody saying, "Ask the boss."

He looked at Taylor who pointed back at Woody. Tommy called out to Woody asking, "Can I lead the trail Boss? I mean Woody Boss?"

Everyone laughed because Tommy seemed so happy when Woody said, "You can lead the train, but keep both eyes open and let us know if you see any signs of trouble."

Hours later Tommy's head hung down as he'd fallen asleep on top of the paint. Taylor still riding his horse, reached over and took Tommy handing him to Woody. Holding Tommy in his arms, he slipped into a daydream, Like once laid in Frank's lap listening to stories of his younger days. The daydream quickly turned into a nightmare, flames in the night from gunfire lit up the circle of wagons as everyone had been put to death. Opening his eyes, he handed Tommy to the women in the back of the wagon. Leaping onto his paint, Woody rode ahead of everyone leading them to safety.

Felix Flores, Jr.

CHAPTER TWENTY-SEVEN

Heat waves full of dust hit Woody's face as blankets of wind tossed about the open country. Wiping away beads of sweat, Woody could see streams of smoke in the sky coming from the town up ahead. The town called Horseshoe sat alone in a valley with patches of grassy fields and a lake to its side providing water.

As the wagons made their way closer to Horseshoe, Woody let everyone know that they would soon be back home.

Roxie held on to Tommy as she whispered a prayer for everyone. Bo and Taylor rode beside Woody while Jack pulled back riding tailgate. Both Marshal Stone and Deputy Dune rode up ahead into Horseshoe. Seeing to it everything would be all right for the wagons of women to ride in. The town was quiet as they rode in. But, the sound of music from the saloon meant someone was getting drunk.

As the swinging doors flew open, the town drunk rolled out onto the wooden porch. Stepping outside, the bartender said, "I told you to stay out. Now get going. He stood up slow only to take a step off the porch, falling onto the rutted road in front of Woody, Bo and Taylor.

Dismounting his horse, Woody helped the town drunk sit on the porch.

Two more cowboys came outside with the bartender.

One was slim packing .44 pistols, wearing a low holster tied to his legs. Woody took one quick glance at him then sized up the other one, who seemed to follow the first one's lead.

Turning around Woody mounted his horse to move on, but the slim cowboy told him, "Hey stranger. You must not have heard what the bartender told this drunk." He put his boot on him and kicked the town drunk off the porch.

In a low voice, Woody told his paint, "Whoa boy." Woody slid off the other side, he motioned Bo and Taylor to stop. Walking up to the town drunk, Woody helped him get up and told the slim cowboy, "How long you been pushing people around in this town?"

The slim cowboy smiled at Woody and stepped off the porch. The sounds of spurs broke the silence. Marshal Stone, Deputy Dune and the Horseshoe sheriff, Tex, walked up. Looking at Woody from head to toe, the slim cowboy told him, "We'll meet again boy."

"Indeed we will," Woody said smiling as he touched his hat with two fingers and nodding. Bo and Taylor removed their hands from their guns as they looked back at the women who were now climbing off the wagons.

The slim cowboy patted his guns looking at Woody with a smile promising a duel. He then walked back into the saloon with the other.

The bartender looked at all three lawmen and Woody as he cut his eyes across Bo and Taylor saying, "They got a mind of their own." He then disappeared into the saloon; the music continued to play.

Seven years ago, Horseshoe was known for trouble, but the men who built it, weren't the ones who caused it. The turmoil began when the women had been taken away and no one did anything about it. Now, any kind of outlaw roamed the only street in Horseshoe as it had become a nesting place for killers. Tex, the sheriff, was the only one who would do nothing to stop them.

Woody looked at Tex and told him, "Take these ladies to the hotel and get them cleaned up." As Tex stood still, Woody kept staring at him and it seemed that Woody's stare had frozen him on the spot. Reaching on Tex's chest, Woody ripped the tin badge off his vest saying, "Spread the word there's a new sheriff in town." Tossing the tin badge to U.S. Marshal Trent Stone, Woody said, "Make sure you tell them his name is Trent Stone. And that he's got back up."

Leading the women towards the hotel, Tex no longer called any shots in Horseshoe. As the women walked towards the hotel, the town's people stepped outside onto the wooden porch. Suddenly a yell here and there called out to the women as each ran towards someone who knew them. Roxie looked across the street to the General Store holding Tommy's hand in hers. The door opened up, a man stepped outside. Roxie took a few steps as he did the same. He called out to her, his voice made her fall to her knees. Running towards her he asked, "Roxie, is that you sweetheart?" Tommy looked towards Woody then back at the man, who'd fallen in front of Roxie hugging each other real tight.

Roxie pulled Tommy next to her and told her husband, "Jerry, this is Tommy, my son,"

Jerry looked down at Tommy for a moment and back at Roxie, whose eyes told him a story and said, "Any part of you is a part of me." Standing up, Jerry and Roxie walked hand in hand as Jerry held Tommy. Tommy looked back at Woody wave goodbye.

"I'll come by later to see you," he waved at Tommy then smiled again just as before.

As the sun set on Horseshoe, the women were reunited with their families and friends. But, safety wasn't promised until the town was cleaned up a bit of outlaws. Woody, Bo, Taylor and Jack, along with Marshal Stone and Deputy Dune Would have their hands full, just like in most parts, the outlaws themselves didn't always fight together and seldom did they even like one another.

The jail building had been built with rooms above it to house the town's sheriff: and guests if it ever came to it. Woody and the rest of the men with him would take turns relaxing. But, when the sun hit Horseshoe come morning, it would spell trouble for Woody and his friends.

The stillness of the night brought Woody to the edge of dreaming, but drifting off into a deep sleep only pushed nightmares into his mind. Tossing and Turning, Taylor looked on with curiosity thinking of how much Woody had been through. Horseshoe would become a testing ground for survival or just another graveyard for bad outlaws. The lantern lights went out in each building.

But, you could rest assured eyes beamed out into the only road which was only about four wagons wide.

With only a few hours sleep, Woody's eyes opened up and stood up checking his guns first. Strapping on his holster he reached for his Bowie knife, that was in its leather sheath.

Reaching for his hat, he made his way outside as the moon gave just enough light to see. In the middle of Horseshoe, a water well stood alone. Walking over to it, he washed his face with his handkerchief. Tying it around his neck, he took a glance at the saloon. A bottle of whiskey would be nice to have, but stepping into the saloon alone would be foolish. The sound of spurs made Woody spin around, with his hand on the butt of his gun. A voice followed as he spun around, "It's okay son, It's me Taylor."

"Need to go into the saloon for a bottle of whiskey," Woody said taking a few steps towards Taylor.

His smile could barely be seen as Woody looked towards the jailhouse. Bo, Jack, Marshal Stone and Deputy Dune came outside as Taylor said, "We need a few drinks ourselves." Each man was ready to back Woody's play no matter where or when it came about. In the wee hours of the night, the saloon was the only place to grab a drink.

Behind them a voice broke the silence, "You boys headed the wrong way."

All six men turned around straining their eyes to see who it was and where the voice was coming from. "It's me Jerry, from the General Store." Standing on the wooden porch, they all listened as Jerry continued, "Please come in, I got plenty of whiskey and a bite to eat for all of you." Woody was the last to walk inside.

He kept staring into the night making sure no one else had seen them.

In the back room, all six men took sips of whiskey and ate. Roxie moved about saying, "Each one of you deserves more than this and y'all are the bravest men I've ever seen."

Jerry's eyes fell to his plate thinking back to the night Roxie and the rest of the women had been taken away. But Roxie's hand on top of his assured him of a love she had for him. She knew that back then he alone could not have stopped them. "There's only one man out there calling the shots and it's the slim one with guns tied down low," Jerry told them in a low voice.

Taking a bigger swig than before Woody stood up saying, "Jerry and Roxie, we all are much obliged for the meal and whiskey." Placing two fingers to the brim of his hat he nodded, "I kinda figured that much when we last met on our way into this town."

The rest of the men stood up around the table. Marshal Stone looked past everyone into Tommy's eyes peeking around the doorframe and said, "Once we clean this town up a bit, I'll stay here until a sheriff is chosen to keep peace."

Walking over to Tommy, Woody rubbed the top of his head saying, "I'll stick around a long while myself," melting Tommy's heart with a wink.

CHAPTER TWENTY-EIGHT

From the hayloft window of the stable, a rooster's crow awoke Horseshoe once more as it did many times before. But, this morning would be different for the outlaws who nested inside the buildings.

Woody, Bo, Jack and Taylor stood at the opening of Horseshoe with only one thing on their minds. Marshal Stone and Deputy Dune stood on the wooden porch on each side of town. The outlaws would awaken to a duel or peacefully lay down their guns. There was a fat chance that would happen. For seven years, no one had ever questioned anyone of them, unless they had a death wish.

The leader, or so it seemed, stepped out of the hotel doors along with six rugged looking men. He began to smile as he looked towards Woody saying, "Well, well. If it ain't my friend." Stepping onto the rutted road his six men followed side by side facing Woody's bunch.

Woody took the first step as the others began walking with him and said, "I don't have friends the likes of any of you."

The slim outlaw smirked raising one hand motioning another bunch of outlaws to come out the swinging doors of the saloon. Still grinning he raised his other hand as another wild bunch, stepped outside the blacksmith shop. "I had a feeling you'd be calling on me, so I got a head start and invited some of my friends to the party."

Outnumbered at least four to one, Woody and the rest still stood their ground as Woody said, "All you got to do now is figure if you'd like to die first."

The door to the General Store opened up as a shotgun poked out first. Jerry stepped outside saying, "Both barrels are pointed straight to your chest."

"All I need is a clean gunfight with that boy called Woody," the slim outlaw said still smiling.

Without hesitation, Woody said, "Sounds good to me." He walked to the middle of the rutted road and the slim outlaw did the same. Ten feet apart Woody said, "Before I kill you, at least tell me your name."

Smiling at Woody, the slim outlaw replied, "You're the one to die today, but I'll tell you my name anyways." Parting his feet slightly he said, "Name's Joe Black." He tried to draw both guns at once, Woody's lightning quick draw sent his body flying backwards onto the rutted road dead. Then all hell broke loose as the shooting echoed through Horseshoe.

In moments, it seemed that it had happened too fast but all the outlaws lay dead side by side. Woody glanced around and began seeing double as he rocked forward trying to balance himself. Falling to the ground was all he could remember as he went down.

A slug from someone's gun hit him dead center of his chest and came out under his right arm. Quickly carrying him Bo and Taylor took him to the doctor almost bleeding to death. He would live yet another day, but it would be days before Woody would awaken. Taking turns his true friends sat with him as each one prayed for his life. The doctor, a chubby old man was skilled with his hands. He carefully sewed up the wounds. Studying Woody's body, he noticed bullet wounds and scars from knives as well. He spoke to himself, "You been to hell and back son." Taking a swig from a whiskey bottle he answered a knock at the door, "Come on in." At the same time, he covered Woody's body to hide his wounds.

Bo, Jack, Taylor, Marshal Stone and Deputy Dune all walked into the room needing to know if Woody would make it. The doctor spoke up without anyone saying anything, "He'll be okay. Just needs to rest." Taking another swig of whiskey, he continued, "He lost a lot of blood in his life."He removed the covers off to show everyone. All five men stared at Woody for a moment, then at each other.

"I'm pretty sure each wound has its own story, but I'd never imagined this young man had really been through so much," Taylor said.

"When he comes to I think he'll be moving out and something tells me on his own," Bo said sitting next to Woody's weak body. "Story has it he don't stick around long because of wanting to find Danny Moore," said Bo covering Woody back up looking at the rest of the men.

Two days passed and Woody's eyes opened seeing Roxie sitting in the chair next to his bed. "How long I been out?" he asked.

"Well cowboy, you been out a few days and you got to eat," she said digging in a basket of food.

He reached for the food and took a bite, but when he tried to sit up, He fell back down on the bed in pain. "I need a drink of whiskey," he said.

"Careful honey," she said handing him the bottle.

"Did anyone else get hurt besides me?" he asked after taking a couple of swigs of whiskey.

"No honey; only you," she answered standing up. "I washed your clothes and Jerry took care of your horse," she said reaching for his clothes. "We got a corral out behind the General Store, I pray you stay a while."

Looking into Roxie's eyes Woody said, "Jerry seems to be a good man." Taking a swig of whiskey he said, "He's very lucky to have you and Tommy."

Roxie knew the answer to her question would be no. Standing up she walked over to the window looking out, "Your friends out there all speak highly of you; Woody, you should try living a good life instead of hunting down bad men."

"Don't worry, I'll stick around a while," Woody said forcing himself in a sitting position.

Roxie smiled at him, but within her mind, she knew just until he could ride a horse. She looked back at Woody as she left the room saying, "Little Tommy needs to see you. He's been crying for two days now."

Taking a big swig of whiskey to kill the pain, Woody stood up saying, "Send him over to me please."

Roxie smiled again looking at his body because the sheet he'd been trying to hold under his arm, fell when he took a swig. Taking a better look her smile faded as she now stared at his wounds. Dropping her eyes, she could no longer hold her tears, as she'd seen what everyone had been saying. Woody was way too young yet held a reputation as well, as the scars of a man in many battles. As she took a step out the door she said, "I'll send Tommy over, but please don't let him see your scars okay?" He didn't answer as he walked over to a trash basket and spit up blood in it.

Moments later, a knock at the door told Woody it would be Tommy, because of the gentle sound a child would make. Fully dressed, he wore a sling on his right arm and held a bottle of whiskey in his left and said, "Come on in."

Tommy's eyes glowed as he saw Woody, "Boss, you okay?"

Woody smiled kneeling down hugging Tommy, still holding the whiskey bottle and said, "Hey little buddy. How you been doing?"

"Everyone keeps saying you'll be leaving as soon as you get well," Tommy said blinking away tears.

Taking another swig Woody stood straight up, placing the bottle on top of the nightstand. Turning around he put his hat on and said, "Let's go out on the town, but first we got to go get your hat okay?"

Tommy grinned from ear to ear as he spun around heading out the door.

Once outside onto the wooden porch, everyone greeted Woody with a smile and a handshake from the men. Bo, Jack, Taylor, Marshal Stone and Deputy Dune stood beside the General Store as if waiting for Woody and Tommy. After shaking everyone's hands, Woody noticed Tex, the former sheriff, standing beside Jerry and Roxie. Taking a few more steps his way, Woody told him, "You let this town get way out of hand." Tex stood still as Woody thought of falling to the ground two days earlier. In a flash, he could see who pulled the trigger and shot him. Shaking his head to clear his thoughts, Woody held onto the side of the building while Bo grabbed him or he would have fallen.

Everyone thought Woody was too weak to be standing outside, Taylor's wits sent Tex's body toppling over the rail as he backhanded him. Before Tex could speak or try to get up, Jack's boot connected with his chin sending him backwards out cold.

Following their lead, Jerry stood next to Woody asking, "What's the matter Woody?"

"Sometimes body language speaks to us," Bo said looking at Jerry with a gleam in his eye.

Jerry looked at Roxie as she took Tommy away saying, "Come with us Jerry."

Between two buildings, Marshal Stone and Deputy Dune beat the hell out of Tex until he told the truth. Dragging him out back behind the jailhouse, a hangman's gallows on its scaffold still stood true as if ready to use. Quickly Tex tried to get away as the people of Horseshoe gathered around. Betraying everyone years ago by not doing anything, was only part of a reason for Tex to be hanged. But trying to kill Woody only made the hanging a must.

As Tex's body swung, Bo, Jack, Taylor and Marshal Stone all stood in front of Woody as Deputy Dune said, "We had a feeling he'd done something wrong. But when you set eyes on him, it told the story." Stepping closer he held out his hand to Woody, "We will always be your friends for life and any man out to kill you will answer to all of us."

Woody shook hands with everyone once more and said, "Hope my right arm gets well cause using my left one is kinda funny to me."

Everyone laughed as they walked away leaving the dead body swinging with the wind. Before sunset, Tex would be buried and his belongings, guns, boots, hat, pocket watch and money, would provide a few drinks for the town drunk. Hanging Tex, the former sheriff of Horseshoe, sent out a message to the rest . . .

Felix Flores, Jr.

CHAPTER TWENTY-NINE

The setting sun cast its dim yellow and orange glow upon the open country. As Woody made camp for another lonely night searching for Danny Moore. It had been about five years since he'd left Horseshoe. Out in the middle of nowhere, he camped out wherever night fell upon him. Small towns no bigger than the last, promised more bottles of whiskey to take along for the ride. Spitting to one side of the camp fire, blood splattered on a rock as he reached for more whiskey. Determined to find one man he most wanted to kill, at times felt like fate just wasn't on his side. Rumors had it that Moore never stayed in one place too long, but always where Woody had gone.

Unrolling his bedroll, Woody smiled as he grabbed his saddle remembering his father, Frank, say, "Real cowboys do," meaning real cowboys used saddles for pillows. Slipping into a deep sleep he awakened only to stare at the stars above. Tears formed in his eyes as he missed Frank and Maggie.

The distant drumbeats echoed gently through the night and the mountains to his left sparked here and there. He knew his Indian friends sent out drumbeats to lost souls such as his and the friendship he'd made with them would last forever.

In his mind, Woody knew where he was and the circle of wagons that surrounded the shallow graves he'd left behind, would all be there. Come morning, he would visit the sight and camp next to the graves to pay his respects. The howls of wolves in the distance was the last thing he heard, before he slipped into a deep sleep.

The pounding of his paint's hooves on the ground awoke Woody. As the dawn's light rose to its light blue, thick white clouds danced above him. Another day to reckon with had brought him to the point of time, in his life where it had all been turned upside down. No longer the boy he used to be, Woody looked on with the wisdom of a man Frank and Maggie would have been proud of.

Riding his paint through decaying wagon parts, the shallow graves with rocks on top of them still held together. But, the wooden crosses leaned to one side on some and others had fallen down. Dismounting his paint, he stood for a moment looking at the graves of his parents. Scenes of their final night shot through his mind. Blinking back tears, he looked around him as a blow to the back of his head knocked him out cold.

Hours later, the tudding sounds of arrows sticking into the side of a wagon awoke Woody up. He'd been tied up as warriors sent out yells into the sky. They shot arrows riding their horses past him. None tried to hit him; they only needed for him to wake up to a scare of his life. He knew when Indians felt betrayed or an enemy was in their grasp, that punishment came first and death later. As the sun beat down, an Indian's body overshadowed Woody. Looking into his face, Woody could not believe Two Feathers was standing in front of him after all these years. His tall muscular body told the others to stop shooting arrows at the white man. Smiling down at Woody, Two Feathers told him. "Many years I've wondered where you have been and now I've come to see that it is you, my friend." He had arrived just in time to save Woody because only Two Feathers could remember him clean shaved and after 25 years. He was the Chief's son calling all the shots and someday would become the Chief himself.

Untying Woody, Two Feathers told the other warriors stories of how he was the only white friend to them and how he'd taught them the white man's tongue. They were amazed that Woody had left when Two Feathers was only 12 years old. Now at the age of 37 he looked into Woody's eyes and asked him how old he was.

Woody stood next to Two Feathers and said, "I'm 45 now, going on 46." Taking a step forward he spit blood, each time thicker than before.

Two Feathers put his hand on Woody's shoulder asking, "My friend, why is it you bleed?"

"Soon I will come back here, but right now I must leave," said Woody with tears in his eyes, not from a memory but from pain. They hugged each other and Woody rode away through the forest.

Months later Woody found himself camping out inside the stone house that used to belong to Galindo, the old blacksmith in the first town he'd ever visited. More pain shot threw his body as he took yet another drink of whiskey. Inside the stone house, the fire glowed on the walls as tree limbs danced over it. The ceiling had crumbled from the fire, as Galindo had told Woody and the moonlight gently glowed into the stone house. Silhouettes of tree branches moved back and forth on the bare walls. Woody dozed off into a deep hard sleep with a whiskey bottle in his hand. Dreaming of his past life, he always seemed to catch a glimpse of Danny Moore's silhouette in a distant place. Maggie yelling "Run!" rang within each dream and he would awaken with a bigger crave to kill.

Heading into the first town he visited, no name came to his mind. But its whereabouts sat deep within his mind and soul. The night still wore on as Woody took big swigs while he spoke to his paint, "Soon I'll release you into the wilderness." Standing up he held on to the side of the stone house wall and his weight caused it to crumble into the trees outside. He took a few steps only to fall face down. Gathering himself, he knelt on one knee and the other as he coughed up blood. The distant drumbeats could be heard faintly as he rode away on his paint. Pain shot through his body as he slid off his horse onto the ground.

A few hours later after mounting his paint, Woody made his way through the forest. As he took his last sip of whiskey, his body shook from the jolts of pain he felt. He threw the empty bottle against a tree shattering it into pieces.

The dawn's light sent beams of light within the forest.

Hungry Woody dismounted his horse as he pulled out his Bowie knife. With the butt of it he broke up pecans he'd gathered on the ground. The voice of someone close by began to get louder as Woody heard, "We'll split the money later. Right now, I'm keeping it all together."

"Every time we do a job, you say the same thing," another voice said. He watched two men behind some bushes who looked mean and rugged. But, to Woody looks held no prize. He knew anyone could draw a gun, but how quick was the answer he found out a second later. Coughing up blood only gave him away as one man pulled his pistol out shooting towards Woody. Missing him, he shot back as the man toppled over dead. Stepping out from behind the bushes, he pointed his gun towards the other.

"Don't shoot me please mister!" he said shaking from head to toe quickly holding his hands in the air. "Take all of it, just let me go," he said pointing to the bag of money.

In moments, the man rode tied belly down as the dead one did.

To keep him quiet, Woody stuffed a handkerchief in his mouth. Stopping for a moment, Woody listened as the drum beats began to float through the forest. Memories floated to the top of his mind of the moments, he shared with his native friends. Then he thought of the wagon train when he rode shotgun. His daydream slipped into a deep sleep. The paint rode on pulling the other two horses. The cool wind of the night awoke Woody as the paint stood still. Dismounting Woody made a campfire with the flint rocks he received as a gift, from the drummer many years ago. Within the saddlebags of the two robbers, Woody found food and a bottle whiskey. Untying the man, he kicked at Woody as he coughed up more blood. Quickly Woody reached for his Bowie knife and slit his throat. Woody tied him back up and would ride into town with both dead bodies come morning.

While the flames of the campfire danced the night away, Woody drank as he spit up more blood. With the glow of the moon, he used the dead men's bedrolls to roll them up with. Tying the ends up with rope, he threw them back on top of the horses and would get some rest first.

Another night of endless dreams always woke Woody as his dreams turned into nightmares. Sitting up next to the campfire he reached for the whiskey bottle. Shots of pain jerked his body. Struggling to stand up, he coughed up more blood but that did not stop him from taking another swig from the whiskey bottle.

While the flames subsided Woody held on to his buffalo rifle using it as a crutch to stand up with. Blinking away tears from pain, he kicked dirt into the campfire. Mounting his paint, he decided to ride out before dawn. Within his mind, he could feel his time was running out and he needed to go find someone to bury him at the circle of death. But first, he had to find someone honest with a will to kill and pay him with eye size gold nuggets. He'd carried in a leather pouch all these years. Thinking back he wished Bo, Jack and Taylor could do the job, but realized they had already done enough for him. Still in pain, he broke a smile remembering the day he told Bo to keep the buffalo rifle. Coughing up more blood, he fell off the paint as he laid there a while. In the distance of the forest, drumbeats echoed once more. Opening his eyes Woody stood up mounting his paint.

The light of dawn took over the darkness of the night as Woody rode on towards the edge of the forest. Coughing up more blood there would be no more whiskey. He'd run out the night before.

Looking into the opening up ahead, Woody knew it meant that down below a town stood alone. Many years had passed as Woody sat on his paint looking down at the town below. Beautiful meadows as far as the eye could see, along with fields of two story buildings showed how the town had grown. Streaks of smoke told of many people being awake to a new day.

As Woody made his paint move downwards from the forest his mind slipped into memories of his past. Had this town been the promised land that held everyone's hopes and dreams? Would it now have a name for itself?

Felix Flores, Jr.

CHAPTER THIRTY

The long rutted road that headed into the town Woody visited many years ago now had a name. A wagon on one side of the road had "Tiptoe" painted in white, with an arrow pointing in the town's direction. Woody untied the moneybag from the saddle horn and headed towards the front of the bank's porch. Standing there was a fat short clean cut man, wearing a three-piece suit looking at him. "Good morning," Woody said nodding.

He seemed to be the banker as he said, "Morning stranger." Taking a few steps closer to the edge of the wooden porch he told Woody, "Name's Adams and I'm the banker here."

"Well then, this money here must be yours," Woody said smiling as he tossed the moneybag to him.

Adams caught the bag with a grin from ear to ear saying,

"Yes sir. Two days ago we got robbed." Looking at the two rolled up bodies on horseback, Adams said, "Them two must be the ones who did it."

"Then they also belong to you," Woody said tossing Adams the rope tied to the horses.

Pulling the reins on his paint, Woody headed towards the saloon. It seemed bigger from the last time he was there. Tying the paint to the rail, Woody stood at the double doors, turning his head to one side he spit up blood on the wooden porch. Stepping inside his mind went into the memory of how he drank so much.

But, looking at all the whiskey bottles on the wall behind the bar, that memory faded just as fast. Standing next to the bar, he pointed at the whiskey bottles. While leaning his buffalo rifle against it, he placed his hat on top of the barrel then said, "I'll need a room, please."

The bartender looked Woody over for a while then said, "Sure but you need to pay up front for room and board if you're staying for a while."

"I like breakfast warm," Woody said smiling as he dropped an eye sized gold nugget in the shot glass.

He spun around as Adams yelled, "That's him right there!" About eight men went at Woody with fists in the air, but he quickly tossed them about as he heard, "He took some of the money out of the bag."

"That's how I got it!" Woody yelled at Adams looking at him. "Bring him out here so we can hang him!"Adams shouted to the eight men.

Fighting his way through the eight men, Woody grabbed Adams by the throat saying, "You ain't hanging nobody cause you're fixing to die." Pulling out his gun he pointed at the eight men, Some still trying to get up from the floor quickly reached for the sky. Suddenly Woody's world went black; the blow to the back of his head knocked him out cold.

Opening his eyes, Woody laid on his back inside the jailhouse floor. Sitting up he held onto the back of his head. He stood up as the jailhouse door swung open. The sheriff walked out and yelled out,

"Everyone needs to calm down a bit cause ain't no hanging happening and any man tries to come through this door will catch a bullet between their eyes." He stood with his legs slightly apart and his hand on the butt of his gun.

All eight men stood behind the banker as he yelled to the sheriff, "We got every right to hang that good for nothing low life in there."

"Yeah, that's right."The men started getting loud as they shouted, "Hang him before sunset." Many more yells were heard, then everything and everyone got quiet as the sheriff shot three rounds in the air.

"Like I said, no hanging is happening and any man tries to get through this door will get shot between the eyes. Now stay out! "

"Who do you think you are telling us what we can and can't do?" another voice yelled as the sheriff turned around stepping inside.

Slowly turning around towards the crowd studying each man, who held picks, axe handles torches and shovels along with a rope with a hangman's noose at the ready. "My name is Carlyle Winston Causey better known as Woody and like I said, no hangings tonight. Now stay out!" Turning back around he stepped inside as he closed the door behind him and walked over to get a cup of coffee.

Inside the cell, Woody held onto the back of his head with one hand and holding on to the bars with his other saying, "Hey, sheriff."

Not even looking at Woody, the sheriff asked, "What's up, old timer?"

"Why the hell did you tell them cowards my name out there?" Woody asked.

"What do you mean your name?" the sheriff asked turning around smiling at Woody.

"My name is Carlyle Winston Causey, better known as Woody," he answered.

Both men locked eyes for a while and Woody asked, "Who named you like that?"

He looked at Woody for a minute and answered, "My grandfather J. D. Freeman."

"Is Jennifer your mother?" Woody asked staring into the sheriff's eyes.

"She was," he answered taking a step closer.

"What do you mean she was?" Woody said still staring into the sheriff's eyes.

Opening the cell door, he told Woody "Jennifer was my mother and I never got to know her because she died when I was born."

Woody hung his head as memories of Jennifer came to mind of how she used to call him, "Mountain man." After a while, he looked up into his son's eyes and told him, "I'm your father."

"Them men outside all heard stories of you, including me," said the sheriff staring back at his father. "Are they true?" Stepping out the cell door, he reached for his hat and asked "You got any whiskey in here, son?"

Turning towards him with a smile on his face, Woody told him, "About them stories of me, only the good ones are true."

Reaching out to hug Woody, the sheriff took a step toward him, Woody leaned to one side holding the desk coughing up blood and said, "I'm dying and I got two last wishes Son."

Opening the bottom drawer pulling out a bottle of whiskey, he handed it to Woody. He took a big swig as his son looked on and said, "Rumors have it you're quick with your gun and killed a lot of men."

"They all had a choice, but some had to die anyways," Woody said smiling.

Opening the door the sheriff stepped outside and yelled, "Listen up!" Motioning Woody outside he said, "This is my father and if any man tries to hurt him, I'll hunt you down and kill you on the spot."

Adams the banker moved towards the wooden porch saying, "That's fine and dandy, but what about the rest of the money he took out the bag?"

Coughing up more blood, Woody stepped off the porch saying, "You sawed off little fat runt, I told you I didn't take any of it."

Pushing through the crowd, the deputy called out for the sheriff, stepping onto the wooden porch saying, "Found this money in one of the dead man's boots."

Taking the money in one hand, the sheriff walked to the edge of the porch saying, "Now looky here!" Tossing the money at the banker, "That's what you're crying for, ain't it?" he asked.

In seconds, the crowd walked away following Adams to the bank. Woody looked at the deputy with curious eyes asking, "Have we ever met somewhere before?" The deputy took a few steps towards Woody as he noticed his bowlegs and a gun in his britches. Looking closer, he saw the deputy's red hair under his hat and he asked,

"Henry Riggins, is that you son?"

"You got a good memory," he said reaching out to shake Woody's hand. He and his grandfather had come across Woody when Henry was only ten years old. Now he stood tall at age 36 and said, "It's been a long time sir." They shook hands and followed the sheriff inside.

Reaching into his pocket once inside, Woody told Henry, "This belongs to you. It was a gift from your grandfather."

Taking the pocket watch, Henry popped it open. The name "Riggins" was written on the inside lid. "Been here ever since you told us about this town," he said looking at Woody.

"Son, we got to go now," Woody said looking towards his son. "I'm running out of time," he said holding onto the desk and as he coughed, more blood slipped out of his mouth.

"I need you to watch over the town," the sheriff told Henry.

"If I don't make it back, it's yours okay?" Henry had been loyal to Woody's son since he was born, because Woody had helped him and his grandfather years ago. When the sheriff was born, Henry was already ten years old. Even though Woody's son had become sheriff, Henry was actually the one who looked out for him.

Not wasting any more time, Woody and his son headed out of Tiptoe. Heading to the circle of death would be the graveyard, of the wagon train Woody had survived but lost Frank and Maggie.

Riding out of town, Woody began speaking to his son. His first wish would be to be buried at the circle of death. The second wish would be that someone hunt down Danny Moore and kill him on the spot. Handing the bag of gold to his son, Woody said, "This is a lot of money in gold. Take it my son and use it to hunt down your grandparents' killer." Spitting up more blood, he told his son, "His name is Danny Moore, and he has a twin brother." Taking a sip of whiskey he said, "Both of them have a piece of their ear cut off to identify each one. The one who needs killing is the one with a piece missing from his right ear. Untying the leather scabbard that held his buffalo rifle, he told his son, "This was my father's. It belongs to you now." Spitting up more blood, he wiped his mouth on his shirtsleeve and continued, "In my saddle bags, you'll find the slugs for it."

"How far is the circle of death?" his son asked tying the leather scabbard to the saddle horn.

"We'll head into the forest of the mountain and come out the other side where the graves are," he answered pointing to the mountains.

The flames danced in the midst of the dark forest as Woody slept peacefully. His son looked at his father who seemed so young to be dying. He thought of all the stories people passing through Tiptoe had shared with him about his father. Slowly drifting into a deep sleep,

Woody's son could hear the distant drum beats for the first time. He'd heard many stories of his father living with the Indians and learning their ways.

The dawn's light lit up the forest as Woody cooked a meal for him and his son. A good cup of coffee and some food would help get them started, on their journey through the mountain forest. Each night Woody seemed to be getting worse, but he sat with his son telling him his life story.

Days turned into weeks and weeks into months. Woody and his son sat on their horses looking at the decaying wagons. Pointing towards them he said, "My son, this is the circle of death where your grandparents rest in peace." Dismounting his paint, he held onto the saddle horn for a while. Then he began untying the saddle from his paint and said, "I'd like for this paint to roam the wilderness after you bury me, my son."

His son dismounted his horse removing the paint's reins from his mouth. He went around Woody's side and said, "Father, release him now and watch him run into the meadows."

"Why the tears, my boy? I ain't dead yet," Woody asked looking at his son. He could tell his father was only being brave because he was coughing up more blood than before and could barely stand on his own.

Once inside the circle of death, Woody sat against the wagon wheel belonging to Frank and Maggie. Yards away beside the shallow graves was where Woody pointed saying, "Please, my son, lay me to rest on the other side of my mother." Coughing up more blood, he said, "Inside this wagon is a shovel I left many years ago."

"Why don't we wait until morning?" Woody's son asked as he reached inside the wagon picking up the shovel.

Looking into his son's eyes, Woody said, "Bury me next to my mother and promise me you will hunt down Danny Moore."

Stepping outside the circle of death, Woody's son walked over to the paint. Unsaddling it, he slapped it on the butt as he shot one round into the air. It ran into the meadows a free horse. Moments later, he walked back into the circle of death and said, "That paint sure is a beautiful horse."

The silence in the air froze Woody's son and a chill ran through his body. Slowly looking down towards his father, Woody had passed away. Kneeling next to Woody, his son hugged him a while and spoke to himself, "I promise."

THE END OF BOOK ONE

Felix Flores, Jr.

ABOUT THE AUTHOR

Felix Flores, Jr. was born in Lubbock, Texas. From an early age, Westerns have always been his favorite movies and books. Single and in his 50s, it's time to tell the world the Western stories in his mind...

Having lived a life of crime, his craving to write Western books grew even more as he sat alone for many years in prison cells.

He spends his time doing prison duties and making sure he writes each day. He has been in prison for over 20 years and will soon be free. Upon his release, he plans on opening a Wood Shop and writing more western books.

He is the Author of Ring Of Smoke. Now he presents Circle Of Death . Shortly, he will present *Circle Of Death The Promise*.

Felix Flores, Jr.

Felix Flores, Jr.

Order Mr. Flores' first book
Ring of Smoke

Name:_____

Address:_____

City: _____ State: _____ Zip:_____

Total number of books ordered ___ @ $8.95   _____

Shipping/Handling ___ x $3.99   _____

TOTAL ENCLOSED   _____

Send check or money order (no cash or stamps) to:

MIDNIGHT EXPRESS BOOKS
POBox 69
Berryville, AR 72616

Additional books may be purchased from any place
where books are sold

Felix Flores, Jr.

www.ingramcontent.com/pod-product-compliance
Lightning Source LLC
Chambersburg PA
CBHW060404260626
47160CB00006B/2427